HIJACKED IN OCEANIA

KATIE MATISON

Print ISBN: 978-1-66780-700-3

eBook ISBN: 978-1-66780-701-0

PROLOGUE

2019

The young man squinted in the dim light of the filthy room as he studied the ship's line drawings and schematics on the laptop screen. The cramped room in the tenement on the outskirts of Kuala Lumpur was stiflingly hot in the late Malaysian afternoon, and the neckband of his Oxford University T-shirt was drenched. The man, now known only as Five, focused intently on committing the diagrams of the ship to his near-perfect memory. He took no notes but simply analyzed the details of the engine room on the screen. He allowed himself no breaks, except to respond to the call to prayer and to use the toilet. He ate only once a day, usually a meal consisting of fruit or a murtabak from a street vendor in the nearby market before resuming his work. Every night, cloaked in the security of darkness, he attended the clandestine meetings a quarter of a mile from his tenement to discuss the mission to advance the Cause.

He had returned to his homeland of Malaysia a month ago from the remote camp in Yemen. Since his return, he had not bothered to contact his parents or siblings living not three miles from away from his cramped room. Since he had been reborn as Five, he had turned his back on his old life. Besides, he knew that it would be pointless to contact his family because they would never understand the importance of the Cause.

The squalor of Five's tiny tenement room was a sharp contrast to his family's life. His father was a successful merchant who had provided a good standard of living for his family, which included a fine house with domestic servants and a private school education for his children. His father's income had enabled Five to obtain a degree in chemistry from Oxford and a master's degree in chemistry from Berkeley without ever worrying about the huge educational cost. Afterward, he had landed a plum position with a major American pharmaceutical corporation. Five's current endeavors would be incomprehensible to his father. But it would be difficult—if not impossible—to explain to a man who had never left Malaysia the extreme isolation and loneliness he had suffered living in America and the UK.

Five had been blissfully happy during his one-year marriage to Caroline, a pretty California blonde, after graduating from Berkeley. Within six months, however, it had become clear to both of them that the marriage was a mistake. In addition to their cultural and religious differences—she was a Catholic and he was a Muslim—her family despised him. His wife's parents were indifferent to the fact that he was highly educated, remarkably handsome, gainfully employed, and clearly in love with their daughter.

Battling depression, he took a trip to London for two weeks after his wife's father, a prominent attorney in San Francisco, assisted his daughter in obtaining an annulment of the marriage. During a party hosted by an Oxford classmate in a small overpriced Knightsbridge flat, he had been recruited for the Cause. Within a week of returning to California, he had resigned his job, donated all of his possessions in San Francisco to a homeless shelter, and moved to a training camp in Yemen. By that point, he had realized that his hedonistic and materialistic past life had been the source of his unhappiness.

He rededicated himself to his new path with a religious fervor. His sophisticated knowledge of chemistry had proven to be a highly valued skill in creating and designing explosives. He had been welcomed into a wide-ranging terrorist cell. It was then that he became known only as Five. He finally had experienced a rapture he had never known existed before dedicating his life to the Cause.

The cell was simply known as 53. With members in six countries, they never used names and were known only by numbers. Members communicated by disposable cells and through Internet cafés and the dark web. The cell members included a coterie of technicians and professionals, including computer programmers, weapons specialists, electrical engineers, and biologists, many of whom were ostensibly leading normal lives.

It was widely known that 53 had a cache of military weapons that rivaled that of an army warehouse. But most importantly, 53 had a grand terrorist mission to celebrate the Cause and punish the infidels. Five had fortunately been one of the lucky few chosen to implement the plan that would cause the world to sit up and take notice. Five was honored to serve and intended to willingly sacrifice his meager life for the greater good.

The photographs of the *Golden Swan*, the new ship and pride of the Paradise Line, filled the screen of the laptop. The majestic ship was only 750 feet long and could carry five hundred passengers with a crew of three hundred. The brochures promised adventures and experiences of a lifetime on cruise routes to Fiji, French Polynesia, New Zealand, and the Cook Islands for those lucky families who could afford such frivolity. The *Golden Swan* was popular with children and adults alike, offering four restaurants, a fleet of gift shops selling South Seas pearls, a gym, a large swimming pool, master dive certification lessons, adventures for children under twelve, a staff of babysitters, and a luxury spa. This was a suites-only ship. The *Golden Swan* emblem shimmered in brilliant gold paint prominently on both sides of the bow and the stern, beckoning to the passengers of the fun ahead.

Five closed his eyes and imagined the golden paint on the brilliant white hull blistering in a wall of tall orange flames. It was a beautiful sight!

CHAPTER ONE

Temperance Tyler, known simply as "Zip" since childhood, watched the brilliant red sunrise over the verdant hills of Papeete from her business class seat in Air Tahiti Nui. The morning sky promised clear weather. Below them, the waning lights of the city glowed faintly and the runway lights loomed ahead. Zip's daughter, Zoe, slept peacefully in the seat beside her. Zip stroked the five-year old's long strawberry-blonde ponytail and admired her beautiful face as she slept. The child had been a trouper on the eight-hour flight from Los Angeles to Tahiti and had slept most of the evening flight.

Reynolds, his brow furrowed in concentration, sat across from them furiously pounding out a message on his iPhone to one of his colleagues at the software company where he was employed in Seattle. Of course, the moment they landed, Reynolds would press send. The iPhone was seldom out of reach twenty-four hours a day. His pack stowed in the overhead compartment contained a MacBook Air and a newer iPad. At thirty-two, Reynolds was completely immersed in his work. He generally worked seven days a week, occasionally taking a break for an outing with Zip and Zoe, a quick game of tennis with friends, or an afternoon of snow skiing at Alpental located an hour outside of Seattle. Zip had been increasingly worried about Reynolds's inability to relax. She hoped the family cruise to French Polynesia and the Cook Islands would be a nice respite for him. Zip, a part-time graphic artist, had the ability to leave her work behind and dedicate herself to a few discrete projects at a time. It gave her the balance she needed to raise their daughter.

The couple lived in the Madrona neighborhood of Seattle in a small mid-century modern house with fantastic views of Lake Washington and Mount Rainier. The house had been extremely outdated when they had purchased it six years earlier. Over time, Zip and Reynolds, with the help of an able contractor, had converted the property to an open floor plan with a modern, minimalist interior. The house was Zip's pride and joy, and it suited the couple's lifestyle perfectly. Downstairs in the fully renovated basement, Zip and Reynolds each had their own home office, which afforded them the peace and quiet needed to work from home. There was a newly constructed guest bedroom with a spa-like en suite bathroom for those occasional visits from Zoe's maternal grandparents. The house was also within walking distance of Epiphany School, where Zoe attended kindergarten.

Zoe woke up and rubbed her eyes as the captain announced the final approach into Papeete. Zip gave the child a hug and smile. She extracted some sugar-fee gum for Zoe from the case at her feet containing their passports, sunscreen, visors, and hats. Both Zip and Zoe had unusually fair skin and blue eyes. Zip, as a redhead, was particularly susceptible to sunburn, so she had purchased several tubes of sunscreen containing titanium and transparent zinc oxide from her dermatologist for herself and Zoe for the trip. Reynolds, with his dark hair and olive complexion that always tanned and never burned, would not need the sunscreen. The case also contained medications for seasickness, food poisoning, and hay fever, as well as aspirin and a broad-spectrum antibiotic as a precaution. Zip knew that Reynolds, who had never been sick a day in their seven-year marriage, most likely would never need any of the medications.

"We're almost here!" Zip told Zoe, giving her hand a squeeze. Zoe simply looked up and smiled before closing her eyes again.

They went through a short customs line after landing and then went to the business class lounge to wait for their hour-long flight to Bora Bora. The lounge served a pleasant breakfast of croissants, fresh fruit, scrambled eggs, bacon, juice, and coffee. The pineapple was especially sweet; Zip was told it was locally grown.

Zip noticed the cloying humidity and early morning heat immediately. She had lost her ability to cope with oppressive heat and humidity during the six years she had lived in the temperate Seattle climate. Seattle was either cold or cool—and rarely hot. Seattle summers were gloriously sunny, clear, and dry. The temperature seldom climbed above 80 degrees, and a light sweater was often required on a summer evening when the temperature plunged to 60. Mount Rainier, Mount Baker, the Cascade Range, and the Olympic Mountains were rarely obscured by clouds during the summer, when Seattle became a tourist mecca.

Refreshed, they boarded their flight to Bora Bora for a relaxing three-day stay in an overwater bungalow at a chic resort with child-friendly amenities. Reynolds, a longtime scuba diver, had told Zip that the diving and snorkeling in the clear lagoon surrounding Bora Bora was some of the finest in the world. Afterward, they would return to Papeete to board the *Golden Swan*, a family-oriented alternative to the Disney cruise, for a fourteen-day adventure.

As the plane circled above and slowed to land, Zip caught her breath at the site of the dramatic volcanic cone rising from the center of Bora Bora. The aqua waters surrounding the island glistened in the early morning light.

Zip felt herself relax the minute the plane landed. It was going to be the best vacation ever.

CHAPTER TWO

James Brooks walked briskly toward his office on Monday morning in a driving March rain. A fierce wind buffeted his umbrella and his trench coat. He was tired, having spent a late evening with his fiancée, Jennifer, known as Bunny to her friends, and their friends in a trendy bar outside the city. The train from his new modern flat in Cambridge had taken just over an hour and twenty minutes, so he had been forced to rise early to reach his office by 9:00 a.m. He ducked into Café Nero on Leadenhall and ordered a large latte to go before continuing the final city block of his journey toward his office in the towering new sleek glass structure known simply as The Scalpel. The building was well situated on the corner of Leadenhall and Lime across the pedestrian way from the Lloyd's building and diagonally from the glass wedge building nicknamed The Cheesegrater. The Willis Building—on the site of the old 58 Lloyd's structure—was tucked in behind The Scalpel. These stunning buildings were part of the new wave of large iconic buildings in Central London, sprinkled between the traditional lower structures.

James stepped into the expansive lobby that glistened with large tiles of Carrara marble and was furnished simply with low modern leather furniture. Three lovely young women wearing identical red blazers sat behind the long reception desk with a marble waterfall edge. It was located near a glass barrier that restricted entry to the elevator lobby and escalator. Two security guards stood by the front door. James fished his laminated badge out of his coat pocket and placed it over the scanner; the glass doors instantly parted, allowing him access to the elevator lobby. Once in the lobby, he scanned his card again, requesting the twenty-eighth floor. The electronic box directed him to the closest elevator, which whisked him to the reception area of the Lunar Syndicate.

A fashionable blonde wearing a black dress and gray blazer with the Lunar logo sat alone behind the reception desk. A huge painting of the moon and the Lunar logo with the inscription *An Infinity of Possibilities* was displayed on the wall behind the receptionist. Glossy brochures detailing Lunar Syndicate's business were displayed on a quartz-topped coffee table in front of a white leather sofa and matching side chairs. An 85-inch flat-screen television was tuned to BBC. The expansive glass walls offered spectacular views of the Thames, the Tower Bridge, and London. On a clear day, the buildings in the financial district were visible. To the left of the reception desk was an etched glass wall restricting entry to a huge coffee bar complete with a barista, pastries, and juice. There was a large area with ultramodern tables and tall booths offering privacy for business meetings. With the exception of three middle-aged men clustered around a small table near the window intently focused on their conversation, the room was nearly empty.

"Good morning, Gloria." James gave her a generous smile and wave as he headed toward the security area on the other side of the floor to his cubicle.

"Good morning, James!" Gloria chirped. "Have a good day!"

James removed his trench coat and hung it, along with his umbrella, in the large coat closet. Underneath, he wore a black suit, white shirt, and bright-yellow tie. The Lunar Syndicate, like many London insurance businesses, had not embraced the concept of business casual. Only black, navy, and gray suits with black shoes were accepted attire; the trend of brown shoes with dark suits was also eschewed. Brown shoes themselves were generally taboo. Insurance business in London was still traditional, although changing with the times.

James sat at his desk, typed in his password, and logged into the secure Lunar Syndicate system with a portal to the Lloyd's server. Three large monitors sprang to life. The Lunar office was paperless, so the computer system was the lifeblood of the syndicate. Like many larger London syndicates, Lunar had a highly qualified team of IT professionals who monitored and guarded the Lunar electronic network. There was no privacy, and private emails were forbidden. IT professionals were authorized—and often did—drop in to monitor business—providing results biweekly to the board. James had a professional iPhone bought, owned, and provided by Lunar to conduct business, as necessary, 24-7. James was always on call. In addition, he had his own personal cell phone for emails and communicating with his friends. Bunny filled his email account on his personal cell phone with constant communications about their upcoming wedding next August.

At thirty-two, James was like many young insurance professionals in the London market. He was a university graduate and had also completed many of his insurance certifications. James was determined that he was going places. His primary area of focus at Lunar was the mega yacht business. There was an increasing number of uber-rich individuals in the world who could afford oceangoing yachts over 125 feet and up with a full-time captain and crew ever ready for the next adventure. Some of the wealthiest individuals had security on board—often ex-military—to fend off undesirables.

James was a member of an elite network of insurance professionals, including underwriters, insurers, brokers, and claims personnel who met at conferences in Monte Carlo and exotic locales throughout the world. As a claim's professional, James had been fortunate enough to go aboard many incredible yachts through his eight-year stint at Lunar.

Mega yachts, like cruise ships, were often targets of hijackings and ransom demands. A number of the uber-rich and their corporations had kidnap and ransom insurance. The condition of insurance was often secrecy. Six months ago, James had been handpicked by the Lunar board to participate in a task force at Lloyd's that handled the occasional crisis of a hijacked vessel. The team was simply called K&R, an initialism for kidnap and ransom. Other team members included members of the protection and indemnity clubs—otherwise known as P&I Clubs—and the London Company market. Since James had joined, there had been only two detentions of smaller yachts. The K&R team had dispatched its paramilitary professionals to handle the crisis and pay small ransoms. Of course, the activities and operations were all private and top secret. The K&R Team had a meeting next week. James was sure there would be little activity. All had been quiet in the world recently.

James opened an email with information about a claim that had come in the previous week. He had a lunch meeting scheduled with two brokers at Chamberlain's in Leadenhall Market and a tennis match with a friend after work before heading home to enjoy a quiet evening in with Bunny. She was a wonderful cook, and she had promised to cook lemon chicken. With the caffeine from the latte coursing through his system, he no longer felt tired. He began the process of carefully reviewing the documents on his screen to evaluate the new claim.

CHAPTER THREE

Zip squeezed the salt water from her long hair and secured it with a dark plastic scrunchie. She slathered sunscreen on her face, shoulders, arms, and neck before smearing the white liquid on Zoe. Afterward, they sat back on the lounge chairs under a covered awning enjoying their lemonade and waiting for their lunch of fish tacos to be delivered poolside.

The infinity pool at Hotel Saint Arc sparkled in the intense March sunshine beneath the towering dark cliffs of Mount Paihia and Mount Otemanu. The two mountains were the only existing remnants of the extinct volcano on Bora Bora. The island was situated in the leeward group of the western segment of French Polynesia. Bora Bora, cocooned within a lagoon and a long barrier reef, was about 143 miles from Papeete, Tahiti, which was the capital of French Polynesia. Along with Moorea, Bora Bora was considered one of the crown jewels of French Polynesia and all of the South Pacific.

Two giant tiki heads anchored the pool on either end. There was a swim-up tiki bar, a tanning shelf under less than a foot of water, and a small bridge connecting the kiddie pool to the adult area. Flowering shrubs and bedding plants in brilliant hues proliferated around the pool deck. The resort was a fairyland of exotic color. A long stretch of white sand, visible beyond the pool area, wrapped along the aquamarine ocean. Gentle waves lapped the shoreline with soft white foam. A sailboat with an alabaster hull floated past in the dark water beyond the lagoon.

The area was impossibly beautiful, and Zip decided from the first moment that no Internet photos or travel brochures could do the South Pacific justice. Over the past two days, she, Zoe, and even Reynolds had become noticeably relaxed. Their fast-paced lives in Seattle seemed practically nonexistent now.

Reynolds and Zip had splurged and booked an overwater bungalow for their three-night stay on Bora Bora. The bungalow had two bedrooms, two bathrooms, a large living room furnished with a 75-inch flat-screen television, a sectional sofa, and a large marble-topped dining table. In addition, the luxurious structure had an efficiency kitchen with high-end appliances and a deck with stairs leading into the water. The bungalow was as well-appointed as any five-star resort. A large sheet of glass was inserted in the living room floor over a small coral garden, which afforded them views of the sea world beneath them. A small school of parrotfish often frequented the area, along with an occasional ray and sea turtle. A sulfur-yellow clown fish lurked in the coral head below their bungalow. Last night, they had seen two immature blacktip sharks no less than two feet long trolling the area.

Every morning and late afternoon, Zoe, Zip, and Reynolds had gone for a quick swim in the lagoon around their bungalow. The water was warm, crystal clear, and only about six feet deep. Zoe always wore a life preserver and had learned to tolerate the snorkel mask so she could delight in the sea life beneath them.

A soft-spoken young woman with a French accent delivered Zip and Zoe's fish tacos and fresh glasses of lemonade on a large tray. The two savored their early lunch while watching tourists frolic in the water. Reynolds had gone scuba diving that morning and planned to join them at

12:30 for an afternoon snorkeling cruise. Bora Bora was rated among the most spectacular diving locations in the world, and Reynolds had made it a point to dive at least once a day since their arrival. He had explored the wonders of Motu Tapu and had even experienced the wall of sharks at the Fakarava South Pass. Reynolds was living the diver's dream.

After lunch, Zip gathered their canvas bags with towels, sunscreen, extra suits, cover-ups, extra shorts for Zoe, and her wallet. Together, they walked down to the resort dock where Reynolds, talking with the boat captain, was waiting for them. Upon spotting her father, Zoe dropped her mother's hand, ran onto the dock, and jumped into her fathers' arms.

"Dad! Are you ready to go on a boat ride?" she squealed.

"Of course, sugar dumpling! Are you sure you will not melt?"

Zoe giggled. "Dad, you are so silly."

"How was it?" Zip asked him.

"Fantastic. The coral garden was spectacular, and we dove with a school of hammerheads." He grinned, exposing his flawless white teeth, and shook his head. "It did not even seem real."

Zip was terrified of sharks—even the little ones that sometimes circled below the bungalow. She shivered involuntarily. "I can't believe you lived to tell about it."

Reynolds smiled and gave Zip a squeeze with his free arm. "Life on the edge."

Zip was glad that Reynolds seemed so relaxed. Over the past two days, his olive skin had gained a soft tan, setting off his dark hair and beautiful smile. As a software engineer heading a large innovative team at the tech company, Reynolds seldom thought about anything but work when they were in Seattle.

They waited less than five minutes on the dock before boarding a forty-foot catamaran that whisked them off on a snorkeling adventure. It was an intimate luxury affair with only ten passengers. Zip, Zoe, and

Reynolds snorkeled for less than an hour above a sandbar studded with coral gardens and brilliant neon fish. Their guide identified small schools of Napoleon fish, damselfish, angelfish, and butterfly fish. Afterward, the first mate served them snacks before bringing them back to their resort dock. Exhausted and content, Zoe slept on the ride back to the Hotel Saint Arc.

The three of them had gotten into the habit of stopping by to watch the dolphin show at the hotel every afternoon at 4:00. A big saltwater enclosure with four young dolphins performed for the crowd of onlookers. Zip had promised Zoe they would spend their last morning at the hotel dolphin encounter. Children and adults were allowed to pet and feed the friendly dolphins under the supervision of a trainer. The dolphins also would pull an inner tube with a maximum of two riders around the shallow enclosure.

"Is it tomorrow, Mommy?" Zoe asked her mother, looking with wonderous eyes at the dolphins.

"That's right, 10:00 a.m. tomorrow after breakfast. We will have to get up early to pack before we fly back to Papeete."

"I can't wait, Mommy! It's going to be so wonderful!"

"Yes, it will be an adventure!" Zip told her, stroking her hair. "But we need to go back to our room for a last swim and then shower for dinner."

The family went for a quick swim off of the bungalow deck before showering and dressing for dinner. Zip had booked the Tahitian feast at the resort, complete with entertainment, for their last evening. She wore her yellow sundress, which set off her red hair, along with gold sandals. She secured her hair in a long ponytail with a bright-gold clasp. Reynolds dressed in shorts with a floral shirt from the hotel gift shop. Zoe insisted on wearing her Tommy Bahama dress with the starfish print and matching sweater.

The hostess escorted them to a table on a stone patio beside a stretch of white sand. The ends of the white tablecloth danced in the soft wind, and a bouquet of fresh flowers decorated the center of the table. Three Tahitian headbands made of flowers rested at each place setting. Zip slipped her floral headdress on before helping Zoe with hers. Even Reynolds placed the floral band around his head.

"Mommy, I feel like a princess. And you look so beautiful."

Zip rubbed Zoe's back. "And you are beautiful! Isn't this fun?"

Dinner was served buffet style, with fantastical food stations offering authentic Tahitian dishes: roast pork cooked in an underground oven, newly caught fish prepared with fresh coconut, chicken with Tahitian spinach cooked in coconut milk, shrimp seasoned with fresh pineapple, and steamed taro. There was a beef station with strip steaks and a made-to-order Asian stir-fry station. The three of them sampled many of the delicious dishes. Even Zoe, who was usually a finicky eater, was enthusiastic about the food. Dessert consisted of French pastries and fruit-based ice cream. By the time the floor show began, Zip and Reynolds had already consumed one bottle of French sauvignon blanc.

The entertainment featured traditional Tahitian dancers and music that had been a significant part of the local culture for nearly 1,000 years. The dances—known as *Ori Tahiti*—had been banned as being lascivious by the colonialists. But in the twentieth century, the old cultural traditions had been revived. The women were dressed in grass skirts that showed their bare midriffs and floral headdresses. Men wore a sarong skirt and shorts with headdresses. Instruments, including the nose flute, ocarina, and conch shells, accompanied the dancers. Despite the fact that it was clearly geared toward tourism, the floor show was a spectacularly beautiful and memorable event.

Zoe, exhausted from their busy day, fell asleep at the table before the show had concluded. Reynolds carried the sleeping child in his arms as he and Zip strolled back to their bungalow. The air was soft and fragrant with the scent of tropical flowers. The gentle lagoon waves lapping at the shore shined in the moonlight.

"Our last night," Zip mused. "I really hate to leave. This has been an incredible beginning to what I am sure will be the best vacation ever."

"I am not wild about the idea of a cruise. I wish we could just stay here," Reynolds replied.

"A cruise is the best way to see all of the islands and to go to the Cook Islands. It is geared toward families, and Zoe will be entertained. Besides, there will be more dive adventures."

"I can always go for more diving," Reynolds laughed. "I am ready to see the giant clams in Aitutaki."

"And our friends will be there too. You will see. Everything will be perfect," she assured him as they closed the bungalow door behind them. "I can't wait."

CHAPTER FOUR

Five flew to Bangkok from Kuala Lumpur four days before the scheduled sailing of the *Golden Swan*. He wore a gray tailored suit from Oxford Street in London with a Lanvin tie and carried a forged United Kingdom passport issued to his alias, Clive Featherstone. The passport, which looked perfectly legitimate, reflected that he lived near the beach in a fashionable area of Brighton and owned a very successful antique shop in The Lanes. The evening before his trip, he had tinted his hair slightly with silver streaks and wore a false graying mustache. The passport listed Clive Featherstone as being forty-seven years of age. Five had also placed a foam insert under his shirt to give the appearance of having a middle-aged paunch. A new cell phone was safely stowed in his jacket pocket. His leather briefcase was equipped with a MacBook Air and a brand-new iPad. He also carried a Burberry wallet containing ten thousand pounds in cash and a credit card issued by the Royal Bank of Scotland. By all indicia, Five was the quintessential businessman.

Five was constantly amazed at the efficiency of 53. The plane tickets, hotel reservations, credit cards, cash, preprogrammed electronic devices, and passport had arrived at his squalid apartment by messenger the day before his journey. He spent the night at the Mandarin Oriental Hotel in

Bangkok, a lavish establishment along the Chao Phraya River. He dined on the balcony of his room, wanting to attract as little attention as possible.

The following morning, Five took a private car to the airport where he was booked on a flight to Los Angeles. As a business class passenger, he easily passed through security without much scrutiny and waited in the Delta lounge until it was time to board. He ate a plate of fruit and drank a large glass of orange juice. Five ignored the scent of espresso that pervaded the lounge. He rarely drank coffee or alcohol, desiring to keep his body clean.

The flight was easy and uneventful. Five entertained himself by watching two popular comedies on his individual screen. He was too excited to sleep, so he also played a video game to pass the time. His seat was strategically located near the front of the cabin away from most passengers. The flight landed at 11:30 a.m. Despite the lack of sleep, Five felt refreshed and alive. He smiled warmly at the cabin attendants and thanked them profusely as he exited onto the Jetway.

He had been given a Fast Track pass for the quick access line through US Customs. A bored Customs agent asked him a few questions, merely glanced at the forged document, and stamped his passport.

"Welcome to the United States," the agent told him before motioning the next passenger in line to come forward.

After Five collected his luggage, he hired a car to take him to the Hyatt Regency in Century City. It was a business hotel, which was consistent with Five's alleged purpose for traveling to the US. He was booked for only one night. The king business room seemed pedestrian and plain in comparison to the Oriental, but Five hardly noticed. He carefully unpacked his suit and two clean shirts before taking a long refreshing shower. After a quick salad in the hotel restaurant, he took a taxi to a nearby office building. The facility rented offices on an as-needed basis to maintain the appearance of a business presence.

The six companions who would accompany him on board the ship had been strategically booked at other business hotels in the Los Angeles metropolitan area. He had met the three men and three women who would be posing as married couples aboard the ship at their meetings in Kuala Lumpur. The team consisted of a computer programmer, two weapons specialists, an engineer, a nurse, and a former tug captain. All three of the men and one of the women had undergone plastic surgery to change their appearance. Each of the women had fair complexions and dyed blonde hair. They had been carefully vetted to blend in with the typical affluent passengers on the *Golden Swan*.

The instructions from 53 had been clear. The team would stay separated until they met on the ship. This was a security precaution. In the unlikely event that one of them was apprehended or detained, he or she would be ignorant of the movements of the other team members. In addition to the team members, Five had learned that the organizer of the mission—an American—would be on board. The American's identity had not been disclosed to Five.

In addition to Five's team, the tentacles of 53 had efficiently made arrangements in Papeete for the *Golden Swan*. The usual ship's doctor had recently had an unfortunate automobile accident in which he had sustained severe injuries. He had been strategically replaced with a Harvard-educated physician who had been selected by 53. Pursuant to the plan, the doctor had recently acquired a small case with enough neurotoxin to quickly paralyze and kill 250 people. The doctor had also reported that he had secreted canisters of the gas sarin in his cabin, which would be used to flood the HVAC system in the crew's quarters. More than six months of careful planning guaranteed that Five and his team would not encounter any resistance from the passengers and crew. Finally, an exorbitant bribe paid to five Indonesian stevedores had enabled 53 to have plastic explosives, hidden in Louis Vuitton suitcases, delivered to the cabin of each team member. The process had taken careful planning, and Five was confident that they were fully prepared.

There would be no survivors. The Cause would be duly served.

The middle-aged woman at the front desk of the center begrudgingly lifted her gaze from her iPhone and handed Five an access card to a third-floor office. Her forearm was elaborately covered in tattoos.

"Says here there is a FedEx package for you upstairs. I left it in the room," she said absently as she typed a message on her phone.

Five opened the thin parcel that contained a credit card from the Royal Bank of Scotland and HSBC, both in the name of Ian York. A flaw-less-looking passport was also enclosed inside the envelope for one Ian York, a thirty-two-year-old stockbroker working in London's financial district. His address was listed as a flat in a posh new building on Canary Wharf. Five stuffed the documents into his briefcase.

He opened the burner cell phone and typed an encrypted message in code. The text—when translated—was simple:

I am here—we are ready.

Five remained at the business office for less than three hours. Before he left, he used the document shredder located in the common office space on the third floor to destroy the documentation pages of Clive Featherstone's passport and two credit cards. Afterward, he returned the key to the receptionist and booked a car service to a nearby restaurant before returning to the Hyatt. He watched CNN for a few hours before falling asleep. The jet lag was finally catching up with him.

He woke up at 4:30 a.m. feeling refreshed. Someone had slipped the hotel bill under the door as he had slept. He had already settled the bill, and there were no additional charges. This was the benefit of staying in a business hotel.

He prayed for nearly two hours. He went downstairs before eight and bought a bottle of orange juice and a croissant from the coffee bar in the lobby. A number of the hotel guests were already checking out.

Upstairs in his room, Five applied a soft brown dye with a brush to the gray streaks on his temples and sideburns. He removed the mustache and concealed it inside a bag the concessionaire at the coffee stand had given him and placed it in the trash bin in his room. He also shredded the foam and placed it in the trash over the dye packaging. He was not worried about attracting attention. Los Angeles was clearly the land of vanity, and surely no one would think that a container of men's hair dye was odd.

When the dye dried, he took a long hot shower with the fragrant hotel soap and washed his hair with the complimentary bottle of salon-grade shampoo. He used a bit of conditioner as well, noting that it made his full head of hair soft and shiny. Today he wore a simple Brooks Brothers oxford shirt, plain brown slacks, and Gucci loafers. The new credit cards stowed in his wallet and Ian York's passport were carefully placed in the inside pocket of his jacket.

Five studied his reflection. He had regained his youthful appearance and could not be recognized as the middle-aged man who had come to America the day before. He was pleased with the result.

He left the room a few minutes before eleven. Five easily rolled his own luggage and briefcase down the hallway to the elevator. The lobby was mainly empty. He dropped his key in the lobby drop box and headed toward the line of taxis parked in front.

He strategically placed what remained of the passport cover in a garbage bin reeking of spoiled food before getting into the taxi in the front of the line. Clive Featherstone had ceased to exist.

Five gave the driver the address of a Marriott Hotel. Then he sat back and enjoyed the ride to his next destination.

CHAPTER FIVE

Upon arriving at the next hotel, Five arranged a late checkout from the Marriott for the following afternoon. He had his hair trimmed and styled at a salon recommended by the concierge. He also treated himself to a manicure. Before checking out the next day, Five took a long shower and dressed in a Burberry shirt, Armani slacks, and Italian loafers for the flight. He then hired a car service to transport him to the Tom Bradley International Terminal at LAX for the Air Tahiti Nui business class flight to Papeete.

Check-in was painless, and the security line was very quick. There were few passengers traveling on a Tuesday evening at 8:00 p.m., and the terminal was nearly deserted. He was admitted to the business class lounge, where he watched CNN and snacked on a salad. In less than ninety minutes, he boarded the flight with the other members of the business class cabin. The interior of the aircraft was decorated in an uplifting color of aqua. Five took this as a good sign.

He noticed two other members of the team already seated in the business class cabin. The woman wore a coral polished cotton dress with a matching cotton sweater and flats. The man traveling with her was completely bald and had an athletic build. They were a striking couple. The remainder of the team was traveling coach. Five ignored them and allowed the young attendant to show him to his seat for the overnight flight.

Despite his excitement, he fell asleep after dinner for a few hours. He awoke, slightly groggy, before breakfast and went into the washroom to brush his teeth and wash his face with cold water. After the light meal, he watched as the sun rose in the distance over Papeete. A few thunderheads loomed on the horizon, but the early morning air was smooth. Streetlights still glowed in the dim light as the plane circled to land.

Once he cleared customs, Five was escorted by a ship representative, along with the rest of his group, to his hotel room at the Intercontinental Tahiti Resort. He would remain at the hotel until he was escorted to the ship at 4:30 that evening. Other tourists had opted for a tour of the city, but Five had decided that he would prefer to relax at the hotel. There was a fantastic pool abutting the beach. In the distance, he could see the outline of Moorea in the faint morning light.

Five spent the morning swimming and sunning on the beach. He ate a delicious seafood salad in the open-air restaurant above the pool. Afterward, he swam laps in the pool and fell asleep for more than an hour in the afternoon sun. Now that he was finally in Tahiti, he could relax. He was gently awakened by a member of the hotel staff.

"Sir, I apologize, but the sun is very strong here, and we do not want you to get burned." The young man smiled at him timidly. "Would you like some complimentary sunscreen?"

Five shook his head and gave him a five-pound note. "Thank you for waking me. I do not want to get burned. This is for you."

"No sir—it is not necessary."

"I want you to have it." Five smiled warmly. "Again, I appreciate your helping me. The last thing I need is a bad sunburn."

He went back to the room, showered, and dressed. At 4:30 sharp, a small *Golden Swan* shuttle picked him up from the hotel open-air lobby for the short trip to the port.

Within moments, the *Golden Swan* was visible, towering over 100 feet above the dock below. Five sharply sucked in his breath and felt his heart pounding with excitement. It was beautiful! Neither the photos nor the vessel schematics had prepared him for the scale and beauty of the ship. The hallmark logo—a golden swan—shone brilliantly in gold paint on the alabaster hull. A few passengers could be seen on the top deck, sipping fruity beverages and gazing at the fabulous views of the Tahitian port.

Five knew it would have been impossible to take over a cruise ship of this size by sea. The tactics pirates used to overtake cruise ships in the Gulf of Aden would not work with a ship of this size. Those pirates hijacked, targeted, and captured boats by the use of small fast ships and rocket-propelled grenades. The movements of the ships were monitored from shore until a target was selected. Despite the prolific number of attacks, however, quite often they were unsuccessful. Because the number of attacks along the shipping route had become a threat to maritime trade, Western government military vessels now patrolled the area, offering protection to commercial vessels off the coast of Africa. Many commercial vessels now used fire hoses and had highly trained armed guards on board to fend off attacks. Most of the attacks in that area targeted container and other cargo ships.

But the geography of Oceania—a vast watery wilderness—did not provide the same opportunities for a land-based attack as the Gulf of Aden. Given that the deep water was littered with small islands, many of which were uninhabited or extremely remote, the chances that a hijacking operation could go undetected were slim. On the other hand, the sheer isolation of the South Pacific made it a fantastic location for the hijacking of a passenger-based cruise ship. The closest nation to the attack would be New Zealand—several thousand miles away from the *Golden Swan's* route.

There would be little—if any—opportunity to thwart a hijacking aimed at the destruction of the vessel and the death of all aboard the ship.

Five had placed the suite luggage tags on his bags before leaving the Intercontinental that day. Three crew members in white uniforms began unloading the luggage and placing it carefully on a dedicated cart. Five tipped the attendant and driver before walking toward a tented area on the dock.

The check-in station teemed with well-heeled, smiling young families, children, and middle-aged couples. Nearly everyone was expensively dressed in designer sportswear in cheerful hues. The excitement and anticipation of the adventure to come was palpable.

Two uniformed security guards were positioned at the far end of the tent. Five caught sight of four more men in the crowd who he knew were likely plainclothes security. Each of these men was a paramilitary type with the familiar bulge of a weapon at his waist. Five watched the men carefully, noticing how they were scrutinizing the crowd. These men would be traveling aboard the *Golden Swan* for the sole purpose of averting a hijacking of the ship, and Five knew that all would need to be killed and thrown overboard after the ship left Rarotonga in the Cook Islands.

Five was ushered into an air-conditioned building that housed a metal detector and luggage scanner. He gave his tickets and passport information to a lovely young woman dressed in a brilliant white uniform with the *Golden Swan* logo. She completed the check-in process, which included taking his digital photograph and issuing an electronic boarding card.

"Welcome, Mr. York, to the Paradise Line," she said sweetly. "Your luggage will be delivered to Suite 1010. In the interim, we are serving refreshments in the lounge on Deck Eleven. See you on board."

Five thanked her and proceeded to an attendant who scanned his access card. He emptied his pockets and walked through the metal detector. The guard gave him a wide smile and directed him toward the security door. He noticed the cameras mounted on either end of the room in the exact location shown on the vessel schematics. Five had memorized the location of the cameras located throughout the ship in all public areas. The team had a plan to disable the cameras in a few days to allow them to prepare for their attack undetected.

Things were going well. He walked through the glass barrier, took the elevator to the Princess and the Pea lounge on Deck 11 floor where he would meet the team.

CHAPTER SIX

James enjoyed a long business lunch at Giorgio's in Leadenhall Market before returning to his office. Business lunches in London generally began at 1:00 and ended at 2:30 p.m. Wine was often served, but James was always careful to limit his consumption to a single glass of wine. He kept a collapsible toothbrush and a small tube of toothpaste he had purchased from Boots in his desk drawer. It would not do to have alcohol breath at work.

James spent his afternoon dealing with a claim for hull damage to a mega yacht that had occurred the week before in Monte Carlo. A comparably sized vessel had struck the insured boat during a berthing operation. He studied the electronic photographs of the damage. The flawless hull of the insured vessel, which had often glistened like fine porcelain, had been badly marred and would be dry-docked. Situations in which a moving vessel strikes a stationary object were known as allisions, and fault was presumptively that of the moving vessel. It would be an easy claim, and a simple resolution would be forged between the insurers of both yachts. James could handle this claim himself, and it was probable that there would be no need to hire outside counsel. Of course, simple did not mean cheap. According to the marine surveyor's reports, the insured vessel would need to be dry-docked and repairs could exceed two million pounds.

Before he left the office for the day, a broker presented a new electronic claim for engine shaft damage. Years ago, claims were presented in person by the London broker, but now they were often presented electronically due to Lloyd's new protocol. This was a more difficult claim, requiring appointment of a marine surveyor and immediate repairs. An engineer would be needed as well to assess the damage. There was also a question concerning coverage under the Inchmaree clause of the hull policy. James sent an email to outside coverage counsel he had used in Long Beach asking him to check for any conflicts of interests. There was an eight-hour time difference, and although it was 4:30 p.m. and near the end of James's day, it was only 8:30 a.m. in California.

James arrived at the Lloyd's building a few minutes before 5:00 p.m. to attend a K&R Team meeting. Completed in 1988, the structure was another iconic London building and affectionately known as Inside-Out. The ultra-modern steel structure rose twelve stories above Lime Street. Inside was an immense twelve-story atrium that housed the original Lloyd's Lutine Bell, which was rung for all major casualties. Underwriting desks for all of Lloyd's syndicates transacting business at Lloyd's filled the second and third floor. The underwriting desk for the Lunar Syndicate was located on the second floor prominently near the escalators. Historic artifacts associated with Lord Nelson were tastefully displayed on the ground floor near the library from the old Lloyd's building, which had been preserved and reconstructed inside the new Lloyd's building.

Business had been conducted at Lloyd's for over three centuries. Lloyd's genesis was not auspicious; it had begun inside a simple London coffee shop frequented by brokers and individuals who had insured vessels and marine cargo. Today, business at Lloyd's encompassed a large range of risks and constituted 25 percent of the world's insurance market.

A glass elevator whisked James to the twelfth floor. A boardroom, complete with wood paneling and a priceless chandelier, had been removed from the old Lloyd's building and installed there. The room seemed incongruous in the modern structure, but was nonetheless impressive. James was always excited to attend meetings at the Lloyd's building board-room. Few insurance claims professionals were admitted to this private domain. James realized that he was privileged to have been selected and promoted by the Lunar Syndicate to participate on the K&R Team. For that reason, he made it a point to never be late to a meeting.

Twenty men attended the gathering that afternoon, all wearing dark suits. A uniformed attendant served wine and sparkling water and passed around puffed cheese pastries and a charcuterie plate. James declined the food and opted for a lemon sparkling water instead.

The meeting began promptly at 5:15 led by Chairman Martin Braden, who was a member of the Lloyd's board. Representatives of three English P&I Clubs and two members of the London company market attended. This was a multidisciplinary group, and neither the P&I Clubs, which were insurance mutuals, nor the London Companies transacted business at Lloyd's. The purpose of the group was to orchestrate a response to a large casualty, such as the regular hijackings off the coast of West Africa. There was also an ancillary strike force of paramilitary professionals used for res-cue attempts. This strike force had not been used since James had joined the team.

The meeting was relatively short, just slightly more than an hour. A large yacht insured by a competitor of the Lunar Syndicate had been detained off the coast of Indonesia. The assailants had robbed the owner and his girlfriend of ten thousand pounds of cash and more than two hundred thousand pounds of jewelry, including a 5-carat diamond neck-lace. There had been rumors that the yacht owner had fallen on financial hard times. A discreet investigation to rule out insurance fraud would be launched, and a report would be given at the next meeting.

Cargo insurers attending the meeting described an attempted hijacking off the east coast of South America. The hijackers had been easily defeated with high-pressure hoses and tear gas.

There was a discussion about a recent scare on a high-end ocean-going cruise line when "*undesirables*" armed with firearms had tried to slip through security. The onboard security and armed guards had easily disabled the would-be assailants before detaining them and surrendering them to the local authorities. These were the types of events that made James incredibly nervous. People on vacation let their guard down and were oblivious to the dangers that awaited them in ports. Like everyone else in the room, James knew it was simply a matter of time before a major catastrophe occurred. The job of the K&R Team was to recommend new protocols to vessel owners and operators to avoid tragedy.

The meeting ended at 6:30 p.m. Martin Braden reminded everyone that their next meeting would be in two weeks, absent any unusual event requiring an emergency meeting. Outlook meeting requests had been circulated at the beginning of the year, and the meetings were prominently marked on the calendars of every member present. Anyone who was unable to attend was expected to notify the chairman.

The members of the group exchanged gracious pleasantries before departing for the evening. A few of them were heard making plans to have a drink at The Lamb Tavern in Leadenhall Market. Of course, this was a shift in habits from years before. Based upon the stories James had routinely heard, thirty years earlier, a large contingent of insurance professionals would go out to dinner and drinks for a late evening. But the Lloyd's market—while still very social—was becoming increasingly work-driven. Gone were the days of three-hour alcohol-infused lunches with raucous American lawyers. The insurance professionals of those days had long since retired, and many of those less serious American attorneys no longer traveled to London. Lloyd's was a serious business conducted by sensible, well-educated, serious, and hardworking men and women.

It was sprinkling lightly as James walked toward the Liverpool Street station for his train back to Cambridge. James had time to check his work emails before the train left. The California lawyer confirmed that he had no conflicts of interest that would prevent him from undertaking his assignment. James promised to send him the documents the following day.

James switched to his personal cell and sent Bunny a text. He let her know he would be home by 8:15. They would meet at the nearby Indian restaurant for a curry and glass of wine. There was still time to enjoy the evening before work the following day.

CHAPTER SEVEN

Zoe could hardly contain her excitement as the airport taxi approached the quay. The three of them had spent a delightful morning at the dolphin show and having one last swim at the resort. Afterward, they followed their adventure with a leisurely swim near their bungalow and a light lunch in the open-air pavilion before their late afternoon flight from Bora Bora to Papeete. It had been a wonderful day.

The brilliant hull of the *Golden Swan* soared above the dock, glistening in the blinding sunlight. From their vantage point, they could see a number of tourists already seated in lounge chairs near the pool on the top deck. The golden swans painted on the hull were not as garish as Zip had expected. In fact, they were quite pretty and distinctive. The vessel was a true work of art.

"Mom, it's beautiful!" Zoe said, leaning forward in her seat to get a better look out of the window.

"It's huge," Reynolds agreed, patting his daughter on the back.

"I can't wait to see our room! Mom booked us on the Ugly Duckling floor—which is the best!" Zoe told him importantly.

The *Golden Swan* had been designed to feature the fairy tales of Hans Christian Andersen, the beloved nineteenth century Danish author. The public spaces and activities had been named after some of his most famous works, such as the Snow Queen Dining Room and the Little Mermaid Theatre. There was a Fairy Tale Activity Center for young children with games, movies, and readings every hour of fairy tales and, of course, the obligatory fairy tale costumes worn by many of the cruise line employees. The Paradise Line promised engaging activities for children and adults alike calculated to surpass any other cruise line. Zip had selected the line when she found out it offered not only a serious adult diving center for Reynolds, but also provided activities geared for their young child. Although Reynolds had been skeptical at first, he had finally succumbed when he had learned about the quality of the diving excursions. As a thrill-junkie, Reynolds had already booked and paid for his shark cage dive. The Paradise Line had seemed to offer the perfect blend of activities to appeal to their family.

After they had booked their trip, Zip and Reynolds had convinced their friends Carla and Wilson Sinclair to join them on the cruise. Wilson was also a software engineer who designed video games, and his wife, Carla, was a yoga instructor. Their daughter, Poppy, attended the same kindergarten class as Zoe. Zip and Carla—both extremely compulsive—had planned all of their activities two months earlier. They were determined it would be a perfect vacation.

The taxi pulled up on the tarmac next to a large tented enclosure manned by uniformed cruise employees. While Reynolds paid the taxi driver, a team of cruise porters surrounded the car and efficiently unloaded their luggage. The cases had all been tagged with their suite number on Deck 10. The cabin was located midships near the Red Shoes Library. Zip had been convinced by the cruise line that midships was best for people like Zip who were prone to occasional seasickness.

"Your luggage will be waiting for you in your suite, madam," the more senior porter told her. "Enjoy your trip."

They breezed through the check-in process under the tented structure. Zip and Reynolds had paid for a significant cabin upgrade, so they were given priority boarding. In the adjacent building, which was thankfully air-conditioned, they were greeted warmly by a beautiful Polynesian woman in a dazzling gold uniform. She expertly took their photographs, issued their boarding card, and guided them through the glass enclosure for the final security screening.

"Heavy security," Reynolds whispered to Zip as they walked away from the x-ray machine. "Impressive."

"I am glad," she told him, clasping Zoe's hand. "It makes me feel safe."

A glass-caged elevator whisked them up to Deck 10. Below them, they could see the impressive atrium in the center of the ship.

Their luggage had already been delivered to the suite. The cabin was gorgeous, with a small living and dining room, and a master bedroom and bath adjoining a balcony. Zoe's room was decorated for children, with watercolor paintings of the Ugly Duckling and white swans. Decorative pillows with fairy tale themes covered the bed. An en suite marble bathroom was situated near the closet.

Within moments, a young man knocked lightly on the door. It was obvious he had been watching their room to greet them upon arrival. He appeared to be about twenty-seven years old. He wore a pale-yellow short-sleeved uniform with a white swan embroidered over his right breast pocket. His name tag identified him as Antoine, a butler. Reynolds shook the butler's hand and introduced Zip and Zoe.

Antoine gave them all a generous smile as he came inside the cabin, explaining that he was their designated butler for the entire cruise. Antoine told them that he was from Bali and had worked for the Paradise Line for five years. It was evident that Antoine was proud that he had achieved seniority in his job.

"How often do you get back to Bali?" Zip asked.

Antoine continued to smile broadly. "I am working for six months, and then I will have a month off so I can go home to see my wife and new baby girl."

"It must be difficult to be away so much," Zip mused.

"The Paradise Line has been good to me—good benefits and I have been able to give my wife a nice home in Bali."

He assured them that he wanted to provide them everything they needed to make it their best vacation ever. "I am here to help you," he said politely. "I will make sure you have fresh fruit every day and cold drinks of your choice. If you would like to have breakfast in your room, please let me know. I will also help you with the laundry service every day. The laundry will wash your swimsuits as well so they are always fresh and dry. Your cabin steward is called IMade, and he will clean your room two times a day. Also, if you do not like the way the cabin steward cleans the room, or if you want privacy or to take a nap, please let me know. My extension is programmed into your phone, so you can reach me 24-7."

"Thank you, Antoine. We will look forward to getting to know you," Reynolds said. "And we promise not to call you in the middle of the night."

Antoine looked at the suitcases near the sofa. "Do you need help unpacking? I can help you put your clothes away and store the cases for you."

Zip smiled. "I think I can do it, Antoine. But if it proves to be too much work, I will call you."

"Well, I will let you get settled." Antoine gave them a shallow bow and big smile before he left.

Reynolds grinned. "I am glad I got a big raise this year," Reynolds said after Antoine left. "This is unbelievable. These people cannot do enough for you. I will have to give Antoine a big tip at the end of the trip."

Zip smiled. "It costs less than you think. And it is the trip of a lifetime."

"I think you are right."

Zip noticed the blinking light on the phone indicating that there was a message. She listened to Carla's recording stating that they had arrived that morning and had changed, and they would wait for them poolside by the Nightingale Snack Bar. Wilson had a work commitment, so they had opted not to go on the pre-cruise excursion at Bora Bora.

Reynolds and Zoe went upstairs to meet Carla, Wilson, and Poppy, while Zip stayed behind to unpack and put away their clothes. Twenty minutes later, she slid the last suitcase into the closet, locked the room, and turned down the hall toward the elevator sign. On the way, she saw Antoine greeting other passengers in the hall, and she gave him a friendly wave before heading upstairs to explore the vessel.

CHAPTER EIGHT

Zip emerged from the atrium into a small lobby separated from the upper deck by glass hydraulic doors. There was an adult pool and hot tub area positioned in front of a garden wall that was covered with scarlet bougain-villea. The entire pool area was enclosed with tinted glass. Two uniformed attendants served strawberry daiquiris in thin glasses to guests relaxing in lounge chairs snuggled up with their electronic readers. Zip emerged from the pool area onto a lush grass lawn adjacent to an open-air restaurant. Two couples were engaged in a friendly game of croquet. Beyond the lawn was another large pool and hot tub area surrounded by lawn chairs. A large emblem of the golden swan had been painted on the tiles on the bottom of the pool.

Zip spotted the Nightingale Snack Bar sign hanging in front of a covered portico draped with flowering hibiscus and bougainvillea. Carla, Wilson, and Reynolds were near the front sipping mojitos. A plate of fresh fruit and fried calamari was in the center of the table near a small vase that held a purple orchid.

Carla looked fresh and relaxed in white cotton slacks, sandals, and a floral shirt that accentuated her perfectly toned figure. Her waist-length blonde hair was pinned in a chignon. She wore no makeup except lip gloss and a bit of sunscreen. Wilson, like Reynolds, wore a T-shirt and shorts. A baseball cap covered his curly blonde hair. Together, Carla and Wilson exuded good health and contentment.

Carla and Wilson were a typical active Seattle couple: camping and long hikes in the summer, snowboarding in the winter. Wilson was a member of a dragon boat crew that rowed daily in the summer at 5:00 a.m. He also was an enthusiastic mountain biker. The two owned a small bungalow, which Carla had lovingly restored, in Madison Park near Bert's Red Apple Market. She had converted the detached garage into a yoga studio and taught several classes a week at her home in addition to her morning classes at a local tennis club. Carla and Zip had met at an Epiphany fundraiser for the kindergarten class and were excited to find they had so much in common. Since that time, they had become fast friends.

Zip gave Carla and Wilson a friendly hug. "Where are the kids?" she asked Reynolds, scanning the room for Zoe and Poppy.

"The Snow Queen came and whisked them away to the Fairy Tale Center for games. The girls were enchanted by her and her costume."

"The Center is on the deck above the adult pool. They will bring the kids to their spot at the safety drill at 6:00," Carla chimed in. "This ship is just as advertised—great activities for adults and kids."

"How was your flight?" Zip asked as she sat down.

"Long," Wilson replied. "But we took naps and managed to get a few hours of sleep. Poppy seemed to sleep well and, of course, Carla is blessed that she can sleep anywhere. I am glad we splurged for the business class upgrade. It made the trip tolerable."

Carla grinned. "This ship is beautiful! It is really better than I ever expected. And I am glad we upgraded our cabin too, so we are down the hall near the stern on the Ugly Duckling deck."

"Do you have a butler too?" Reynolds asked them after ordering Zip a strawberry daquiri from an attentive waiter. "Our butler is Antoine from Bali."

"Alistair from Kuala Lumpur," Wilson replied. "He told us that it is his adoptive name because no one from the US could pronounce his real name. He is a really nice guy, unbelievably professional and eager to please. I could get used to this."

Carla stretched. "Me too. This is the life. I checked the weather in Seattle, and it is unseasonably cold with light snow flurries. It is good to be here."

"It has to be hard for the crew," Zip commented after sipping her mojito. "Antoine only sees his family every six months or so."

"But he probably lives better than everyone around him. This is probably one of the best jobs he could get, other than working at a resort in Bali. We will just make sure to give him a big tip," Reynolds said between bites of calamari.

Wilson ordered another mojito. "Ready for the shark cage dive tomorrow, man?"

The first port of call the following day would be Moorea, one of the other acknowledged jewels of French Polynesia. Zip had booked Reynolds and Wilson on a shark-cage adventure. It had been exorbitantly expensive, but it certainly would be memorable. It had always been on Reynolds's bucket list.

Reynolds nodded. "I am ready. Can't wait. I can tick that off my list."

"What are you two doing again?" Wilson asked Carla and Zip.

"The kids are booked on a youth beach adventure and barbecue with games with fairy tale characters. Carla and I are going out on a sandbar off Moorea to watch the local guides feed rays and baby sharks. We will hook up with the kids at the barbecue on the beach," Zip told them.

"Sounds terrific," Wilson replied. "A big adventure."

Carla raised her glass. "Here's to an incredible day tomorrow."

Smiling, they clinked their glasses and sat back to watch the magnificent roseate hues cast over the Pacific in the late afternoon light. Life was good.

CHAPTER NINE

The Princess and the Pea Lounge was bright and spacious, decorated with comfortable low sofas and chairs. The area was enclosed with floor-to-ceiling panels of glass affording amazing views of the verdant mountains surrounding Papeete.

The closed-circuit cameras were scattered throughout the room to monitor activities in all public areas. Five was acutely aware that passengers were always being watched. Most travelers were unaware that bad behavior occasionally occurred on cruise lines, mainly because it was always handled as quietly as possible. Five and the team had been trained that they must at all costs appear to be normal vacationers on a bucket list trip lest they attract the kind of attention that could impair their mission.

Five ordered a strawberry lemonade and selected a seat in a large horseshoe sofa near two team members whom he had recognized as fellow travelers from the business class cabin. The couple gave him a knowing look, and the two men shook hands. Five nodded to the woman politely. They had met for a forty-eight-hour interval in Yemen one month earlier, but their transformation into Westerners was remarkable. The couple introduced themselves as Jason and Ruby Lombard from Toronto. Ruby stated that she was a biologist, and her husband was a computer programmer. Ruby was strikingly beautiful, with professionally dyed long blonde hair. She wore white slacks and a fashionable floral summer blouse. The Lombards, originally from Saudi Arabia, had undergone intense training for their roles. The elocution lessons had been successful—they were convincing affluent Canadian citizens with appropriate pronunciation and mannerisms. In fact, if Five had not known them previously, he would have believed them to be Canadian.

The group made small talk and pretended to introduce themselves, mainly for the benefit of the service staff and the cameras. Although the staff was solicitous, Five and the others knew they had been trained to report anything suspicious. The staff might have low-level positions, but none of them were stupid. Each member of the crew wanted to protect his or her job and the ship.

Five rubbed the gold wedding band on his left ring finger so it would be visible. It was unusual for any man to be traveling alone on this vacation. He made it a point to tell the group, as the server placed their drinks on a low coffee table, that his wife, Julianne, a British solicitor, had been forced to change her plane ticket for their trip at the last minute because of a large business deal.

"I hope she will be able to join the ship in the Cook Islands," he told them. Of course, it was a lie serving only to provide him a convenient excuse for traveling alone. Although he had come under enormous pressure from 53 to travel with a woman, Five could not stomach the thought after his marriage had ended. He was no longer interested in the pleasures of the flesh, and he now only strived to serve the Cause.

Jason explained that he and Ruby were traveling with two other couples who were getting settled on the boat. The Lombards, discovering that Five was traveling alone without his wife, invited him to join the group for dinner at 7:30 in the Golden Swan Dining Room.

When he had finished his lemonade, Five got up to leave. There was no ticket to sign—the Golden Swan was an all-inclusive line.

"Great to meet you, Ian," Ruby told him brightly.

"See you at dinner at 7:30," Jason said, smiling warmly.

"I am looking forward to it," Five replied, giving them a friendly wave. He smiled at the waiter on the way out of the lounge.

There was a large staircase near the rotunda outside of the lounge. Five opted for the stairs down one level in lieu of the elevator. He did not need to consult the map of the interior spaces on the wall. He had, of course, memorized the entire layout of the ship.

Five inspected his suite on the Ugly Duckling deck. It was luxurious beyond measure, with a small refrigerator stocked with snacks and cold beverages in a corner of the living room. A large sectional sofa had been strategically placed in front of a flat-screen television. Sliding glass doors led to a spacious private verandah with deck chairs and a table. His luggage rested on a thin bench near the walk-in closet in the adjoining bedroom. The white Carrara marble bathroom contained a cavernous shower enclosed with rimless glass and body sprays. Fresh-scented toiletries had been carefully displayed on the counter beside a stack of fluffy white towels.

The entire setup reminded him of the condo he had shared with his wife in the Bay Area before their marriage had ended. It was also reminiscent of the high standard of living his parents had finally achieved.

Greed! So much of the world was starving while a frivolous few lived like kings. He had realized in Yemen during his training that one needed much less to be fulfilled in life.

Five unpacked his suitcases and stored in the extra-large safe in the closet some valuables he would use to advance the Cause. Alistair, his butler, came into the room to greet him just as he was sliding the suitcases into a corner of the closet.

"Brother," Alistair said as he warmly embraced Five. "The time is finally here."

"Brothers in the Cause," Five replied, returning the embrace.

The two of them had met a few times in Kuala Lumpur during the small meetings held between a few of the members of 53. Alistair had been instrumental in organizing 53's mission aboard the *Golden Swan*. Five's cabin had been strategically selected so that Alistair would be his assigned butler. Five could meet with the other team members and maintain his documents without fear of discovery. Of course, the cabin steward, IMade, was not part of the Cause. It would be necessary to kill him before they launched the mission. It would be easy. Alistair had stowed large knives in the safe as well. Alistair would handle the cabin steward quickly and toss his body overboard.

The two men talked for a few minutes, discussing several predeparture details. They had arranged a large meeting with the team in Five's cabin on the upcoming sea day. The takeover of the vessel would not occur until after the vessel left Rarotonga in the Cook Islands heading toward French Polynesia. The South Pacific region—known as Oceania—was a vast, empty landscape. It was the ideal setting for the hijacking. They could sink the boat before any unlikely military intervention from either New Zealand or Australia could be mobilized.

Shortly after Alistair left to greet his other assigned passengers, the captain announced the mandatory safety drill. The Safety of Life at Sea Convention, known simply as SOLAS, required that all passengers report to their muster station near their assigned lifeboats before the cruise began. In the unlikely event of a sinking or other marine disaster, all passengers and crew would report to their muster station and board their lifeboats. SOLAS, enacted after the *Titanic* disaster, required that all vessels carry enough lifeboats to accommodate all passengers.

Five grabbed his life jacket and reported to the port side of Deck 4 as reflected by the stamp on his access card. He opted for the stairs and was one of the first passengers reporting to the assigned area. SOLAS protocols were established by the International Maritime Organization, known simply as the IMO, to save lives. Five knew that he needed to listen carefully to the instructions given to the passengers. All efforts to ensure survival and safety would need to be thwarted.

The goal of 53 had been clear: There must be no survivors in order for the Cause to be served. When the time was right, Five and the team would be certain that all lifeboats were disabled and unusable. It was important to ensure that no one could escape alive. He could feel his heart pounding in his chest with excitement. After all of the planning and sacrifice, their time for implementation was nearly here.

CHAPTER TEN

Zip rested her hands on Zoe's shoulders as they waited patiently at their assigned muster station on Deck 4, Station 11, for the safety drill to begin. Carla stood beside her with Poppy near the front of the gathering crowd so they had an unobstructed view. The two women, relaxed after their refreshments on the top deck, chatted while waiting for the drill to begin. Reynolds and Wilson stood in the shade against the plate glass window, deep in conversation about their planned shark cage dive trip the following day.

The assembly of passengers grew to approximately twenty people, mainly consisting of small family groups and couples, all well-dressed in designer casual clothing. Zip recognized the attractive middle-aged couple from the suite next door.

The bright sun edged low in the sky near the horizon, making the cluster of passengers uncomfortably warm. Zip wore her life jacket loosely and eyed the two officers in crisp white uniforms with the golden logo above their pockets. The two young men, who appeared to be Scandinavian, calmly surveyed the small group, seemingly oblivious to the heat. A covered orange tender suspended by cables alongside the vessel was painted prominently with an Arabic number 11—Ugly Duckling Port Side.

One of the officers, introducing himself as Officer Damian Oliver, took a quick roll call of the passengers assigned to cabins on Deck 10. Everyone was present and accounted for, and Officer Oliver seemed pleased.

"Ladies and gentlemen, thank you for attending this drill. This drill is mandatory and required by international law before every cruise. It is like the safety drill on an aircraft before takeoff. I am joined here by my colleague, Officer Angus Green. Both of us have an Unlimited Masters License and will be your assigned crew in the event of an emergency." He smiled at the crowd before continuing. "An emergency is unlikely. The *Golden Swan* is a new vessel and has only been in service for six months. She is equipped with state-of-the-art electronics, and her hull is nearly impenetrable. The *Golden Swan* is an extremely stable vessel and was designed for these very waters in which we sail. I do not want you to worry that she will sink. The chances of that are extremely remote. In fact, I have a greater chance of winning the lottery by buying only one ticket."

Soft laughter murmured from the crowd, and Officer Green grinned widely. The well-rehearsed speech was calculated to put the passengers at ease.

"But it is always important to be prepared for the unexpected. There could be situations that the captain deems an emergency requiring you to leave this ship. So, we need to be prepared. You are all assigned to cabins on the port side of the Ugly Duckling Deck. You will notice that your access card is marked with Boat Number 11. Number 11 is our tender number. In the event that there is an emergency, the captain or crew will make an announcement and you will go to your cabin—if you have time—pick up your life vest, and report here to board the tender. Do not try to pack clothing or empty your safe. Remember that the captain will only announce an emergency in a serious situation. Report immediately to Deck 4 in front of our tender. Officer Green and I will load you on board, the tender will be lowered, and we will leave the ship quickly."

Officer Green demonstrated the right way to secure the life jackets. Zip and Carla each helped their daughters before securing their own vest. Like most kids, Zoe and Poppy thought it was all a fascinating game.

"French Polynesia and the Cook Islands are in the region of the world known as Oceania, an area south of the equator that includes the South Pacific tropical islands and atolls, Polynesia, Micronesia, Melanesia, Australia, and New Zealand. While there are many islands, this is a remote area of the world. We have a special lecturer on board who will talk to you, if you are interested, about this wilderness. You will notice as we near Rarotonga that there are few airplanes overhead, and we will rarely encounter other shipping traffic. This is a desolate area, so we want to be prepared for anything." Officer Green scanned the crowd, gauging their interest in his talk.

"The Paradise Line wants to be sure that your trip aboard the *Golden Swan* is the best trip of your life," Officer Oliver added. "I really appreciate your attention and help today. For that reason, Officer Green and I have gifts for all of you."

The two men, assisted by a young woman with dark hair wrapped into a crisp bun, began passing out small gift bags decorated with the *Golden Swan* logo. Inside was a new snorkel and goggles for the small children and coconut candy. The adult bags contained sunscreen and a wine stopper with the *Golden Swan* logo. It was a nice touch and certainly beyond what was expected.

"Finally, there will be a party on Deck 14 tonight to celebrate our departure. It is always an exciting evening, and we look forward to seeing you there at 8:00," Officer Green announced.

After all the gift bags were distributed, the crowd disbursed. Zip, Carla, and the kids went upstairs to freshen up before dinner. Zip had decided to wear the Tahitian pearl necklace Reynolds had bought her from the Robert Wan boutique on Bora Bora. It would be a perfect match for her black-and-gold sundress. Reynolds had given Zoe a small inexpensive necklace as well. In less than an hour, Zip and Zoe met up with Carla and Poppy, and the four of them headed upstairs to meet their husbands in the Golden Swan Dining room for dinner. They would finish dinner early just in time to enjoy the sailing party that evening. It would be the perfect start to their trip.

CHAPTER ELEVEN

After a lovely dinner in the Snow Queen Dining Room, Five and his companions joined the crowd on the top deck for the evening voyage to Moorea. There were many young families and middle-aged couples spilling out of the snack bar and the crow's nest above them. They found a sectional sofa by the railing and drank virgin strawberry daiquiris.

The atmosphere was electric with anticipation and excitement. The soft breeze cooled the humid air, and there was a pervasive scent of tropical flowers. Five noticed that the dock below them was now empty. The captain made an announcement, and the ship's horn bellowed loudly to announce their departure from the dock. It would be a short trip. Moorea was often visible from Papeete and was serviced by daily ferries from the island of Tahiti.

The Lombards' companions had joined them and Five for dinner. Christian and Bridget Valcourt, originally from Syria, were residents of Nice. Christian was a general surgeon, and his wife, Bridget, was a nurse. The Valcourts, were dressed in designer clothing and made an elegant couple. They seemed unlikely recruits for the Cause. But after an hour or so, Five noticed that Christian had a compelling, angry intensity that was barely under control. He freely discussed the discrimination he and Bridget had suffered in France. Christian had scores to settle and was adamant that he was prepared to die for the Cause. Five hoped Christian could contain his rage so that the mission's success would not be jeopardized. When the time was right, Christian and Bridget would assist the ship's doctor in dispensing with the senior officers. They were critical members of the team.

Mark and Lauren Jensen carried Canadian passports that listed their home as Toronto. They were ostensibly friends of the Lombards, although the couples had never met. Mark and Lauren, both engineers, had been born and educated in Istanbul before joining the Cause. They claimed to have immigrated to Toronto, where they had become Canadian citizens and Anglicized their names. Lauren, who was small and fair, was flawlessly beautiful. Five noticed that the serving staff was extremely attentive to her and seemed almost awed by her presence. The Jensens spoke rapidly in heavily accented English and exuded high energy.

The group stayed on deck for nearly an hour during the leisurely voyage to Moorea. Then Mark, Christian, and Jason joined Five in his cabin to discuss a few logistical details. They were careful to announce to their wives within the hearing of other passengers that they were going to play a few hands of poker.

The cabin steward had serviced the suite during dinner. The king-sized bed had been turned down, and the drapes had been drawn in both the bedroom and living room. A bath towel shaped like a swan rested on the marble vanity in the bathroom, and chocolate candy wrapped in gold foil bearing the Paradise logo had been placed on the bedside table. A Paradise Line daily newsletter was left on the bed, detailing activities and information about Moorea. The flat-screen television had been muted and displayed breathtaking photographs of Moorea, a prize of French Polynesia.

Alistair had thoughtfully set out a tray of Mediterranean light refreshments and lemonade on the coffee table for them. The food remained untouched as the men focused on their plans for the mission.

Mark, Christian, and Jason left Five's suite before 10:30. It was important that none of them disturb the other passengers on the floor or attract unwanted attention. The mission had to be protected at all costs.

"You are a great poker player," Jason told Five as they entered the central hallway. He was careful to turn his head away from the camera angle.

The hallway was empty except for two middle-aged couples returning from dinner. Five gave them a friendly wave.

"Tomorrow before dinner, let's play a couple of hands in the cardroom," Five replied as he shut the door.

Alistair appeared less than five minutes later to remove the tray and pitcher of lemonade with the aid of a small cart.

"Was all well?" he asked Five as he placed the tray on the cart.

Five watched as Alistair stir the appetizers with a knife, shoving some food onto serving plates to make it appear that it had been eaten. It was an important detail that Five had ignored. It would not do to have any server questioning why they had ordered food and then not eaten any. He could never forget that they were posing as tourists.

"It was all perfect. Everything is on track," Five assured him.

Alistair smiled. "Enjoy your evening, sir," he replied as he left the room.

Five set his alarm for 7:00 a.m. and retrieved his checklist from the safe. He reviewed the document until he felt his eyelids become heavy with exhaustion. The traveling and jet lag were finally taking their toll on him and he needed rest.

He and his new companions had all signed up for a Jeep tour of Moorea, followed by an encounter feeding rays and sharks on a sandbar, and concluding with a barbecue lunch on a small nearby island. Despite his need to serve the Cause, Five found himself looking forward to the excursion. His life had been filled with intense studies and work, and besides his honeymoon and short trip to the UK, there had never been much time to enjoy the hedonistic pleasures of the Western world.

The bed was soft and luxurious, and the down pillows perfectly conformed to his neck, head, and shoulders. It was a pleasant experience and a sharp contrast to the fetid mattress and old sheet he had slept on for months in Kuala Lumpur. He closed his eyes and thought of Moorea.

CHAPTER TWELVE

James and Bunny took the train to Terminal Five and stayed in a king-sized room at the Sofitel London Heathrow. The hotel adjoined the airport and was accessible via a walkway. Their large room was quiet and modern, with a flat-screen television integrated into the bathroom mirror and a reasonable number of amenities. They had a drink and appetizers in the bar before retiring for the evening.

After a buffet breakfast early Sunday morning, James and Bunny flew directly from Heathrow Airport to Miami International Airport. James had a mediation on a case involving a collision of two large yachts in a Miami marina. The Lunar Syndicate, of course, was paying all of his travel expenses, including his stay at a chic boutique hotel on South Beach, to attend the mediation. At the last minute, he and Bunny had found a cheap ticket for premium economy, known as World Traveler Plus, on British Airways so Bunny could accompany James on his business trip. It would be a welcome perk for her. The weather in the UK had been unusually wet, dark, and dreary, and Bunny was excited about basking in the sunshine. It would be a short trip—less than seventy-two hours with a five-hour time difference—but certainly worthwhile.

James, of course, flew business class. Luckily, the airline upgraded Bunny as well when they checked in. Bunny was elated, spending the flight watching new release movies, sipping champagne, and taking an occasional nap. Bunny loved the flight so much that she informed James that the two of them would need to book business class tickets to the Maldives for their honeymoon.

After James and Bunny had cleared US customs, they found a driver holding up a placard that displayed James's name. They followed him into the airport garage, which was already warm in the midday sun. Palm trees swayed in a gentle breeze as the Lincoln SUV headed to the exit.

Bunny put on her sunglasses and sat back in the black leather seat of the SUV. "The light is brilliant white. I had almost forgotten what the sun is like," she told James. "And it is deliciously warm!" She removed her wool jacket and stowed it in her small carry-on in the seat between them.

James put on his sunglasses and took in the view from the back seat. His briefcase containing his iPad and laptop, loaded with electronic documents for the mediation, rested in his lap. Across the water, he noticed a large berthing area accommodating a strand of glistening pearlescent cruise ships. The water was a lovely aquamarine color.

"It is beautiful," James remarked. "I forget how lovely it is here every time I come back." James had already traveled to Miami and Fort Lauderdale six times on business for the Lunar Syndicate. It was one of the benefits of his position.

The driver dropped them safely in front of an exclusive boutique hotel in South Beach. Generally, James preferred the larger resort hotels on Miami Beach, but Bunny had been insistent that this was *the place*. It was quite expensive, but no one at Lunar seemed to notice the cost, which had been a relief to James.

Although it was only 1:00 p.m., their room was available for an early check-in. The ultramodern room was oceanfront on the sixth floor, offering expansive views of the beach and large waves. There was even a small covered balcony, accessible from a set of sliding doors. The two of them quickly changed into their swimsuits, grabbed beach towels from the marble bath, and went out for a swim and walk on the beach.

The waves were surprisingly large, and a few surfers tried their luck. The beach was full of tourists and locals, who reclined on colorful towels and lounge chairs, enjoying the brisk wind and afternoon sun. James charged the fee to his room for a space on two cushioned lounge chairs carefully positioned under a blue-striped umbrella that offered protection from the glaring sun. A uniformed attendant brought them two vodka Collins flavored with grenadine. After their drinks, they took a brief swim in the crashing surf. James managed to swallow a mouthful of seawater, which he found disgustingly salty. Afterward, they returned to their beach chairs and napped peacefully.

A few minutes before 5:00, James nudged Bunny, who was snoring softly next to him. Bunny was the typical "English rose" with long sandy-blonde hair, blue eyes, and alabaster skin. James often marveled at how angelic she looked when she slept.

"Bunny, darling, it is time to wake up. We need to shower and dress for dinner."

Bunny groaned, rubbing her eyes. "Gosh, James, I was fast asleep. I have not felt so relaxed in a long time. I think I needed this trip."

"I know. It is nearly 10:00 p.m. in Cambridge, and your body clock wants you to sleep. But we promised Noah and Tracey that we would be there at 6:30."

Noah Esposito was the senior defense lawyer representing the Lunar insured client at the mediation. It was the first time that Noah, who worked in a good-sized Miami firm of about 100 lawyers, had handled a case for Lunar. Noah and his wife had invited James and Bunny to their home for a casual dinner in Coral Gables.

James, who was feeling jet-lagged as well, stood beside Bunny, took her hand, and helped her to her feet. Before they left, he tipped and thanked the attendant.

Less than an hour later, they were showered, dressed, and waiting for their Uber under the awning of the hotel lobby. Bunny wore a sundress with a matching floral cotton sweater and sandals. Her waist-length blonde hair was pulled away from her face with a seashell headband. James, as always, swelled with pride as he noticed the admiring glances from the hotel staff as Bunny walked past. The name Bunny suited her: she looked as harmless, lovely, and as innocent as a white rabbit.

The sun was low in the sky as they hopped into their Uber and headed toward Coral Gables. Traffic was heavy for a Sunday evening, and the trip was longer than James had expected. As they entered Coral Gables, Bunny was entranced by the Spanish stucco homes and lush flowering gardens. Extreme wealth and privilege were on fine display in the prestigious neighborhoods. The car took the traffic circle from Le Jeune and turned onto Old Cutler. Within a few short blocks, the car took a right turn onto a quiet street with well-manicured lawns before stopping in front of a low ranch-style house with two banyan trees in the front. Flowers spilled from large concrete planters near the travertine entrance.

"Jesus Christ," James told Bunny as they slid out of the Uber. "I picked the wrong profession."

This was Bunny's first trip to America, and she was awestruck with the display of wealth. "It's brilliant," she said. "And it fits all of the American stereotypes."

"Noah is a nice guy," he told her. "Fairly down-to-earth. We met once in London."

Noah and Tracey greeted them warmly at the front door. They were in their mid-forties and showed the signs of too much sun. Noah's grandparents had immigrated from Cuba to escape Castro and had prospered in South Florida. Tracey explained that she had grown up in the house. After her parents had passed away, she and Noah had gutted and redecorated the home. James drew in his breath. The travertine extended throughout a large open-plan room with low Italian furniture overlooking a magnificent pool, hot tub, outdoor kitchen, tiki bar, and tennis court. Garden lighting accentuated the oasis.

While they enjoyed a glass of prosecco outside by the pool, the group chatted amiably. Tracey informed them that their children were on a skiing trip in Colorado, so it would only be the four of them for dinner. Their cook, an older man who spoke only Spanish, worked in the outdoor kitchen preparing their seafood over the open grill. Before dinner, Tracey gave them a tour of the house, discussing the changes they had made.

Dinner was a delicious feast of stone crab, shrimp, and paella at a glass-topped table overlooking the pool. It was a magical evening. After dessert, Noah arranged for a car service to take James and Bunny back to their hotel. They were in bed and asleep by 10:30.

James met Noah at his office at 8:30 the next morning for a quick Cuban coffee before the mediation began at 9:30 in a nearby office building. The conference rooms where the mediation was conducted offered staggering views of Miami Beach.

The lawsuit between both boat owners was pending in federal court and set for trial in less than ninety days. It was a mutual fault collision, but the lawyers for both parties had conducted scorched earth discovery, exchanging voluminous electronic data and conducting twenty depositions. Motions for summary judgment were pending, and the case was ripe for settlement. The Lunar Syndicate had insured the more culpable party, and James was prepared with primary policy limits authority of five million dollars. As with all mediations, there would be the predictable posturing of the parties and their respective teams of lawyers, but after a suitable interval, James would be certain that a settlement was reached. Legal fees for his client alone now exceeded four hundred thousand dollars. Moreover, the expert fees for all three specialists Noah had hired mounted daily. Lunar and all concerned needed to cut their losses.

Noah handled the mediation skillfully, and the proceeding was concluded by 5:00. To his credit, Noah and his associate had prepared a complex release that was amended and signed by all parties before the group dispersed. James reported the results on his iPhone to the head of claims, a pragmatist, who was pleased with the result. Noah had made James look good to his manager, and James knew that he would use Noah on future cases.

It was after six by the time James returned to the hotel. Bunny, who had spent the day shopping and later swimming in the hotel pool, was already showered and dressed for the evening. She wore a new dress she had bought at Neiman Marcus that morning, looking beautiful as ever. James showered and changed before dinner. Bunny had booked a reservation at a trendy place close by called A Fish Called Avalon. They had a pleasurable evening and walked back to their hotel happy and relaxed.

"Thank you for taking me with you," Bunny told him as they took the elevator back to their room. "This was wonderful!"

James gave her a warm hug and kissed her on the forehead. He was lucky to have Bunny.

"It was wonderful to have you here with me. It made the trip much more fun."

"It was brilliant," she said, smiling broadly. "And I want to invite Noah and Tracey to our wedding. They made me feel so much at home."

"Of course, as you like," James replied. Ordinarily, he was reluctant to mix business lawyers with his personal life. But Noah and Tracey had been great and might appreciate the invitation. Privately, he hoped they would not come. Even though Bunny's father, a surgeon in Canterbury, was funding the wedding, it was burgeoning into a huge affair. But more than anything, James wanted Bunny to be happy. She was really the best thing that had ever happened to him.

Bunny squeezed his hand lightly as the elevator door opened on their floor. "You are the best," she told him sweetly, typing a reminder note on her iPhone. "I will put them on the list."

The next day, they flew back to London. James stayed in the city in a hotel in Central London, again courtesy of the Lunar Syndicate, while Bunny returned to their home in Cambridge.

James arrived at The Scalpel bright and early Wednesday morning. The March morning was dark and dreary, and the trip to Miami now seemed almost like a dream. He fired up his computer, noticing three new claims had been submitted by the local broker. As promised, the pdf of the fully executed settlement from Noah was in his in-box. James sipped his extra-large cappuccino in the Costa Coffee plastic cup and settled into work. It promised to be a long day.

CHAPTER THIRTEEN

Zip, Zoe, and Reynolds went to an early breakfast at the Little Match Girl Cafe on the top deck. It was a clear morning, and the floor-to-ceiling windows in the restaurant offered staggering views of the rugged, verdant mountains of Moorea. The outline of the island of Tahiti was visible in the distance eleven miles away. The brochure left in their room the night before detailing the activities available had explained that the name Moorea actually meant yellow lizard in the Polynesian language, and that Moorea was part of the Windward Islands of the Society Islands archipelago. It had been settled over one thousand years ago by the Polynesians and explored by the Spanish as early as 1606. Samuel Wallis, Captain James Cook, and even Charles Darwin had all found inspiration and beauty on Moorea. According to the brochure, the University of California at Berkeley currently operated the Richard B. Gump South Pacific Biological Research Station overlooking Cook's Bay. The island was impossibly gorgeous with sheer cliffs covered in tropical vegetation and seemed to float in the aquamarine water of the lagoon surrounding the coral atoll. Arthur Frommer's travel books named Moorea the most beautiful island in the world.

Zoe sipped her mocha latte while admiring the view as Reynolds tapped on his iPhone. He had been up at dawn, typing furiously on his laptop computer. He had barely noticed her as she walked into the living room of their suite and poured herself a cup of hot tea. It was as if the relaxed person he had become over the last few days had evaporated in minutes. There had been a crisis at work that required his attention. Frankly, there was always a crisis at work, and she wished that for once, they would let Reynolds have time away. It was one of the downsides of technology. People were always available 24-7.

Zip chatted with Zoe, who was picking at a stack of pancakes shaped like a swan and lightly coated with strands of fresh honey. The kids were going for a swim in the pool of a large resort on the shores of Moorea. Zip and Carla had booked a tour of the island for themselves, followed by a small shark and stingray feeding encounter. Later, the entire group would meet up on a small island nearby for a leisurely barbecue and swim. The trips were designed to give the parents their "away" time, all the while knowing that their kids were safely supervised.

Reynolds had shut down his phone by the time Carla, Poppy, and Wilson arrived.

"Ready for the big adventure man?" Wilson asked. "Another shark cage dive."

"Can't wait," Reynolds told him, as he took a bite of his ham-and-cheese omelet. "Need to get my strength up with this ploughman's meal."

"I am going to have something light. We meet at the diving center at 9:30." A smiling server appeared at their table wearing a crisp white uniform with the *Golden Swan* logo. Wilson and Carla ordered fruit, juice, yogurt, and croissants.

"I will have to go on a diet when I get back to Seattle," Carla told them. "The food on this boat is incredible. I have never eaten like this on vacation."

"I know what you mean. I am trying to remind myself with every meal that I need to fit into my swimsuit." Zip drained the last bit of cranberry juice from her glass and sat back in her chair.

Carla giggled. "Maybe we can buy an extra seat on the plane so we will fit."

"Good plan," Zip smiled. "I might join you."

Wilson and Carla's food appeared in record time. Poppy and Zoe chatted with excitement about their upcoming excursion. "Mom bought me a new beach bag for my towel, hat, and shorts," Zoe told Poppy proudly. "It has starfish all over it."

"We picked it up at the resort in Bora Bora," Zip told Carla. "They had the most amazing stores, as you might expect."

After the kids had finished eating, Zip and Carla took the kids back to the rooms to grab their bags and brush their teeth. They were scheduled to meet at the Fairy Tale Activity Center so they could depart with their respective groups. Zoe was beside herself with excitement. Zip accompanied her and checked her in with the supervisor of the children's center. The attendants at the center were enthusiastic and chatted amiably with Zoe as if they had known her for years. Zip felt relieved as she watched Zoe giggling with the attendant and another little girl from North Carolina. If Zoe had not been happy, Zip would not have been able to leave her. After she hugged Zoe goodbye, she headed to the Little Mermaid Theatre, which was the adults' meeting spot.

The theatre was teeming with activity by the time Zoe arrived. She signed in with the group and sat down near the entrance so she could see Carla when she came in. She placed her bag with her hat, glasses, and beach towel in the seat beside her. Carla arrived shortly afterward, wearing a tropical print cover-up and shorts.

"Reynolds and Wilson are on their way to the dive center," Carla told her. "I don't know how they do it. I have seen reports on TV that occasionally a shark will wedge into the cage with the divers."

"Well, Reynolds assured me that there is a dive instructor with them and the cage has a camera, so they can be lifted immediately if there is a problem."

"I hope it is safe," Carla said as she pulled her hair into a ponytail.

"Well, they won't have anything on us. Today we are having our own shark and stingray adventure. We will officially be as macho as our husbands."

"True. We will have bragging rights," Carla replied smugly.

Within minutes, a young Indonesian man wearing a pressed white uniform with shorts called their group and escorted them from the theatre to the security gate. A young woman scanned their ship access card before they were ushered to a small line of Jeeps waiting on the tarmac.

The young man from the ship divided them into small groups of four per car with an assigned driver and guide. Zip and Carla were paired with a Toronto couple, Jason and Ruby Lombard. Giroux, their driver/guide, politely introduced himself to the group, enthusiastically explaining that he would give them their tour of Moorea. In less than ten minutes, the caravan of Jeeps left the area and headed toward the tall cliffs. They spent about two hours on the tour as the line of Jeeps circled the islands and headed into the mountains. They visited a pineapple farm, Magic Mountain, and the Belvedere Lookout perched high above the adjoining cliffs and the glistening sea below. In the distance, a pod of spinner dolphins was frolicking in the waves. It was stunningly beautiful. Finally, they stopped for a glass of fresh-squeezed pineapple juice at a small restaurant perched on a sheer cliff face overlooking the water. The surrounding garden was filled to capacity with an explosion of fragrant tropical trees and flowering plants. Zip felt parched, and the pineapple juice was refreshing in the warm climate.

They sat at a small table with Ruby and Jason. Zip marveled at how impossibly beautiful Ruby was and how she barely seemed fazed by the hot, humid air. Zip and Carla chatted amiably with the couple as they drank their juice. Ruby explained that the Canadian winter had been particularly brutal that year, and they had been yearning for a sunny vacation to rejuvenate themselves.

"I love Toronto," Ruby told them. "But it has been so cold and gray lately that we needed a change. I have been suffering from cabin fever this year. It is such a shock to see flowers and green grass, and to be able to swim. Jason and I have been so excited about this vacation."

"We understand completely. Seattle is cold and wet in March, so this is a good break for us, too," Carla replied, smiling broadly.

By the time the Jeep had reached the dock of the Intercontinental Hotel, Zip felt that she and Carla had made new friends. The temperature had soared into the low nineties, and Zip decided that a swim would feel delicious.

Giroux stopped near a long dock lined with boats with a covered canopy top to take them to the sandbar to feed the rays and sharks. "The boats have a shallow hull because you will go onto the sandbar," he explained.

Zip thanked Giroux as she pressed a $10 tip into his hand. "It was really a fun morning," she told him as she and Carla waived goodbye.

The boats each carried about fifteen people. Their guide, Austin, wore floral swim trunks and a T-shirt with the *Golden Swan* logo. Zip and Carla sat near the front across from Ruby and Jason as the remaining passengers found their seats. Once the boat was full, the captain piloted the small craft out toward the sandbar.

Zip easily spotted their destination, which was dotted with boats of a similar size moored in waist-deep water in the lagoon. The water was as clear as glass. A throng of tourists stood beside the vessels clustered around their guides. Zip was nervous. She hated sharks, and she was not sure if she could get into the water. As the boat pulled near the others and dropped anchor, she noticed that the sharks were barely two feet long and were dwarfed by the magnificent rays.

"These are blacktip reef sharks," Austin told them, his voice punctuated by a French accent. "These sharks are quite young. You do not have to be afraid, but do not try to pet them, and do not follow them into the deep water. Generally, they are very afraid, and it is important not to splash around in the water. I will feed the sharks and rays and you can watch. The rays are very gentle, and they are waiting to be fed."

Austin grabbed a bag of fish before leading the group down the steps into the warm water. The passengers followed him like a flock of sheep.

Carla put on her snorkel mask. "Wilson said I should look at the fish underwater as they feed them. Bring your mask, too."

Zip slipped the mask over her head and let it drape on her neck. "Got it," she told Carla as she waded into the water.

Within minutes, the rays and sharks surrounded Austin. The crowd of tourists stroked the rays as they came up to Austin to be hand-fed. The sharks were wary scavengers, circling past Austin and grabbing any errant piece of fish that was not consumed by the rays. The sharks were small, about two feet in length, and their bodies were a sandy beige. The tip of the dorsal fin was ebony as if it had been dipped in black paint.

Zip felt herself relax as she stroked the back of one of the giant rays. Only the skin on the area near the tail was rough. The giants were gentle and soft—almost like a neoprene wet suit—as they glided slowly past in the direction of Austin, who was passing out the food. The largest of the rays stayed near Austin, pestering him to be fed. It was an amazing experience.

Zip noticed Jason and Ruby talking with two other couples and a single passenger they called Ian. Clearly, they too were enjoying the encounter with the gentle giants of the ocean. Another man they identified as the ship's doctor was with them as well.

After forty minutes, Austin gathered the group and they boarded the boat for a short ride to the beach of a deserted island less than a mile away. The Polynesians called the beaches on the small islands a motu. The water was calm as they entered a narrow channel between two small islands. The captain pulled the boat onto the shore into water less than a foot deep and tied up.

Reynolds and Wilson were playing ball with Zoe and Poppy in a shaded field beyond the barbecue pits. Three uniformed attendants were cooking chicken, fish, and hamburgers over a charcoal grill. Platters of fruit, including slices of coconut, awaited the group on a cluster of picnic tables near the water. Drinks and fresh-squeezed juice were displayed on a small tiki bar. The air was scented with the aroma of grilling food. Zip suddenly realized she was hungry.

She gave Zoe a big hug and Reynolds kissed her on the cheek. "How was it?" he asked her.

"Actually, you know I was nervous, but it was wonderful. The rays are amazing creatures. The sharks were kind of creepy, but they were quite small, so I felt alright once I realized that they were really just babies. Apparently, the big sharks eat them, so they stay in the shallow water. But now I have bragging rights."

"That you do," Reynolds smiled. "My brave wife."

"How was the cage dive?" she asked him.

"Two big gray reef sharks came close to our cage and were trying to find a way in. I have to admit it was heart-stopping."

"Have you had your shark fix for the trip?"

"I think I have had enough. Next port, I think I will just enjoy the coral and tropical fish."

"Good, then I will not worry."

They played ball with the kids, Carla, and Wilson until the food was served. They ate their lunch at a solitary picnic table by the narrow channel. The food was fresh and delicious. Warm chocolate chip cookies were served after the meal, much to the delight of Zoe and Poppy. The girls devoured two large cookies each, dripping strands of warm melted chocolate across their paper plates. The kids could not have been happier.

Afterward, Reynolds and Wilson took the girls into the water on a blow-up raft. The kids each wore a small life vest and floated easily on the water.

Zip watched her husband frolic with the kids in the shallow lagoon. Reynold's obvious stress from earlier that day had dissipated, and once again he was relaxed. The trip had been a fantastic family outing.

The tourists spent a lazy afternoon on the island. One of the ship's employees demonstrated the process of extracting coconut milk from one of the plentiful coconuts on the island. He then made a ceviche with coconut milk as a snack for the group. As the passengers gathered for the demonstration, Carla and Zip introduced Wilson and Reynolds to Jason and Ruby. Wilson and Reynolds seemed to instantly hit it off with Jason. They all promised to get together for a drink before dinner that evening at the Emperor's Lounge. Of course, making new friends was one of the benefits of cruise travel.

Zip and Reynolds went for a quick snorkel in the narrow channel of the lagoon while Carla watched the girls. Massive coral heads populated with neon-colored fish littered the sandy seafloor. The beauty of the scene below the water's surface was magnificent. When they finally surfaced, Zip realized she had not felt so relaxed in years. It had been a perfect day—one of many more she hoped they would enjoy before returning to their busy lives in Seattle.

CHAPTER FOURTEEN

Five shaved and took a long tepid shower when he returned to his suite after his adventure in the port of Moorea. His olive-skin cheeks were tinted pink from the brutal sun and its reflection off the water. He had to admit it had been a wonderful experience, and despite his underlying mission, he had enjoyed himself immensely.

He and the others in 53 had been trained to assimilate well so they would not be easily suspected or detected. Because he had lived in America for a few years, it had been easy for him to casually mingle with the other tourists in his group. He had mentioned that he enjoyed vacationing in the Bay Area and could carry on a conversation about interesting sites or restaurants. Most of the Americans he had met were extremely friendly and open. If any of them had harbored any resentment toward him because of his nationality or religion, they had concealed it very well. Since he had left the US, he had almost forgotten the friendly acceptance he had experienced when he lived on the West Coast. On one level, it was sad that all of the families he had met on the ship would have to die in a few days. Yet, he assured himself that all of them would become martyrs and die for a good purpose. There was no better sacrifice any of them could make than to serve the Cause.

He felt utterly relaxed as he said his afternoon prayers. Afterward, he dressed in a Tommy Bahama shirt, tan slacks, and Gucci shoes. The dress code for dinner was business casual. Five noticed that the brilliant aqua shirt complemented his complexion. Of course, he could not take credit for the tastefulness of his wardrobe. Someone affiliated with 53 had purchased all of the clothing that was packed away in the Louis Vuitton suitcases he had picked up in Los Angeles.

After he had dressed, Alistair and the ship's doctor paid him a visit. Five was already prepared for them, with the line drawings and schematics of the ship laid out on the coffee table. Five put the Do Not Disturb sign on the door as soon as the two had arrived. It would not do to have the cabin steward interrupt them; it would be a problem they would need to deal with immediately. Alistair had already emphasized that it would be reckless and would arouse suspicion if they had to dispatch the cabin steward prematurely. The shipping line would immediately replace him, and his replacement might not be as intimidated by Alistair as IMade was under the circumstances.

Alistair brought in a silver tray holding three tall glasses filled with fresh squeezed fruit juice and a small plate of berries, setting it on a nearby end table. Five noticed that Alistair's starched uniform still looked like new even after a long day at work.

The doctor, George Bishop, was in his early forties, with a slight paunch and receding hairline. He spoke with a beautiful English accent and was well dressed in an oxford cloth shirt with the classic Brooks Brothers sheep logo and casual slacks. He had been educated at Harvard Medical School and completed a neurosurgical residency at Massachusetts General Hospital. Dr. Bishop shared a nice home in Boston with his young wife and two daughters, seemingly living the American dream as an upstanding citizen. But like Five, George Bishop had become disaffected, angry, and covertly radicalized. He had carefully kept his views to himself but was eager to serve the Cause. The doctor had been chosen by 53 for the mission and was the last-minute replacement for the *Golden Swan's* regular doctor who had been in a serious car accident a few weeks earlier.

George smiled broadly at Five, picked up his juice with a slender hand, and leaned back comfortably on the sectional sofa in the living room.

Five consumed the drink quickly, savoring the flavorful liquid filled with pulp. It was extremely refreshing after a hot day in the sun.

"I did not realize how thirsty I was," he told his colleagues.

"The sun," the doctor replied. "You need to remember to drink plenty of water and stay hydrated. We do not want you to fall ill. We have work to do."

"It is surprising because Kuala Lumpur is hot. I lived in a place with no air-conditioning and it was a virtual sweatbox."

"Salt water and physical activity—it does it to all of us. Drink water," George chided him as they got down to the business at hand.

"It was a pleasant day," Five told them as he set his drink on the tray. "I think I needed the relaxation. We need to be relaxed so we can focus."

"It was wonderful," George agreed. "And we assimilated well with the others. I do not think that anyone would have any suspicion of what is to come. Things are going well."

They turned their attention to the sheaf of plans covering the coffee table. The plans, created by a naval architectural firm, were detailed drawings of the *Golden Swan's* decks. One of the tech-savvy members of 53 had hacked into the architectural firm's computer system, bypassed numerous firewalls, and downloaded the plans. They had been delivered to Five on a JumpDrive, and paper copies had been judiciously distributed to the final team. A final set of plans had awaited Five in his suite's safe.

Five passed out color-coded pens to each man: red for explosives, blue for weapons, and green for biological weapons. A few strategic bribes and alliances with local suppliers, stevedores, and lower-level ship employees had ensured that the ship would be loaded and prepared before any of the passengers embarked. This plan obviated the need for any team member to carry any item aboard. Of course, with its usual efficiency, the tentacles of 53 made sure there were no witnesses. With the exception of the customs agents, every person who had provided assistance had suddenly disappeared or met with an untimely accident.

Sarin and a toxic cocktail of bacteria guaranteed to disable anyone in hours were carefully stowed in the medical suite on Deck 4. George took a green pen and marked the areas on the plan with green ink. He had already confirmed the presence of the weapons that would be ready to use when the time was right.

Alistair marked the location of the machine guns and assault rifles in blue. There was a stash near the captain's quarters in a locked crew cabin on Deck 13 and another stash near the Fairy Tale Activity Center. Children would be some of the first targets of the attack.

The plastic explosives had been placed on Deck 3 near the engine room in several discrete locations. A blast of that magnitude would be guaranteed to rip a large gash in the hull, creating rapid water incursion and a quick sinking in less than an hour. Five's colleagues had performed mathematical calculations to determine the size of the blast needed to sink the vessel before help could arrive. New Zealand was over four hours away, and even rescue attempts from American Samoa would be too late.

There would be no escape for anyone in the deep water south of Rarotonga. Those passengers who decided to brave the desolate seas would become easy prey for the vicious oceanic whitetip shark. This shark, a member of the requiem shark group, patrolled the deep waters of the tropical seas, causing death and devastation. The oceanic whitetip shark had killed hundreds of soldiers after the sinking of the USS *Indianapolis* in World War II and had been designated by the famed Jacques Cousteau as "the most dangerous of all sharks." It was an exquisitely planned mission guaranteed to leave no survivors.

Like nearly all major cruise lines, the Paradise Line had six plain-clothed armed guards. Alistair and George marked their staterooms with a lavender highlighter. Alistair had given the team digital photos of the men, and they had easily identified them over the last twenty-four hours. The guards spent most of their time in the security room scanning the multiple banks of monitors from the cameras strategically placed throughout the ship. They were trained to watch for sexual assaults and the occasional murder on the high seas. Of course, these men would be disabled when the attack began. The team would use the security cameras to monitor the passengers before the ship sank.

The men lingered for a few more minutes discussing last-minute details. When they left, Five wrapped up the drawings and stowed them in the safe. He then carefully brushed his hair and grabbed his key card. He was meeting the team and some of the Americans in the Emperor's Lounge before dinner. He did not want to be late.

CHAPTER FIFTEEN

After departing Moorea, the *Golden Swan* sailed to a small island owned by the cruise line near Bora Bora. Six of the lifeboat tenders ferried the passengers from the deep water surrounding the lagoon to the dock on a sandy beach. The island was surrounded by a lagoon brimming with magnificent coral gardens lining the seafloor. Tropical fish in neon colors darted between the coral fans and formations. Zip, Reynolds, Carla, and Wilson went for a long snorkel and swim, exploring the beauty hidden beneath the surface, while Zoe and Poppy played children's games supervised by cruise line employees in a corralled enclosure underneath a large pavilion. When Zip went over to collect the kids for lunch, she observed Zoe and Poppy engaged in a competitive game of hopscotch with some girls near their own age.

"Hopscotch!" she remarked to Carla as they escorted the kids toward the shaded picnic table where Wilson and Reynolds waited. The two men looked relaxed, nursing tall glasses of draft beer.

"I know. So many kids today are glued to their iPads and computers. It is great to see the kids outside playing old-fashioned games."

"After lunch, we need to go back and finish our game," Poppy told Carla. "And then Miss Lillian is going to take us for a short swim."

"We promised we would be back in an hour," Zoe agreed. "We don't want to miss our fun activities, and you can do your adult things."

Zip laughed out loud. "Of course! We will be certain that you are back in time to participate in everything." It was wonderful that the girls had their own activities and were having such a good time. The trip would not have been nearly as relaxing or enjoyable if the parents had not been able to have their *adult* time.

Zoe gave Reynolds a big hug when they arrived at the table. The air was cool in the shade, fanned by a soft sea breeze. "Daddy, I placed second in hopscotch," she told him importantly. "Poppy and I need to be back in an hour so we can finish."

Reynolds tickled her under her chin. "Bunny, my little social butterfly."

"Let's get something to eat," Zip told her daughter. "But first, sunscreen."

"I hate sunscreen," Zoe pouted. "Jenny told me that it makes me look like a ghost."

"Who is Jenny?" Reynolds asked. "And what does she know?"

Zoe giggled. "A girl in the activity center. She said my skin is too white and I should get some sun."

"Tell Jenny I said you have red hair and must wear sunscreen. If she has an issue with that, tell Miss Lillian I would like talk to Jenny's mother."

Zip pulled out the large tube of sunscreen with zinc oxide and slathered it onto Zoe's shoulders, arms, neck, face, and legs. Zoe squirmed, but Zip was not deterred.

"It's cold," Zoe complained.

"Believe me, you will thank me when you are thirty. Sunburn hurts, and it would ruin your trip, so let's be cautious."

Zip smoothed the sunscreen onto her own face, neck, arms, and shoulders in the areas that were exposed. She gathered her wet hair into a scrunchie and put on her sunglasses before heading over to the enormous buffet. Uniformed employees of the cruise line served burgers, fish, chicken, and beef dishes on silver trays and chafing dishes. An entire table was dedicated to an assortment of salad dishes, cheese, and freshly baked bread. An ice cream trolley, manned by a cruise employee, served soft-serve ice cream and gelato in waffle cones. Employees dressed as characters from Hans Christian Andersen's stories strolled through the picnic area, much to the delight of the children. Zoe and Poppy seemed enthralled.

By the time that Zip returned to the table with plates for herself and Zoe, she saw that their new friends, Jason, Ruby, and Ian had joined them. Reynolds and Wilson were in deep conversation with Jason and Ian. Ruby was devouring a large hamburger, and her plate was heaped with onion rings. Her wet hair was pulled back into a ponytail and she wore no makeup, but she still looked gorgeous.

Zip smiled broadly. "Hello. Did you have a nice day?"

"It was wonderful!" Ruby replied. "And now we want to crash your party. I hope it is OK."

"It makes it more fun," Carla told her. "We are glad you could join us."

Carla and Ruby chatted amiably over their lunch. Poppy sat quietly beside her mother and picked at her chicken fingers and french fries. A cruise line employee came by with a pitcher of lemonade to wash down their meals.

Zip sat beside Zoe and coaxed her to eat a decent lunch. Like most children, Zoe was a picky eater, but she loved salad. Zip cut up her lunch, a lemon chicken breast, and Zoe's hotdog without the bun, as Zoe began eating her salad. Poppy, on the other hand, would eat only chicken fingers, which the cruise line had thoughtfully provided on the buffet.

Satisfied that Zoe would eat well, Zip turned her attention to her own plate of grilled fish, potato salad, and sliced tomatoes.

"According to the brochure left in our room, tomorrow is a sea day," Ruby told them. "I am going to be good to myself and booked some treatments at the spa. Care to join me?"

The *Golden Swan*, among its many high-end amenities, was equipped with a luxurious spa, offering skin care, massages, microdermabrasion, full salon hair and nail treatments, and even acupuncture.

Zip was not really the spa type. She had her long hair trimmed every twelve weeks at a salon in Madison Park but had never availed herself of spa treatments. Carla, on the other hand, frequented a spa at the University Village shopping mall twice a month.

"Let's book a facial and a massage, Zip! I will book the appointments when we get back to the boat." Carla said. "And the spa will serve us a salad for lunch."

"How much will it cost?" Zip asked. She was reluctant to incur too many more expenses. The cruise and trip to Bora Bora had been the most expensive vacation splurge she and Reynolds had ever made.

"It is part of the all-inclusive fee we paid," Carla replied. "And the girls will be fine. The Fairy Tale Center has something fun planned for them."

Zip decided that Carla was right, and she could not refuse. "Fine. You know that I have never even been to a spa."

"You will looooove it!" Ruby assured her.

"Okay, I am convinced," Zip replied.

"Where are we sailing tomorrow?" Carla asked, taking a bite of her cucumber salad.

"Cook Islands, the Aitutaki Lagoon," Ruby replied. "It will be a highlight of the trip. But it takes a day to sail there. It is very remote."

Aitutaki was a low coral atoll surrounded by a shallow lagoon filled with exotic fish and unique coral formations. It was considered another jewel of the South Pacific and was a tourist mecca. Reynolds had been eagerly anticipating the Cook Islands leg of their journey.

"So, it is a sea day—with time to ourselves—which we rarely ever have in Seattle," Carla said as she finished her salad.

Zip had to admit that it all did sound heavenly. Reynolds would hit the gym and swim tomorrow, and Zoe would no doubt be engaged in another fun adventure in the Fairy Tale Activity Center. Zip could have a spa treatment, relax, and read one of the best sellers she had loaded on her Kindle Oasis.

"I am in," Zip agreed. "And maybe I can have my hair trimmed. All of this salt water and chlorine is taking its toll."

"I will see what is available," Carla promised.

After the girls finished lunch, Zip took them over to the ice cream cart for chocolate gelato. Even Zip, who was usually very diet-conscious, ordered a small cone of strawberry gelato for herself. Both girls finished their waffle cones in record time. Zip dabbed the ice cream from their faces with a damp napkin and took them to the restroom before bringing them back to the outdoor pavilion.

Miss Lillian, despite the humidity, still looked fresh and crisp in her white uniform. Her hair was swept into a bun at the nape of her neck. Speaking in a soft French accent, she told Zip that she had grown up in Nice. Clearly the girls loved Miss Lillian. The woman gave them a big hug before they rushed back to resume their game of hopscotch.

Zip watched the girls play for a few minutes, intrigued by their seriousness and intensity. Zip remembered well the level of competition among her childhood friends in the games they played. It was always important to be good at games, and it made things so much fun. Zoe and Poppy were fully engaged in their game and clearly were having a good time. As she turned to rejoin the adults, she was again glad that she had booked the trip. And she was secretly looking forward to her spa day.

CHAPTER SIXTEEN

Zip gazed at the royal-blue waves of the South Pacific Ocean through the plate glass windows of the spa. The luxurious facility was located in the stern of the vessel, offering fabulous views of the endless watery landscape, as well as the endless ribbons of churning water from the ship's wake. At the oceanographer's brief lecture, which Zip, Carla, and Ruby had attended earlier that morning, he had explained that this area of the ocean was a vast wilderness with little ocean or air traffic. They had encountered no other ships or even small boats since leaving the western edge of French Polynesia. It was also immediately apparent that they had not seen any jets overhead. The passengers on the *Golden Swan* were all but alone.

The manicurist buffed Zip's fingernails with a clear, shiny buffing solution. Her nails looked both well-groomed and professional. Zip hated nail tips and the brilliantly colored fake fingernails sported by so many women in Seattle. She looked over at Ruby in the manicure station beside her. Ruby's fingernails were painted hot pink, but somehow it suited her.

Earlier that morning, Zip had treated Zoe to a pedicure. The nail specialist had painted their toenails a matching soft-blue color. Carla and Poppy used the same blue polish, so they all matched. Afterward, the attendant from the Fairy Tale Activity Center had escorted Zoe and Poppy back for the remaining activities planned for the children. Since it was a sea day, there was a special hamburger, hot dog, and fish and chicken finger dinner for the kids. Sea days were treated as special days, and the girls would not be ready to return to their room until 8:00.

Zip, Carla, and Ruby each had an hour-long massage followed by a facial and a steam bath. Ruby had regaled them with stories about her last trip to Banff and Jasper National Parks in Canada. Ruby's stories of the wildlife they had encountered were so wonderful that Zip promised herself that she and Reynolds would take Zoe there next year. At the end of the treatment sessions, Zip could not remember the last time she had felt so totally relaxed.

When Zip returned to the suite to take a nap before dinner, she found Reynolds feverishly typing on his laptop. He barely seemed to notice when she walked over and gave him a kiss on the forehead.

"Are you working?" she asked, noticing his furrowed brow, which always indicated that he was concentrating deeply.

"Yes. It is another work crisis. I have attended two conference calls since breakfast," he told her without lifting his eyes from the screen.

"I am taking a nap. Wake me in an hour so I can shower before dinner," she said.

Zip slept soundly and was still dreaming when Reynolds gently put his hand on her shoulder. "Time to get up, beautiful," he said, sitting down on the bed beside her. "It is almost 5:00 o'clock."

Zip rolled over and gave him a groggy smile. "I need to take a shower and wash my hair before dinner. I still have that sticky cucumber mask in my hair from my facial."

"Your skin looks smooth," he said, running his hand across her cheek.

"I hope so. The spa treatments are not cheap, but it was a fun girls' day." She sat up and swung her legs over the side of the bed. They still felt like jelly.

"We need to talk," he said softly. "Something has come up."

Zip recognized the signs immediately. He was not looking at her directly. Reynolds was going to tell her something he knew she would not like.

"What is it Reynolds? What is wrong?"

"I need to go back to Seattle. There is a crisis at work, and Jim is putting pressure on me to come back early. I am worried that if I don't, it will impact my job."

Jim was Reynolds's work supervisor from hell, a man without a life or interests beyond work. Jim considered anyone who had a family or interests outside of work to be a slacker. Zip could see the concern etched in her husband's forehead. She was furious with Jim. This was their dream vacation, but she knew it would be wrong to talk Reynolds into staying on the trip. The pressure from Jim at work would certainly negatively affect Reynolds if he did not return. The trip was ruined now. Reynolds would be panicked if he stayed, and she would feel guilty if she badgered him to stay. The situation was a dilemma and Jim, as usual, had won as he had so many times before. Reynolds had made so many sacrifices in the past for his job and, once again, Jim was ruining a once in a lifetime family trip.

"Is there anyone else who could handle this? Jim knows we are on a family vacation."

"Zip, he is a fucking ass, and we both know it. He is demanding that I come home."

She chose her words carefully. "It seems that he has left you no choice."

Reynolds shook his head. "There is no choice if I want to keep my job. I will make it up to you and Zoe, I promise. I am so sorry."

"When would you leave? We are essentially in the middle of nowhere. We have not seen any other ships since our last port, and there aren't even any planes flying overhead. Even the lecturer this morning said we were in an area less frequented than the North and South Poles."

"The cruise line told me there is a flight from Rarotonga to Auckland. From there, I could fly directly to Los Angeles on Air New Zealand and then on to Seattle. Jim said the company will cover the extra expense."

"So less than forty-eight hours?"

"Yes. Our port tomorrow is Aitutaki. It is a small place, so I will need to wait until Friday morning to leave from Rarotonga. There is a larger airport there."

"Well, we will at least have tomorrow, one of the highlights of the trip."

"I am sorry, Zip. But we can still enjoy another full day of fun and adventure together."

Zip was livid with Jim, but she could not be angry with Reynolds. "Well, I suppose we are lucky that he did not demand that you come home earlier."

Reynolds gave her a hug, and she could feel his relief that she was not angry with him. She hugged him back.

"You are the best, Zip."

"Zoe will be disappointed. She is such a daddy's girl."

A cloud passed over his face. "I know. I feel guilty about it. But I know the two of you will have a wonderful time. And maybe we can do something special this summer to make up for it. What about a week-long cruise to Alaska?"

"You are on, mister. I will hold you to it. I am just glad we have already had so much fun."

"And tomorrow is the fabled Aitutaki Lagoon."

"I can't wait," she agreed as she stood up and stretched.

Reynolds stood up and lifted her off of her feet, causing Zip to giggle uncontrollably. "Let's make the most of the time we have left," he said as he carried her toward the marble bath.

Zip smiled in spite of her disappointment. She would not allow Jim to ruin their trip. There were still exciting days ahead.

CHAPTER SEVENTEEN

The *Golden Swan* had already dropped anchor beyond the vast barrier reef encircling the shores of Aitutaki when Zip and Reynolds woke up the next morning at 6:30. The largest settlement, Arutanga, was visible from the expansive windows of their suite. The lagoon surrounding the coral atoll was a shimmering turquoise rimmed with pale aqua in the shallow regions.

Zip had packed a beach bag with towels, a clean pair of shorts, sunscreen, and their snorkel gear the night before. She quickly freshened up and put on her newest one-piece swimsuit from Nordstrom, a flowing cover-up, and sandals. She brushed her hair into a long ponytail and shoved her hat and sunglasses into the bag. As she dressed, she noticed that her skin still glowed from her facial. She decided to skip makeup for the day and wear only sunscreen and lip gloss. She felt healthy and alive. All of these daily adventures reminded her of her days at summer camp as a child. Life had been so simple then—nothing to worry about except having a good time.

Reynolds helped her get Zoe out of bed to brush her teeth and get dressed. They were all ready and headed out of the door for breakfast by 7:15. They decided to eat a quick meal in the main dining room, which offered fruit, pastries, juice, and omelets made-to-order. Zip prepared a breakfast of fruit, a croissant, and cold cereal for Zoe. She and Reynolds both ate a light breakfast of fruit and oatmeal and made-to-order vanilla lattes. By 8:30, they had retrieved their bag and snorkel gear, dropped Zoe off at the Fairy Tale Adventure Center with Miss Lillian, and headed to the auditorium to wait for their tender to take them ashore to the Aitutaki Lagoon and One Foot Island excursion.

Zip and Reynolds obtained their stickers for the assigned tender to take them to their meeting point on shore and found a seat near the stage. The activities director assured them that there would be less than a ten-minute wait before departure. Zip scanned the crowd. Carla and Wilson had not yet arrived. She noticed Ruby, Jason, and Ian a few rows behind them and gave them a smile and a wave. Ian was deep in conversation with the couple. The room was extremely cool, and Zip shivered.

A PowerPoint with breathtaking images of the Cook Islands played in a loop on the screens located strategically in the main theatre. The underwater shots captured the expansive variety of sea life in the Aitutaki Lagoon. Photographs of the uplands showed small volcanic fields that had been cultivated to grow fruits and vegetables. The area was the proverbial paradise. The Cook Islands were an unspoiled wilderness, first explored by the Polynesians almost eight hundred years earlier. The fabled Captain Bligh of the HMS *Bounty*, forever chronicled in the *Mutiny on the Bounty*, commanded the first European ship to venture into the Cook Islands at the Aitutaki Atoll. According to the maps and captions on the screen, it was an isolated area. Today, the Cook Islands were governed by New Zealand, an island nation below the Australian continent accessible only by more than four hours by commercial jet and across the international date line. The Cook Islands were hundreds of miles from French Polynesia and felt impossibly remote.

Carla and Wilson joined Zip and Reynolds a few minutes before 9:00 with their stickers in hand. "We overslept," Carla explained as she sat down in the seat next to Zip. "After the spa and a few frozen fruity drinks last night, I slept like a baby. Fortunately, Antoine arranged for us to have coffee and a simple breakfast in our room. I just dropped Poppy off at the Fairy Tale Center."

"I feel relaxed, too," Zip replied. "I was thinking this morning that this is like summer camp—divorced from reality in a remote place and every day is a new adventure."

"It is like being a kid again. I have loved it," Carla smiled. "And I am so glad that we all did this."

"It has been wonderful. I just hate it that Reynolds has to leave tomorrow."

Carla gave her friend a hug. "Oh, I know—Reynolds told Wilson. It is awful, and his boss must be a complete jerk. But don't worry. Wilson and I will take care of you and Zoe after he leaves. We will still have lots of fun."

Zip grinned. Carla was such a good friend. "I know. And I will have some good mommy time with Zoe."

The activities director called their number, and they filed in line for the theatre exit. The lifeboats were used as tenders to ferry the passengers through the narrow aperture of the lagoon and through the shallow waters to the dock. The boats were enclosed and stuffy inside. Zip noticed a large mesh netting that enclosed a raft of life vests hanging on the wall.

They arrived at the dock in less than fifteen minutes. Zip noticed that the water was crystal clear. A few yellow tropical fish circled one of the dock pilings in a lazy eight. Their guide explained that the fish were waiting to be fed.

Despite the fact that it was not even 9:30, the air was hot and humid, and the sun was strong. Zip was glad she had brought her sun shirt to protect her back and shoulders as she was snorkeling. She slipped on her wide-brimmed hat, which she pulled down securely over her forehead.

Another small shallow-hulled vessel transported their small group to the Aitutaki Lagoon. The guide pulled the boat onto a sandbar that was covered in less than one foot of water. Less than half a mile away, a glistening beach on an island covered in palm trees was visible. The guide explained that this was Honeymoon Island.

Zip and Reynolds put on their snorkels, masks, and fins before disembarking the boat. The lagoon dipped down suddenly like a large bowl onto a sandy floor about twenty feet deep. There were enormous coral heads covered with giant clams—most more than two feet across—with large siphons. A giant silvery-blue trevally weighing almost seventy-five pounds greeted them as they submerged into the warm waters of the lagoon. Reynolds had explained to Zip that the giant trevally was an apex hunter that followed large predators in the hopes of sharing prey. Zip gazed into the huge eyes of the fish that seemed to anticipate her every move and followed her and Reynolds as they explored the beauty of the lagoon. They continued to snorkel for nearly two hours, discovering the coral heads and tropical fish.

Carla and Wilson were waiting for them on the boat as Zip and Reynolds reluctantly emerged from the lagoon.

"Man, I could have stayed there all day," Reynolds told them as he dried off. "I am glad I got to see it."

Zip knew that Reynolds hated to leave. He was already thinking his vacation was over and was worried about work.

"It was amazing," Zip said. "I could do it all over again."

When all of the passengers in their group came aboard, the guide took them to see Honeymoon Island, where they walked among the palm trees for about thirty minutes. They spent the remainder of the afternoon on One Foot Island, another must-see destination of the Cook Islands.

It was nearly 4:30 when their guide dropped them back at the dock and ferried them to the ship. Upon reboarding the ship, Zip noticed a small throng of passengers surrounding a group of uniformed officers who were pushing a gurney toward a helicopter pad. The sheet cover was stained a crimson color, and the woman lying on the gurney was ashen. Zip was startled to realize that the woman on the gurney was Ruby. Jason was leaning over her talking to her quietly. Ruby's eyes were closed.

"Oh my god, that's Ruby! Look at all the blood! What happened?" Carla covered her mouth with both hands in shock.

An overweight woman from the UK turned to Zip and Carla. "A shark bit her foot off. She was wearing hot pink nail polish, and it thought it was blood. I think he bit her on the leg, too."

"Where are they taking her?"

"I think they are flying her to a hospital in Rarotonga. The ship's doctor is going with her."

Zip felt a sudden chill of terror. This was a vacation. How could such an awful thing happen in paradise?

CHAPTER EIGHTEEN

The ship's doctor sent word to Five that Ruby had died overnight. She had been attacked by a gray reef shark that had found its way into the lagoon. It was an extremely rare occurrence because the gray reef shark generally inhabited the deep waters surrounding the coral atoll. The animal had been huge—about six feet long—and easily overwhelmed petite Ruby. The shark had severed her right foot and had bitten her across both thighs severing her femoral artery. Her injuries were so severe that she had nearly bled to death by the time the helicopter landed in Rarotonga. The doctor and local physician at the small medical clinic in town had amputated her leg and tried to repair the artery without success. Ruby never regained conscious-ness after the surgery.

Ruby's body would be placed in a cadaver cooler on Deck 3 to be sent back to Papeete. The existence of the cadaver cooler was a closely guarded secret by the Paradise Line. But Five knew that coolers to accommodate dead bodies were standard equipment aboard ships. Death, especially of elderly passengers, occurred with regularity on cruise lines. The Paradise Line had an efficient protocol for the crew to deal with death. The deceased were quietly and secretly stowed in the cadaver cooler so as not to spoil the vacation for other passengers. Death was an unwelcome intruder into the continuing excitement of the cruise life.

Ruby's injury had frightened a number of passengers. As expected, several of the vacationers had cancelled snorkeling excursions or other water activities, resulting in a loss of revenue for the Paradise Line. Hiking trips, which had been the least popular activity, were suddenly oversubscribed. People were nervous about killer sharks, and several passengers could be heard loudly complaining that they were anxious to return home because the waters were dangerous.

Five sat in his living room suite with Jason, Christian, and Mark eating the breakfast that Alistair had laid out for them. Jason was understandably somber; Ruby was the love of his life. But she had died serving the Cause. She had achieved glory and would ultimately be buried at sea when the ship sank.

There was an air of excitement that practically electrified the room. Today was *the day*. Tonight, after the ship sailed from Rarotonga, the mission would commence.

The jagged, dark-green mountains of Rarotonga arose in the distance as the ship dropped anchor in the turquoise waters. The view was stunningly beautiful, but the team was focused on the last-minute preparation for the evening. Each of them had previously booked a half-day excursion so as not to arouse suspicion. They would each be rested and prepared for the tasks ahead. The mission would commence exactly at 9:00 p.m., three hours after the vessel departed Rarotonga.

When the ship had moored, the process of the lowering the tenders to ferry passengers to shore commenced. Shortly thereafter, a Cook Islands government boat sporting the flag of New Zealand, pulled alongside the *Golden Swan*. Five uniformed officers disembarked and boarded the ship. The crew and any passengers who were witnesses to Ruby's accident would be interviewed. Jason had given a statement to the authorities on the dock in Aitutaki. Any death on a ship was investigated by the vessel flag or local authorities. This was an unforeseen complication that the team had never expected. Their goal was to blend in and appear to be normal passengers. The irony that Jason was interviewed by the Cook Islands authorities as a victim was not lost on any of them. But they were all concerned that they do nothing to arouse suspicion that would interfere with their mission.

Five noticed one of the ship's tenders as it began the twenty-minute journey toward Rarotonga. He knew this was the tender taking Reynolds to Rarotonga. The team had initially planned to kill Reynolds rather than allowing him to return to Seattle. The plan had been simple. They would invite him for a nightcap, drug his drink, and toss him overboard. Their instructions from the Cell had been clear: there were to be no survivors. There could be no witnesses who could provide information to the authorities. Information was power and could jeopardize future missions in serving the Cause.

But Ruby's death had changed things. The officers and crew on the ship were hypervigilant in guarding the safety of passengers and soothing their nerves. The presence of local uniformed authorities on the ship created unrest. Another unexpected death could potentially derail the mission entirely. The team had discussed the issue carefully, evaluating all potential ramifications. Christian had been adamant that it was unwise to allow Reynolds to leave the ship. But Mark and Five had argued heatedly that they needed to be flexible and adapt to the new development. The flight from New Zealand to Los Angeles was almost fifteen hours. By the time Reynolds arrived back in the United States, the *Golden Swan* would be at the bottom of the Pacific Ocean.

Finally, they had agreed that there was too great a risk that a second death would spark yet another investigation once the ship reached Rarotonga. Two deaths in twenty-four hours of young, vibrant people would cause suspicion. Further, unexplained deaths on cruise ships often became the focus of constant news stories. Any risk that could cause the mission to be defeated had to avoided at all costs. For that reason, they had collectively decided that allowing Reynolds to simply leave the vessel unharmed was the best course. Ruby's untimely death would be Reynolds's good fortune. He would be the sole survivor of the cruise.

But after the decision had been made by the team to spare Reynolds' life, Five had received a confidential communication from the Cell that shocked him to his core. He was instructed not to share the message with his team. Five was surprised to learn that Reynolds was *the American* who had been instrumental in planning the mission for the Cause. Yet, despite his involvement, Reynolds was unwilling to die for the Cause. Five felt a wave of disgust and revulsion as he realized that Reynolds was a coward. Solemnly, he watched the tender until it was a mere spec on the ocean racing toward Rarotonga.

CHAPTER NINETEEN

Zoe was inconsolable after she hugged Reynolds goodbye on Deck 4 near the disembarkation ramp. Zip carried her daughter upstairs to their suite to wash her face and calm her down. Zoe was too despondent to go to the Fairy Tale Activity Center, so Zip had promised to spend the entire day with her daughter. They booked a private tour that included a trip to a pearl farm, a beach outing, and a boat ride on a glass bottom boat. After the ship sailed that evening, they would dine on the balcony of their suite, a fine end to a real mother-daughter day.

Rarotonga was incredibly beautiful, with soaring mountains with jagged peaks against a cloudless sky. Zip and Zoe met their driver on the dock tarmac after disembarking from their tender. The driver, Elias, drove them through the area, stopping at a pearl farm that cultivated the coveted South Seas black pearl. The actual farm was located in the northern Cook Islands, but this farm served to demonstrate the process. The oysters were seeded and looped together on a long rope in a saltwater pen protected by a steel mesh enclosure. On a whim, Zip bought Zoe a small peacock pearl drop necklace in the gift shop before returning to the Jeep where Elias waited patiently for them. The prices here for pearls were noticeably cheaper than Tahiti, and the necklace seemed to lift Zoe's spirits. They then took the glass bottom boat ride in a lagoon near a small hotel. Parrotfish could be seen darting among the coral heads and chasing the smaller neon fish. Afterward, they relaxed in lounge chairs placed under a shade tree on the beach, listening to the relaxing sound of the waves. They decided not to go into the water; everyone was on edge after Ruby's shark attack. A hotel attendant served them fish tacos and tall glasses of lemonade before Elias picked them up to return to the drop-off point to catch the tender back to the *Golden Swan*.

Reynolds sent Zip a text from the Auckland Airport. "Boarding flight soon. See you at home next week. Love and miss you. Kiss Zoe 4 me."

The text made Zip miss Reynolds even more. It was not same without him. She and Zoe sent a return text. "We miss you. Zoe cried. Safe travels. Not the same without U. Love, Zip."

The tender ride took only ten minutes to the ship. They took the elevator back to their deck. Antoine had thoughtfully left them a pitcher of strawberry lemonade in the refrigerator along with some lemon cookies. Zip poured them each a glass, and they went out to sit on the lounge chairs on their balcony while getting their last look at Rarotonga. It was nearly 5:00 o'clock, and the sun was starting to edge down the mountaintops.

Zip connected to the ship's Wi-Fi and checked her phone, hoping that Reynolds had sent her another text. There was no other message. He was probably en route back to the US. She sent him a text anyway, letting him know that they had had a great day and asking him to text her when he arrived in LA. On a whim, she checked the weather in Seattle. It was raining and a chilly 38 degrees. It seemed impossible to imagine after the last ten days in the tropical warmth. She plugged in her iPhone to recharge and put her purse on the shelf in the closet.

"I know what we should do," she said brightly to Zoe, mustering all of her enthusiasm.

Zoe looked at her patiently. Zip knew that Zoe still thinking about Reynolds.

"What, Mommy?"

"Let's get cleaned up and go shopping on the ship! I will buy you something fun to remember the trip."

Zoe furrowed her brow. "I want the nightshirt with the big green sea turtle on the front."

Zip smiled. "If they have it, I will buy it."

Zoe grinned and clapped her hands. Zip was relieved that Zoe was recovering from Reynolds's sudden departure. Children were nothing if not resilient.

They showered, and Zip washed and dried her long hair. She washed Zoe's hair and pulled it into a ponytail with a yellow rose on the clasp. Afterward, they changed into Tommy Bahama cotton slacks and shirts in a tropical flowered print from the store in University Village. Zip slipped on her gold sandals and surveyed their appearance. She realized how they had adapted to the tropical life. This had been so enjoyable. Maybe on their next trip they should go to Maui, she decided.

They perused the shops, and Zip bought Zoe two sleep shirts. Afterward they found a shady spot on the top deck as twilight appeared. The peaks of Rarotonga were dark shadows in the waning light. The captain announced that the anchor had been pulled up and they would be heading back to Papeete. Tomorrow would be another sea day. The engines sprang to life with a dull, audible hum, and a strong breeze buffeted Zoe's hair as the vessel commenced its voyage.

"We're off! Are you hungry?"

Zoe grinned. "Starving."

"What would you like to do? Go into the dining room and meet Poppy, Carla, and Wilson?"

Zoe shook her head persistently. "No. Let's have a girl's night like you said on the balcony."

"Sounds great."

They enjoyed the fresh air on the top deck and then returned to their suite with Zoe's packages. After scouring the room service menu, they ordered a light dinner: salad, fish and coconut rice, with lemon meringue pie for dessert. Antoine delivered their meal in less than thirty minutes, setting the table in the large dining room of their suite before excusing himself.

"I could get used to this," Zip told her daughter as they ate their meal. "It is such a luxury to have someone prepare our food and serve it. And there is no mess to clean up."

"Tell Daddy we need a cook when we get home," Zoe replied in a matter-of-fact tone.

Zip touched the tip of Zoe's nose. "You are so silly!"

The young child giggled. "Then we could just play all the time."

Zip grinned, thinking about the simplicity of how a child views the world. "It would be fabulous, but it would be too expensive. And besides, I do like cooking. Just not every day. I have no complaints at all." Zip did like to cook, but she hated trips to the grocery store. Her idea of luxury was home delivery of groceries from Amazon Fresh. And there were a number of fun restaurants in their neighborhood. Reynolds was good about taking them out to eat often.

Zip phoned Antoine after dinner to thank him for the meal. Within five minutes, IMade came and removed their dirty dishes. He was unfailingly polite, as always, asking them about their day.

Zoe told him about the pearl farm and proudly displayed her necklace. Zip was glad that despite the earlier trauma of Reynolds's departure, the child was enthusiastic about their day.

"Let us know if you need anything else. Have a good evening," IMade told them as he wheeled the cart away with the dishes.

Zip and Zoe brushed their teeth and then settled down on the couch to stream one of the many children's movies available on the flat-screen TV in their suite. Within minutes, both of them had fallen asleep.

Zip awoke to the sound of gunshots and screaming in the hallway. The clock face on the end table was not illuminated.

She rushed over to the suite door, peering through the safety peephole out into the hallway. She felt a surge of absolute terror and panic as she watched Alistair, one of the butlers assigned to the port side of the vessel, casually raise a handgun and shoot Antoine in the head. The shot was so forceful it blasted a large cavity above Antoine's right orbital area. The butler, still wearing his impeccably crisp *Golden Swan* uniform, fell backward onto the carpeted floor of the hallway. Blood gushed from the open wound, and Antoine's eyes were frozen in a state of shock. As she looked in the other direction, Zip could see the feet of an elderly couple crumpled on the floor at an impossible angle. She watched in horror as Alistair turned away from Antoine and fired the gun toward the couple. The woman whimpered in protest followed by a deafening blast.

What was happening? Was this a dream?

Zip drew in a deep breath and quickly engaged the safety lock on the door. She had to get to Zoe! On impulse, she grabbed a paring knife and her phone. She flipped off the television, turned off the lamp, and carried Zoe, still asleep, to the closet.

CHAPTER TWENTY

By 8:30 p.m., the ship was in the open water, at least fifty miles from Rarotonga. The vessel was now on the high seas in international waters, beyond the control of any local governmental authorities in the Cook Islands. The waves were noticeably higher, and the air was heavy with humidity from an approaching squall line. As planned, the team had disabled the security camera system aboard the ship at 8:45. The security detail monitoring the system was easily overtaken. All six men were quickly killed with automatics fitted with silencers. Once the security crew was dispatched, the team was free to move about the ship without fear of detection.

George had incapacitated most of the crew with the sarin that had been piped into the crew's quarters at 9:00 p.m. Sarin had been developed in Germany in the 1930s and had been refined during World War II. Today, the gas had been used as a powerful nerve agent, and most recently had been used in Syria. The chemical weapon smuggled aboard by the well-paid team of stevedores was known to be more than twenty times as powerful as cyanide. Sarin was clear, colorless, tasteless, and odorless. The team had determined it would be ideal for their purposes because by the time it was detected, it would be too late. The gas attacked the central nervous system, often paralyzing lung function and rendering its victims comatose. Studies had shown that death from sarin inhalation would occur within ten minutes from exposure.

Jason, Mark, and Christian, with the assistance of Alistair, had diverted the air intake of the HVAC system servicing the crew quarters, flooding the air with the poisonous gas. They had also activated automatic locks on the access holds. Most of the crew's quarters were inside cabins without portholes or access to fresh air. There would be no escape. By 9:00 every evening, the quarters were nearly full, except for the cooks, dinner servers, and bartenders. By that time, most of the cabin stewards had cleaned the passenger cabins before the guests returned from dinner. Most of the crew servicing the vessel had excruciatingly long hours, rising well before dawn. The crew took every available opportunity to sleep before another grueling day.

Death had been painful but reasonably swift. The team's best estimate was that at least three hundred crewmembers had perished. There would be no survivors. Christian sent a video clip to Five's tablet. It showed several of the crewmembers were dead in the hallway trying to open the locked door. The operation had been efficient.

There were still more than fifty crewmembers who would need to be dealt with individually over the evening, excluding the performers in the theatre. But the disabling and death of the majority of the crew was a real milestone for the mission.

Five accompanied George, Christian, and Mark to the bridge of the vessel at 9:45. They were dressed casually as if they had just come back from dinner. The three men waited discreetly in the vestibule to wait for George to enter the bridge.

Because George wore a uniformed shirt of the *Golden Swan* line, the captain, first and second mates were not initially alarmed as he entered the restricted area. The man Five knew was the second mate was busily studying some electronic instruments.

"Good evening, George," the captain said, greeting him with a smile. He had a strong Scottish accent. "The security system and cameras are off-line. I sent someone to check on the problem."

George returned the smile and walked toward the captain. "Excellent. I am sure you will get the problem under control. What is our next port?"

"Bora Bora. It is a long trip. Tomorrow is a sea day."

"It will be a busy day for me," George replied. "People always want to see the doctor on a sea day."

"Sea days are always busy for the crew," the captain replied. "The times when passengers are relaxing the most are the busiest days for the crew."

George gave the captain a friendly grin. "I am learning that. Actually, being a passenger on a cruise is certainly different than working on a cruise."

The captain and first mate turned their gaze toward Five, Christian, and Mark as they entered the bridge area. "May I help you?" asked the captain?

Five noticed that the captain looked younger than he had expected, maybe early forties, and was obviously very fit.

The first mate glanced at the captain knowingly before he approached the men. Five estimated that the young man in the perfectly pressed uniform was in his mid-thirties. He was impeccably groomed and wore a gold wedding band on his left ring finger. His brass name tag identified him as Ivan Kiev. His tone was firm but yet friendly, probably the result of rigorous training in passenger relations by the cruise line.

"I am sorry, gentlemen, but the cruise line does not allow us to entertain passengers on the bridge while the vessel is underway. But I am happy to arrange a tour of the bridge at the next port."

Without a word, Christian raised his left hand and shot the first mate point-blank in the chest. The golden swan on the officer's breast pocket immediately turned a brilliant red as his lifeless body sank to the floor, his eyes wide-open with a look of perplexed shock. The noise of the gunshot had been deafening.

Christian aimed his weapon at the captain. The second officer blanched, and he pressed up against the counter with the bank of electronic navigation systems.

"What the fuck are you doing?" the captain shrieked. "You have killed him!"

Five stepped forward calmly. "Captain Fortenberry, we are taking over your ship. There are some things that we need you to do, and you need to follow our instructions very carefully." Five paused allowing his words to sink in.

"What do you want?" the captain replied defiantly.

Five felt adrenalin coursing through his system. He had not felt so exhilarated or on high alert in his life. "First, we are going to turn the direction of the ship due south."

Captain Fortenberry's brown eyes widened. "South? There is nothing south of us but Antarctica, other than a small island or two. The farther south we go, the worse the weather and sea conditions will get."

"That's exactly right," Five replied. "Due south, 180 degrees. My colleagues will help you."

"You people are insane." Captain Fortenberry shook his head in resignation. From his demeanor, it was clear to Five that he knew there was no escape. They were in such a remote part of the world and they did not stand a chance of escaping.

Five approached the captain, watching his every movement. The man was cornered, and like a wild animal, this was when people were the most unpredictable. Five knew that there was a gun on the bridge for just this occasion. He needed to be careful.

"Captain Fortenberry, keep your hands where I can see them. You need to forget about the .45 in the compartment by the window. Now, I want you to follow instructions. Here is what I want you to do. It is all very simple, and we just want three things from you." He waited, scrutinizing the captain to be certain he understood his instructions. "First, we are going to turn the vessel due south. You will give your second mate the go-ahead to help you."

The captain nodded without a word, angrily staring Five.

"Second, we want you to call a meeting of the crew and senior officers. Third—and finally—we have an email we want you to send to the head office of the *Golden Swan* in Miami." Five gave the man a warm smile. "See? Easy."

The captain glared at him, never breaking eye contact. Five noticed that George had drawn his handgun that was aimed toward the captain. Of course, the captain knew he was powerless to overcome the armed men, but there was no guarantee that he would not try. Most men under these circumstances would wilt in fear, but Captain Fortenberry was a fighter, and he was visibly enraged.

"Are you going to cooperate with us, or do we need to kill the other officer now to make our point?

"I will do what you want," the captain replied angrily. "What choice do we have?"

"Good," Five said calmly. "You are right. You have no choice. We are in control."

Five nodded to Mark and Christian. Both men had received intensive training in vessel operation in preparation for the mission. Before they dispatched with the captain, it would be important to have his assistance in setting the vessel on the proper course. Mark and Five walked over to the second mate, who was still cowering in the corner. Five noticed that he had soiled his uniform, a yellow stain now appearing on his white slacks.

Mark patted the shoulder of the second mate. "What is your name?"

"Kirby Daniels," he replied in a tremorous voice. "I will do whatever you need. Please—I have a wife and two young kids."

Mark continued to rub the young man's shoulder, trying to calm him. "Everything is going to be fine, Kirby. Let's just do what we need to do. First how much fuel do we have?"

Kirby pointed toward the blue light of the electronic fuel indicators. "We have not consumed much. We picked up fuel in Rarotonga for the trip back."

"Good. Let's program our course and turn this bad boy around so we can head due south. I have always wanted to visit Antarctica. Deal?"

Kirby stared at the instrument panel silently, tears running down his face. "Deal," he said softly.

CHAPTER TWENTY-ONE

Zip's mind was racing, and she was consumed with a fear she had never known existed. She heard someone, who she recognized as Alistair, try to open the door to the suite. Instinctively, she ducked into the large walk-in closet of their suite.

She had to think! At all costs, she needed to protect Zoe.

She could hear a man yelling in the hallway, his cries punctuated by gunshots. Zoe was awakened by the noise and looked up at her mother quizzically.

"Mommy? What is happening?"

Zip gave her a daughter a squeeze and cupped her face in her hand. "Zoe, I do not know. But there is a bad man outside of our room doing bad things and hurting people. We have to hide."

"Why would he do that, Mommy?"

"I don't know, baby. But we need to hide. And we need to be quiet. You cannot say a word. That is the most important thing!"

Zoe began to cry. "I'm scared, Mommy! Let's hide under the bed."

Zip held the child close and whispered. "Zoe, there is no need to cry. We will be fine. I just need you to be a big girl and be quiet. All we have to do is hide until someone from the cruise line comes and takes the bad man away. Can you do that?"

Zoe sniffed and wiped the tears from her eyes with the back of her hand. "OK," she said quietly.

Zip's mind was buzzing. They had to find a safe spot. Underneath the bed was too obvious. There had to be someplace better. As her eyes adjusted to the light, she noticed the 32-inch suitcase that zipped up on three sides. Zoe could easily fit inside the case. It would be the perfect hiding spot. She reached for the case. Her hand trembled with fear as she unzipped the side.

She cupped Zoe's chin again and talked to her sternly. "Baby, I need you to listen to me. You will just fit into this suitcase. I will leave the side against the wall slightly unzipped, and I will be here behind the shoe rack. Can you be a big girl? Can you help me?"

Zoe shook her head. "No, Mommy. I might smother. I can't do it."

"Please, baby, please. I will be right here. After the man leaves, I will take you out! I don't want him to hurt us!"

She felt the child's heart racing. She was tired and confused. "Promise, it will be just for a few minutes?" whimpered Zoe.

"I promise. I will be right here. Nothing will happen to you. And when it is all over and we go home, I will tell Daddy what a big girl you were!"

Zoe looked dejected. "OK, Mommy."

"I will be right here. I promise."

Zip slid the little girl inside the case and shoved it against the wall. "I am here, baby. Just be quiet no matter what. I don't want that man to find us. This will be just like a game of hide-and-seek. Can you do that?"

"OK, Mommy," the child replied, her voice slight muffled from the canvas case surrounding her.

Zip wedged herself behind the shoe rack in the walk-in closet. It was not the best hiding place, but she needed to be close to Zoe.

"I am right here, baby. Mommy is right here, just a foot away," she whispered.

She heard the door to the suite swing open. Of course, the butler would have a master key to every room. Through the crack in the closet door, she could see that he had flipped on the living room and bedroom lights. She heard what sounded like someone opening the sliding doors to the balconies and a search of the interior of the cabinets near the bar. Suddenly, the lights in the dressing room were illuminated, casting a circle of light toward the closet. The man she had recognized as Alistair slid open the closet doors, scanning the floor. He stopped and jiggled the big suitcase.

Zip's heart jumped into her throat when she heard Zoe sneeze. Alistair knelt down and began unzipping the case. Zip could hear Zoe's muffled voice.

"Mommy, is the bad man gone?"

Her instincts to protect her daughter were swift and predatory. She dropped her cell phone, and with all the force she could muster, she raised her hand and buried the paring knife into the side of the butler's neck. She was amazed that it almost felt like cutting butter. She began tugging on the knife, slicing open a gaping hole in his neck. Blood spurted like a fountain as the butler dropped the gun and placed his hand over his wound.

Zip could feel the knife, slick with blood. She buried the knife again in the area she thought would be his right kidney. Instantly, she removed the knife and sliced his Achilles tendon. The butler turned his head and reached for her arm.

"You fucking bitch! I will kill you and your kid!"

Zip pulled her arm away and kicked the kneeling man as hard as she could in his lower back. He fell over onto his side. She stepped over him and kicked the gun into the dressing room before jumping on his back and stabbing him repeatedly below his left shoulder blade. It was as if she were on autopilot. She was only vaguely aware of Zoe's muffled crying from inside the suitcase. After what seemed like an eternity, the man stopped moving as he bled out onto the carpet. She dropped the paring knife beside him, thinking how just yesterday she had sliced a pear with the same knife for a snack.

Zip reached into the case and pulled Zoe out. The blood spatter had gone right through the canvas case covering Zoe in blood.

"Stay here, baby," Zip said, as she ran toward the suite door and locked it. With horror, she noticed the telltale footprints of the butler's blood on the carpet.

They could not leave a blood trail. Instinctively, Zip knew there were probably other killers on board. It was unlikely Alistair was acting alone. She and Zoe needed to stay hidden, and their bloody clothes would make them an easy mark. They needed to rinse off and change clothes. With a speed she did not know was possible, she removed their clothing, tossing everything on top of the butler. They hosed off quickly with the hand-held shower hose before quickly putting on clean slacks and T-shirts. Zip grabbed a small pack, filling it with snacks and her phone. She lifted the butler's gun, flipping the safety switch up, and placed the gun in the pack. Zip's father had worked for the FBI and had taught gun safety to all three of his daughters.

She had killed a man! How could that have happened? But it had been self-defense. She and Zoe would need to get to a safe hiding place to wait. This could not go on for long. These things did not happen on cruise lines. Someone would catch the killers and then they would be safe.

She carried Zoe through the sliding glass doors onto the balcony.

"Where are we going, Mommy? I'm scared," the child cried.

Zoe hugged her. "Don't be scared, baby. Mommy is going to take care of us. The bad man is gone. But I want to make sure there are no other bad men. OK?"

They managed to climb over the partition to the balcony of the adjoining suit. They would need to get as far away from the butler's body in their cabin as they could. The process was time-consuming with a child, but they finally found a quiet spot on a balcony three suites away. Zip cradled Zoe like a baby as they lay on a lounge chair wedged against the wall. The air had chilled, and a soft rain fell. She refused to allow herself to think about the emotional damage this experience would have on her daughter. Right now, they needed to simply survive.

Zoe stared out at the cool rain. The ocean had become choppy, and the waves were higher than they had been earlier in the day. And they seemed to be going in a different direction as well.

Something was drastically wrong.

After what seemed like forever, Zoe fell asleep in her arms. Careful not to wake her, Zoe powered up her cell phone, tapped in her password, and sent Reynolds a text.

"Boat hijacked. Zoe and I are OK but hiding." She pushed send. The message showed it was delivered. She tapped out another message. Before she could send it, however, the display showed no cellular data was available. Wi-Fi was unavailable. Instinctively, Zip knew that someone was jamming the signal.

Through the glass door, she could hear an announcement from Captain Fortenberry asking all passengers to come to the theatre. It was nearly midnight. None of this made sense to her. She could not comprehend why anyone would demand that families with children report to the theatre in the middle of the night. Besides, the crew always identified the ship room by name. She had observed that referring to locations on the vessel by name seemed to be a cruise line protocol. The announcement did not specify the Little Mermaid Theatre.

Was that really the captain, or was it someone masquerading as the captain? This all seemed wrong.

Zip weighed their options. On the one hand, the theatre might be the safest place. But the announcement from the captain could be a trap. There could be other killers trolling the halls who could ambush her. For the moment, she and Zoe were safe. She decided to stay on the balcony for now.

CHAPTER TWENTY-TWO

Five watched as Mark gave the captain the script email message for the ship's officers. The missive was perfect in its simplicity.

"There has been an emergency event this evening. Please proceed to Officers' Muster Station behind the Snow Queen Ice Bar at 10:15 p.m. We do not want to alarm any passengers or the crew. I am counting on your discretion so we can deal with the problem quietly. I will meet you there."

Mark proofed the email to make sure it was verbatim. The last thing he needed was for the captain to send an encrypted message or code to the crew. When he was satisfied that the email was correct, Mark pressed the send button to distribute the message to the LISTSERV of ship's officers.

George, as a senior officer, was on the distribution list for emails of this nature from the captain. George's ship-issued cell phone buzzed, indicating that he had received a message. He checked the screen and reviewed the message carefully before nodding to Five and Mark. "It's done," he said simply.

Captain Fortenberry looked at George with disappointment. It was clear to Five that the man's resolve was gradually crumbling. Clearly, he now recognized that the situation was hopeless. Five noticed that occasionally the captain allowed his gaze to drift over to the body of the first mate, crumpled in a large pool of congealing blood near the entrance to the bridge. The coppery smell of blood was pungent in the air, and what had been a work space of rigid organization had dissolved into chaos.

Officer Kirby, the second mate, continued to pilot the vessel due south. The young man stood at attention, quiet and compliant. Five had been taught during his training to recognize the variety of predictable human responses to a deadly crisis. In situations like this, some men, like the first mate, became defiant and confrontational. Others, like Officer Kirby, became extremely cooperative, hoping against hope that they would be allowed to live. Of course, Officer Kirby was simply kidding himself. There would be no survivors, and the young man would be dead within the hour.

Five typed the simple email for the captain to send to the Paradise Line's corporate office in Miami. Their plan was to send the email at precisely 11:30 p.m. By that time, the vessel would be more than eighty miles south of Rarotonga, far away from any adjacent island or landmass, and nearly all of the crew would be dead. The situation would be impossible.

Five stepped to the side of the computer so Captain Fortenberry could read the screen. The captain's face visibly blanched as he read the message.

"I know you have a code word to show that this is real. You need to tell us what it is." Five glared at the captain, his patience wearing thin. This was the only thing he needed from the captain.

The man stared at his shoes, which were polished to a high luster. Despite his desperate circumstances, he was still impeccably groomed.

"Don't make me shoot you in the kneecaps. Eventually, you will tell me. Why put yourself or Officer Kirby through that agony?"

Captain Fortenberry's shoulders visibly slumped. He took a long look at the first mate and then turned to Five. He gave an audible sigh, and a tear escaped from his right eye, slowing running down his cheek.

"Odense. It is the birthplace of Hans Christian Andersen," he said softly. "O-d-e-n-s-e."

Five studied the man's facial features carefully, looking for telltale micro-expressions that would show he was lying. But the captain was finally beaten. He knew that further fighting would be useless.

Five gently placed his hand on the captain's shoulder. Then he changed his tone as if he were talking to a friend.

"Thank you, Captain. Is there any special sequence of placement of the word in the email that is critical?"

"It should always be the first word of an emergency email."

Five typed the word Odense into the email. It was another simple missive:

Odense! At 23:30 the *Golden Swan* was taken over to serve the Cause. All crew is lost. Sinking imminent. Praise Allah!"

He turned the screen so the captain could easily read the text.

"Jesus Christ," the captain said softly.

"Is that all that is needed?" Five pressed him.

"Yes, they will know it is real," he replied, obviously overcome.

Five patted the captain on the shoulder. "I know this is hard, but it is a worthy sacrifice."

Before the captain could reply, George walked up behind him and slit the captain's throat with a scalpel. The captain grasped his neck and turned toward George. A torrent of blood poured from the gaping wound in his neck. The doctor shoved the man toward the body of the first mate.

"It will take him a minute or two to die. But he always has been an arrogant bastard. A bullet was too good for him," George said with a grin.

Five looked at George with distaste and disapproval. Without a word, he removed the automatic pistol from his waistband and shot the captain in the heart to end his suffering. He would deal with George later in the evening after the email was sent to the head office. The faithful did not engage in sadism to serve in the virtue of the Cause. But for now, he had to arrange to dispatch the senior officers. He needed to focus on the task at hand.

"Alright. The email is ready. We will send it at 11:30. Let's go down and take care of the officers."

CHAPTER TWENTY-THREE

By 11:30, the small group of ship's officers had gathered in the muster station behind the Snow Queen Ice Bar. There was a shiny brass plaque on the door in bold font stating, "Officers Only." Inside there were four large flatscreens mounted on the walls. Two of the screens contained navigational images and sea conditions. The other two screens were dark.

All eighteen officers were seated dutifully in the overstuffed sofas and chairs waiting for the captain's arrival. Because the officers' quarters were on Deck 6, separate from the crew's quarters on the lower decks, the officers had not been impacted by the release of sarin earlier that evening. Four of the officers were young women. Two of the young women were more junior officers and worked in the catering division. One was a blonde with her hair coiled carefully into a chignon. She was obviously less than thirty and her uniform, even after a long day, was creased and fresh. The young woman seated next to her was Asian with lovely porcelain skin.

Five, Mark, and George filed into the room. Five had memorized all of the officers' identities before he had boarded the ship. The quality of information available on the Internet was accurate. Five noticed the bleary eyes of several of the senior officers, who obviously had been awakened from a sound sleep. The man in charge of housekeeping was noticeably absent. Five knew that Alistair had managed to quietly deal with him while the man was working in his office on the sixth floor earlier that evening.

The group stopped talking immediately, their faces registering surprise at the arrival of the passengers. None of the officers were armed. They relied on the ship's security team who, unbeknownst to them, had been killed earlier that evening. When they had originally boarded the *Golden Swan*, the officers had relied completely on the security scanners and metal detectors on Deck 4 as a guaranteed safeguard against the entry of weapons. But the security protocol of the Paradise Line and the Port of Papeete had discounted the possibility of a security breach by the stevedoring team loading the vessel stores. A few well-placed bribes had assured that the sarin gas, handguns, assault rifles, and the plastique explosives would be easily loaded onto the ship. Security breaches were always best accomplished by those who were generally viewed as invisible: the cleaners and manual labor crews. These people often had access to areas that were viewed as safe. It was a clear gap in an otherwise vigilant security protocol.

Hans, a Danish officer who looked to be over forty years old, was seated in the front row. He stood up and gave the three a practiced smile. Five estimated that he was over six feet tall.

"This room is for officers only. It is off-limits to passengers," the man said imperiously to Five and Mark. He then looked pointedly at George. "George, you know that. What is the meaning of this?"

As the ship's doctor, George was considered an officer. He had been in the officers' muster station on several occasions on this voyage.

"They are friends of mine, Hans," George replied evenly.

"The captain will be angry, and they must leave now." Hans took a step towards Mark and Five. "Here, I will show you out."

Before Hans closed the short distance between them, George pulled an automatic from his jacket and shot Hans through the heart. The gun was equipped with a silencer, and the only sound emitted was a soft pop. Hans put his hand over his chest before falling forward in a crumpled mass near the doorway. He was clearly dead.

Most of the assembly of officers were transfixed by the spectacle. The two young women seated in the back suddenly leapt from their seats, seeking refuge under a large desk in the corner. They were still partially visible, flattened against the wall. Five thought almost remorsefully that it was a sad attempt to hide, something a child would have done to escape. He did not relish the thought of killing young women, but it had to be done. It was necessary to serve the Cause. He decided to deal with them last.

With military precision, the three men began systematically shooting the officers at point-blank range. Most of them did not struggle, surrendering to the inevitable. Within mere seconds, they had murdered fourteen of the officers. Only the women hiding under the desk and two younger officers were left.

Suddenly, the two men rushed Mark, knocking him to the floor behind the row of chairs. The heavier of the two men sat on top of Mark, slugging him repeatedly in the face. Five could see that both men were muscular, obviously spending a great deal of time in the gym. Together, they had easily overpowered Mark, beating him nearly unconscious. The smaller officer grabbed Mark's arm with the gun, firing off two errant rounds. One of the bullets hit George, and Five watched in amazement as the entire right side of George's head exploded, embedding bone and brain fragments into the ceiling. Before Five could react, the younger officer wrenched the pistol from Mark's hand and shot him in the chest and head. The other man scrambled towards George's body, grabbing his weapon.

Both men aimed their weapons at Five. The heavier man grinned sardonically. His otherwise perfect uniform was smeared in Mark's blood. His brass nametag was engraved with the name Officer Damian Oliver. Five recognized him as the officer leading the safety drill.

"What are you going to do now, motherfucker? You shoot one of us, the other one will shoot you. There is no way you are walking out of this room."

"Yeah, fucker, you did not count on this. You are toast," the smaller man hissed in what sounded like a Scandinavian accent. "The captain will have you locked up, or we will throw you overboard and feed you to the sharks. You won't last two minutes in that water."

The two young women, emboldened by the turn of events, scrambled out from under the desk, standing to the right of the two men. The women stared at Five with unbridled hatred.

Five's brain raced, trying to assess the circumstances. Clearly, he was outnumbered. They had lost control over this situation. But besides Kirby, there were only four officers left. They had limited ammunition and would be no match for the assault rifles that would be used on the passengers. He decided it would be pointless to fight these men now. Slowly, he backed toward the door of the room, all the while keeping his weapon trained on the two officers.

"Captain Fortenberry is dead. We killed him less than an hour ago. The first mate is also dead." Five watched their faces register surprise and disbelief as he hastened his backward pace toward the open door.

"That is bullshit," spat Officer Oliver. "You are all alone, and we are going to kill you."

As Five reached the door, he fired two shots, killing the Asian female officer. As he slammed the door behind him, he heard a soft pop and felt a sharp sting in his left leg. A large crimson patch bloomed on his slacks. He felt his leg. The bullet had only grazed him, so he could still walk. He managed to slowly run toward the theatre where Bridget and Lauren were waiting for the remaining passengers to assemble.

CHAPTER TWENTY-FOUR

James and Bunny slept in late on Saturday, recovering from their fantastic evening the night before. Two of James's clients from New York had taken them to dinner at The Ivy, followed by a delightful performance of *Tina* at the theatre. It had been nearly 1:30 a.m. by the time their train had arrived at their station. The two of them slept soundly, woke up a little before 8:00, showered, and dressed. James watched BBC News while Bunny finished her morning routine. Within thirty-five minutes, she emerged, her freshly washed hair cascading in long ribbons around her perfectly made-up face. She wore a pair of tight jeans and a sweater under a navy-blue jacket. James marveled that even after a late night, Bunny always looked perfect and refreshed.

About 9:30, they strolled down to the Green Horse and Saddle for a hearty brunch. There was a sharp edge to the wind. The late March sky was dark slate and threatening rain, typical for this time of year in England. Bunny's face turned a soft pink in the brisk wind. The Green Horse and Saddle had been recently purchased by a chain and been completely redecorated. The bar and old floors had been refinished and restored to a glossy mahogany, and the walls were painted a dark green. A large fire roared in the corner of the far wall. It was a cozy and popular place, bustling with locals enjoying Saturday brunch.

They found a table for two beside the fireplace and ordered brunch. James drank two cappuccinos and devoured a full English breakfast. Bunny, as usual, picked at her food, eating only yogurt, fruit, and a croissant with strawberry jam. She was concerned about her weight and fitting into her wedding dress. She had decided that between now and the wedding, she would be on a strict diet.

"The performance was brilliant, wasn't it?" she asked James dreamily. "I wish we could do this every weekend."

James carefully slathered his toast with butter. "It was brilliant but expensive. And I am saving every penny for the Maldives. Besides, going out with clients is business and is not the same thing as going out on a date with you."

She flashed her perfect smile. "I know, James. But you have such an exciting life. I have only been to the theatre in London's West End twice in my entire life, and I have never dined at The Ivy."

He bit into his toast. "Me either. But business is different. And the lawyers have expense accounts. It is not always coming out of their pocket."

"By the way, I heard from Noah and Tracey before I took the train into London yesterday. They are actually coming to our wedding!"

"Fantastic," James replied, still enjoying his toast. "Did you tell your mum?"

"I did. And a reservation was made for them at the hotel in Cambridge for their stay."

"Great," James said with more enthusiasm than he actually felt. The wedding planning was getting old, and every detail was examined and discussed until Bunny and her mother were sure that it would be perfectly executed. The ceremony was in a historic church in Cambridge followed by a reception in the nicest hotel in Cambridge. He knew it would be beautiful, but he was really looking forward to the trip to the Maldives where they could vegetate and relax.

After breakfast, they browsed through a couple of shops along the way home before stopping at the local Tesco. Bunny picked up a freshly made up pizza and ingredients for a salad for dinner. James was looking forward to a quiet evening.

His work phone began buzzing as they left Tesco to head home. The distinct sound of the ringtone had a jarring sound and sent him into high alert. The phone was the Lunar emergency phone indicating that somewhere in the world, there had been a maritime casualty requiring his attention. He shifted the grocery bag to his left arm and answered on the second ring. It was his boss, Reed Coleman.

"You need to come back to London. There has been a hijacking of the *Golden Swan* cruise ship. There is an emergency K&R Team meeting in the Lloyd's Building library."

James tried to ignore the bustling traffic noise and focus on the conversation. He had heard of the cruise line, but hijackings of such large cruise ships were rare. "Where did it happen?"

"Around the Cook Islands. It is an isolated area. It happened a couple of hours ago. Terrorists took over and about three hundred crew were killed. A number of passengers have been killed as well."

"Good God!" He could not imagine such a thing. And he was not sure he even knew where the Cook Islands were located.

"Get back here to London as soon as you can and take a taxi straight to the Lloyd's building. Pack a bag for a couple of days because this will not be resolved overnight. Abbie has booked you a room at the Leonardo. And bring your passport just in case."

"Alright, I will."

"And James, it goes without saying that this is a public relations nightmare. Discuss this with no one. See you soon."

Bunny looked at him quizzically. "Who was that?"

"It was Reed. There has been a work emergency. It is ve [...] have to go back to London for a couple of days. Let's get home. I nee [...] help packing a bag."

The two of them returned to their garden home. Bunny flipped on the BBC as she helped him pack his bag. The newscaster was already reporting the hijacking of the *Golden Swan.*

Bunny's face blanched. "Is that it?"

James shook his head. "Can you check the train schedule? I need to get back as soon as possible."

CHAPTER TWENTY-FIVE

Five took off in a running limp as he headed toward the theatre to meet Lauren, Bridget, and Jason. His weapon was safely stowed in the shoulder holster concealed by his designer jacket. Inside his pocket, he had extra ammunition. Once the passengers had assembled in the theatre, the execution would begin, and a recording would be made with the ship's equipment. Later, before the explosives were detonated, a video of the massacre of the passengers in the theatre and the officers would be emailed to the Paradise Line home office and CNN. Worldwide viewing of the pain and suffering of the infidels was crucial to the Cause and the accomplishment of its mission.

While the theatre massacre was occurring, Christian make certain that the *Golden Swan* continued its course due south. Now that Mark was gone, Christian was the only member of the team who was proficient in operating the ship. The team was counting on him to continue the voyage to the desolate regions of the Pacific. Of course, Christian did not yet know that George and Mark were dead. The team was smaller, but Five was confident the mission would be a success.

The searing pain in Five's leg was relentless. Rivulets of blood streamed from the gunshot wound staining his Nikes. His leg often failed to support him, and several times he had nearly lost his balance. He wondered if the bullet had fractured his tibia or destroyed the ligaments. There was no exit wound, so it was likely that the bullet was still lodged in his calf. But he knew there was nothing much he could do except tie the area with a tourniquet. Now that George was dead, Bridget and Christian were the only ones with medical training. Bridget had given Lauren some basic first aid training. Hopefully Bridget or Lauren could give him a shot. He would have to work through the pain and soldier on until the mission was complete.

Five's mind was on overdrive as he quickly descended the interior stairwell toward the Little Mermaid Theatre on Deck 6. He was still reeling from the fact that both Mark and George had not survived the ambush of the small cadre of officers. Only the team had been armed. Several of the officers had begged for their lives and cried. Others had accepted their fate with a stoic resignation. He had never expected the two younger officers to fight back. Five recalled now that their résumés had indicated that they were former naval officers and had served in the Middle East. Obviously, they had had combat training during their military service. Officer Oliver and his colleague had not been afraid and had easily overcome Mark and George.

The two officers were dangerous. Five had ignored that risk when he had reviewed the officer profiles. Did any of the passengers assembling in the theatre have similar training? The team would have to be more careful and keep their distance from every passenger who could suddenly rush them. The mission was nearly complete. They were so close and could not let anything stand in their way.

Sidestepping the throngs of passengers, he hugged the banister for support and maneuvered his way down the carpeted stairs. The mood was rather somber, and people could be heard questioning the reason for the gathering at such a late hour. Several of the younger passengers looked downright angry. The evening entertainment had ended more than two hours ago, so most of the passengers had already returned to their suites for the evening. Five noticed that many of the passengers had simply thrown on a T-shirt over rumpled shorts. The crowd was robotically following Captain Fortenberry's directive to meet for an unknown reason in the theatre. The crowd reminded Five of the flocks of sheep dotting the English country landscape placidly following their leader.

The size of the crowd was less than expected, but Alistair and his team had quietly dispatched most of the passengers on Decks 10 and 11 an hour earlier. These decks were the closest to the wheelhouse, the pool, and the upper deck areas. It was critical to cull as many passengers as possible so there were no fragmented groups that could surprise the team. As he had just learned, even a few men with misplaced bravery could thwart their efforts.

He wondered how many stragglers had remained on the upper deck swimming or drinking or simply enjoying the night air. They would likely be oblivious to the events going on below deck. After the theatre massacre, the team would sweep the upper deck for any small groups of errant passengers before the plastic explosives were detonated. Those people not killed by the team would perish in the blast and sinking of the ship. The explosives had been strategically placed in the hull of the ship in multiple locations. The placement of the explosives guaranteed that even if one blast were anemic, the collective force of the entire number of explosives would promise a quick sinking of the ship. The ocean depth in the location they were heading was more than 14,000 feet. There would be no survivors.

Five's reverie was interrupted as an older man grasped his arm. "Did you know you are bleeding? Are you hurt?" the man asked, stopping on the stairs beside Five.

"I slipped and fell earlier," he said simply, making eye contact with a tall man he estimated to be in his fifties. The man's ginger hair was thinning on the crown of his head, and Five noticed he had a comb-over.

"I am an orthopedic surgeon," the older man told him. "Why don't we find you a chair and I can take a look at your leg?"

"I am seeing the ship's doctor after the theatre meeting."

"You should not be walking on that leg. You may cause yourself more damage. In fact, you may need to be evacuated off the ship when we get back to French Polynesia."

"That would be a disappointment to my wife."

The doctor straightened his shoulders and grabbed Five's arm to support him down the stairs. "Look, with all due respect, the ship's doctor is just some general practitioner hack. I will come with you to see him."

"I appreciate your concern," Five replied, anxious to get away from the doctor. "I am meeting my wife. I will look for you after the meeting in the theatre." He gave the doctor a warm smile.

"Alright. I can understand why you would want your wife with you. I will sit in the back. Be careful."

"Perfect. See you soon."

Five patted the doctor's arm and grabbed the banister, hobbling toward the theatre. After the group was assembled, the doors would be electronically locked so the execution could begin.

The Little Mermaid Theatre was smaller than the cavernous entertainment spaces of most cruise ships. The theatre was one level and wide, spanning both the port and starboard sides of the ship. It was a unique configuration that offered excellent viewing to all of the attendees for any performance. There were a series of large, overstuffed sofas, benches, and comfortable chairs in lieu of the traditional theatre seating. A few rows of more traditional chairs lined the back of the room. Because it was a small space, the theatre was the ideal location for the planned execution.

Earlier that evening, there had been a spectacular show featuring Tahitian folk dancers accompanied by live music. The stage was now dark and empty, and the curtains were pulled closed. The scent of tropical flowers remained in the air. The cleaning crew had been dispatched as they were vacuuming the carpet shortly after the performance. Several crushed plumeria littered the floor next to an abandoned vacuum cleaner.

The room was eerily quiet as the passengers waited dutifully for Captain Fortenberry to appear. A few children slept in their parents' arms or were stretched out on the sofas. Wi-Fi had been disabled earlier, so those passengers trying to use their phones quickly gave up after a few minutes. Five sat quietly in a short row in the back near the doctor and his wife.

When the last of the passengers entered the space, the door was closed. Five heard a small click indicating that Lauren had engaged the electronic locks on both doors. There would be no escape. The video cameras mounted on the opposing walls sprang to life and projected a red glow. The recorder had been activated, and the event would be filmed.

Finally, Lauren, Bridget, and Jason slipped through the curtains and stood on the stage. Each of them carried a machine gun. A murmur rippled through the crowd. As Lauren raised her weapon, Five quietly unholstered his gun. Within seconds, the deafening sound of the machine guns pierced the air.

CHAPTER TWENTY-SIX

Zoe dozed in her mother's arms, still secreted in a dark corner of the outside balcony. The child had been terrified, and it had taken Zip nearly fifteen minutes to soothe her. They had to be quiet and stay hidden if they were going to stay alive.

Zip was wide-awake and adrenalin still coursed through her veins. She felt a hypervigilance she had never previously experienced. Her life had been very sheltered until that point: private education and living an ideal, safe life in Seattle. At home, there was little to worry about except for shopping for non-GMO foods for her family, getting plenty of exercise, taking Zoe to school, and working with her clients on their graphic arts projects. Things were nearly perfect at home, and she was ill-equipped to deal with a life-and-death situation for herself and her child.

She wondered about Carla, Wilson, and Poppy. Were they safe? If only she could find them.

The air was markedly cooler, and a light rain fell. A strong wind buffeted the canvas umbrella on the adjoining balcony. The sea conditions had deteriorated, and the water illuminated by the cones of the navigation lights was dotted with whitecaps. She could smell the pervasive scent of ozone signaling a thunderstorm.

There was a soft glow from the lights of the open-air pool area two decks above them. The ship's Wi-Fi had been disabled, and she could no longer get cell service. She shoved the phone into the outside pocket of her small pack. Fortunately, she had had the presence of mind to text Reynolds over an hour ago because now the opportunity was gone.

She thought again about the cabin butler she had killed. It had all seemed so unreal. But the man surely would have killed Zoe before her very eyes had she not intervened.

Zoe checked her watch. 12:44 a.m. Reynolds would be landing in Los Angeles in a few hours. The first thing he would do when he landed would be to check his cell phone. He would get her text and call the FBI. Of course, the US government would make a rescue attempt. The world would not allow a cruise ship with 800 people to die.

All she had to do was stay hidden. Help would be on the way, and they would be rescued.

Suddenly, there was a blast of gunfire appearing to come from the pool deck. Zip shivered with panic as she heard a woman's voice begging for mercy. The woman's pleas were cut short by the repetitive blasts of what sounded like more than one gun. These guns were different from the handguns that were used earlier that evening. Were these machine guns? Alistair's gun had been fitted with a silencer, as if he wanted to be as quiet as possible. Now, the hijackers did not care how much noise they made. Zip knew this was a bad sign.

The hijackers were clearly in control. She had to think! The gunfire and screaming were relentless. As soon as it stopped, it began anew.

Zip felt a deep empathy for the victims whose lives were cut short by a group of cold-blooded killers. She determined that the screams must have been from those passengers who were upstairs enjoying the night air, an evening swim, or a relaxing soak in the hot tub. There were a number of young couples on the ship who partied until the late hours. Like Zip, they had been in the prime of their lives. It all seemed so senseless.

They needed to stay hidden. What if someone started checking the balconies? Were she and Zoe safe here? Was it simply a matter of time before they were discovered? There was nothing she could do to protect herself and her child from a maniac with a machine gun.

Suddenly, Zoe startled and sat up in Zip's arms. "Mommy, what is that noise? It's so loud." She rubbed her eyes and yawned.

"Shh. Let's be quiet, baby." Zip stroked her child's hair and kissed her forehead. Zoe leaned back against her mother's chest.

"I'm scared, Mommy."

Zip continued to softly stroke Zoe's hair to calm her. They had to be quiet. "Don't be scared, baby. Mommy will protect you. But you need to do what I say. Can you do that?" She kissed the crown of Zoe's head. "Mommy needs you to be brave. I will not let anyone hurt you."

"I will be good, Mommy."

"That's my girl."

"I need to go potty bad, Mommy."

Zip sighed. She got up from the lawn chair and checked the sliding door. The door was locked. Her only option was to go back to their suite. Zip helped Zoe crawl through the dividers between the adjoining balconies until they reached their suite.

The cabin was dark, except for the lamp in the living room near the sectional. The door connecting the suite to the hallway was slightly ajar. Zip was tempted to close it, but decided it might be a signal used by the terrorists. As quietly as possible, she carried Zoe across the carpeted area through the bedroom into the adjacent bath.

"You go potty, Zoe, but do not flush. I will be right back," she whispered.

The child looked at her quizzically. "But Mommy, you always tell me—"

Zip put her hand lightly over Zoe's mouth. "Quiet, don't flush. You promised to do what Mommy said."

"OK, Mommy."

Zip tiptoed into Zoe's room and grabbed the child's life jacket. She pulled a cotton sweater off the silk coat hanger provided by the cruise line. It was cool outside, and she did not want Zoe to be chilled. Zip wanted a sweater too, but she could not bring herself to go into the dressing area where Alistair's dead body lay on the floor. She decided she would have to manage.

She looked at the marking on the life jacket in the dim light. In plain black writing, there was a label marked: "Deck 4, Station 11, Ugly Duckling Port Side."

Zip clearly remembered Officer Oliver telling them that this was their meeting point in an emergency. Perhaps Carla, Wilson, and Poppy were already there.

Of course, Zip had paid very little attention during the safety drill before the first sailing of the vessel. All of them had been so excited, and no one had ever dreamed they would be victims of a terrorist attack.

She tiptoed back into the bathroom where Zoe stood quietly waiting for her. Gently, she helped the child with her sweater and life jacket. "Here, I want you to wear this."

"It's bulky, Mommy."

"I know, baby. But Mommy cannot carry you, the pack, and the life jacket. Can you help me?"

"OK."

Once the child had the sweater and life jacket on, Zip picked her up and quietly walked to the front door. The life jacket was indeed bulky, but it was lightweight. She peered through the open door, shocked at the carnage and blood in the hallway. She could not allow her daughter to see this path of death or she would be traumatized forever.

"Let's play a game, Zoe. I want you to close your eyes and put your head against my shoulder. Can you do that?"

Zoe nodded. "Yes."

"And you won't peak?"

Zoe smiled. "I promise."

Zip checked both ends of the hallway to be sure none of the killers were waiting for them. Satisfied that the area was clear, she crept into the hall, stepping around the bodies of the elderly couple from next door. The smell of blood lingered in the air.

She needed to avoid the elevators. She would have to take the stairs seven levels down to the emergency station.

As she headed toward the interior staircase nearest to the stateroom, she saw the bodies of what appeared to be a couple and a small child. The woman's beautiful long blonde hair was spattered with blood and spilled over onto the chest of the man lying beside her. The man's body stretched over the child as if he were trying to protect her. Zip shielded Zoe's eyes as she moved in for a closer look to determine whether the little girl was still alive. The child was young, not more than six. Her China-blue eyes were open in a lifeless stare.

She was not alive.

Zip felt a surge of nausea as she recognized their faces. Carla, Wilson, and Poppy were dead.

CHAPTER TWENTY-SEVEN

Although the weekend trains typically ran less frequently, James managed to catch a direct fast train to Waterloo Station. As he hurried toward the exit, he checked his phone. A CNN reporter stood in front of the Paradise Line headquarters reporting on the hijacking. A headline in bold white text on the screen stated: "Estimated 800 passengers and crew die in terrorist attack on cruise ship." The blonde reporter, speaking in a crisp, clear accent, explained that a terrorist group believed to be from Yemen and calling themselves Cell 53 were taking credit for the attack. Videos of the attack had been emailed exclusively to CNN.

"They are calling it Good Friday Justice," she explained. "It is nearly 1:00 a.m. off the coast of Rarotonga in the South Pacific. It is a beautiful but isolated area, a favorite spot for honeymooners and the wealthy. Today, it has become a place of terror. There is no word whether a rescue attempt will be made or whether there are any survivors on board."

James flipped off his phone. The taxi line was nearly empty. He grabbed a black taxi instead of waiting for an Uber and gave the driver the address. The driver was an older, more experienced driver, and eager to engage James in conversation.

"I read on my iPad about a cruise ship in the South Pacific taken o by terrorists. Have you seen the story?"

"I saw it on my phone," James replied, trying to dissuade the driver from engaging in a lengthy conversation. "Terrible thing."

"My wife has been dying to take a cruise. But I don't like the idea. Now that they are terrorist targets, hell will freeze over before I get on one of those death traps."

James tried to appear interested, allowing the driver to ramble about the perils of cruising. As he gazed out of the window, he thought about the passengers' horror and the tragedy that children had been ruthlessly killed. The economic casualty would be extraordinary as well. After the grieving families recovered from shock, a cascade of lawsuits would follow. It was likely that attorneys for the cruise line had already been instructed. The passenger tickets also contained a forum selection clause. The cruise line would make a claim under the hull policy. The Lloyd's kidnap and ransom team, who were all former military officers, would also be involved in the coordinated rescue attempt. The sheer economic cost to the London Market would be felt worldwide.

James arrived at the front entrance of the Lloyd's building at 12:15 p.m. He carried an overnight bag over his shoulder, packed with clean shirts and ties. His laptop and other personal items were stowed in his pack.

The usual security at the front entrance on the ground level had been replaced with officers from Scotland Yard and officers armed with automatic weapons. A crowd of reporters with mobile camera crews gathered on Lime Street. Usually, this area was deserted on a Saturday, but today it bustled with a frantic crowd. He ignored the questions from reporters and entered the revolving doors. Security today was much more stringent. The guards agreed to store his luggage and pack, allowing him only to bring his laptop into the building.

The size of the meeting required that the group assemble in the old Lloyd's library instead of the boardroom on the top floor. The old Library that had been removed from its former location and installed in the modern building. It was a grand historical space with a spiral staircase and priceless paneled walls. The library was located below ground level and was only accessible from the interior escalator of the Lloyd building. It was a secure space with no exterior windows.

In the atrium, there was a display of treasures in glass cases from General Nelson. A small group was clustered outside the library deep in conversation. A few white-coated caterers were preparing long portable tables with white cloths. The meeting was expected to last all hours until the crisis was over. James found a seat near one of the paneled walls in the crowded room.

There was a beehive of activity. The assembly teemed with diplomats, politicians, international law enforcement personnel, members from various branches of the British and the American military, members of the foreign service, insurers, and at least two representatives of the Paradise Line who happened to be in London for insurance renewal. James's boss was seated in the front along with representatives from the British Secret Intelligence Service, also known as MI6, the CIA, INTERPOL, the International Crime Court, the International Crime Bureau of the International Maritime Organization, a general of the US Navy, and three of the P&I Clubs. The ambassador from New Zealand was in close conversation with two military officers and the K&R Team from the London Market. The hijacking of the *Golden Swan* and the ruthless assassination of so many on board was an international crisis of the greatest magnitude. The passengers and crew were citizens of many countries, and the victims' deaths would be felt by a number of nations.

Another television monitor rested on a rack near the corner. The screen conveyed satellite images of the seas below Rarotonga. A large map of Oceania was mounted on a stand near the door.

Simpson Waters, the most senior member of INTERPOL in London, stood on the dais and began the meeting. "Ladies and gentlemen, the area of the attack, as we all know, is in an area of the South Pacific region called Oceania. The Cook Islands are eleven hours behind GMT. It is a desolate area riddled with sharks. Military drones have been launched, and all of the data from the electronics on board indicates that the ship appears to still be afloat. Rescue attempts will be a challenge because of the isolated location. The hijackers have completely taken over the ship. We do not know what has happened to all of the crew, but they are presumed dead. The senior officers, including the captain, were brutally assassinated, and at least four hundred fifty passengers were slaughtered." Waters nodded to his assistant to show the email and the two videos to the group.

James stared in horror at the video screen installed over the dais as he watched the massacre of the hundred passengers in the Little Mermaid Theatre. Two women and two men, each armed with assault rifles, machine guns, and automatic pistols, ruthlessly slaughtered men, women, and children at close range, ignoring their screams and pleas for mercy. Thirty or so women and young children huddled in the back of theatre, scrambling to escape through the locked theatre doors. The two female terrorists savagely stalked the group, spraying them with bullets from their machine guns until every one of the passengers in the huddle had been killed. Chairs, benches, sofas, and chaise lounges in the theatre were riddled with bullet holes and drenched in blood. The gruesome carnage of the dead bodies littered the furniture, floor, and aisles. The atrocity was despicable and unimaginable.

The team of assassins were well-dressed and attractive. From all outward appearances, these people fit the profile of the upscale passengers who were the lifeblood of the Paradise Line. No one would have ever suspected that this cadre of people were stone-cold killers.

The video had been emailed to CNN and the head office of the Paradise Line. The second video attached to the email was a short clip of the execution of the second mate. The camera panned the bridge, capturing the dead bodies of Captain Fortenberry and a man identified as the first mate. The subject line of the email stated only "*Golden Swan* Hijacking." The text of the email was brief:

"The videos attached depict the important work of Cell 53 dispensing Good Friday Justice. Death to the Infidels, Glory to the Cause! There will be no survivors, but their deaths will serve the Cause."

The crowded room was eerily silent as the video ended. Clearly everyone in attendance was shocked by the horror depicted. The scenario seemed almost unreal. Few assassins recorded the murder of their victims in such a callous way.

Henry Pratt, a representative of the American embassy in London, finally broke the silence. The man appeared to be in his late forties with the confident air of a person who had spent his entire career in the foreign service. "Jesus Christ, how could this happen?"

"Do we know if there are any survivors?" asked one woman in the back.

"We are trying to find that out," Waters replied somberly.

A US Navy general stood up to address the crowd. "The ship is apparently headed due south toward Antarctica. Australia and New Zealand have dispatched rescue efforts toward the ship, but it is in a remote area and more than four hours away. The president has ordered a rescue attempt from our base in American Samoa with Navy SEALS. We do not know if there are any survivors."

"Do we know the identity of the terrorists?" asked a member of the Paradise Line P&I Club.

"We have run facial recognition from the video to the security photos taken by the ship and emailed the results to the head office of the Paradise Line. The men and women in the video were all traveling under an alias, as you might expect."

Waters paused and nodded to his assistant. Security photos of the team were displayed on the screen. With a click of the cursor, Five's photograph dominated the screen. James sucked in his breath. The man was obviously fit, youthful, and handsome—an unlikely terrorist.

"The team leader is a man from a wealthy family in Kuala Lumpur with degrees in chemistry from Oxford and Berkeley. His given name is Ashraf Mayang, but he is traveling under the name of Ian York. He was married to the daughter of a prominent San Francisco attorney, but the marriage was annulled. He worked for a big pharmaceutical outfit, but he quit his job suddenly and returned to England. For a while, he was staying in Knightsbridge, where he may have connected to a terrorist group. Somehow, he became disenfranchised and was trained in Yemen. His Cell name is simply Five. He has no criminal history. As you might expect, his parents are shocked and heartbroken."

Without waiting for a comment, he brought up the photos of Ruby and Jason. "The woman was traveling under the name Ruby Lombard. She was from Saudi Arabia, and her name was Mary Shah. Her purported husband had the alias and passport for Jason Lombard of Canada. Jason was from Saudi Arabia; his real identity is Hasim Jehan. Shah was killed by a shark attack after a snorkeling trip in Aitutaki. Her body is aboard the ship in the morgue.

Bridget's passport photo next filled the screen. "This woman is from Syria. Her real name is Layla Kalpar. We do not know anything else about this woman except she was traveling with Imran Rahim from Syria. They are registered under the name Christian and Bridget Valcourt from Nice. We know very little about them yet. They are two of the assassins portrayed in the video with the passengers. Rahim was present for the execution of the officers."

The screen next flipped to Lauren's image. Her face was framed by a cascade of blonde hair around perfect features. "This woman is traveling under the name of Lauren Jensen. We believe her real name is Amayah Zakaria, but this has not been verified. She is believed to be from Istanbul. It is interesting to note that her alleged husband, registered with the Paradise

Line as Mark Jensen, is shown in the video of the killing of the captain but not the passengers. We do not yet know whether there is any significance to this and have not determined his real identity."

"None of them look the part," observed a man seated on the second row.

The American general piped in. "They never do. The video footage of the 9/11 killers shows them as average, reasonably well-dressed people. The most dangerous people often appear to be the most benign."

A woman in the back cupped her hands around her mouth and shouted to Waters. "What happened to the security guards on board?"

Waters shook his head. "No one has been able to contact them. We are presuming they are dead."

The woman from the back stood. James recognized her as an employee from a Norwegian P&I Club with an office in London. Her employer was one of members of the consortium of insurers insuring the Paradise Line. "Is anyone in contact with the ship?"

"The governments of the US, UK, New Zealand, and Australia have attempted to make contact without success. As of now, there has not been a response."

Suddenly, Pratt jumped to his feet, holding his cell phone in the air. "We have a text message from one of the passengers. She is an American citizen. Her name is Temperance Tyler, and she is traveling with her five-year-old child, Zoe. Her husband, Reynolds Tyler, had to return to Seattle for work. He flew from Auckland to Los Angeles and received a text message from his wife when the plane landed. It appears to be a couple of hours old. Tyler's message states that she and the child are in hiding. He immediately reported the text to the FBI."

"Do we know if she and the child were among those people in the theatre massacre?" asked one of the P&I Club representatives.

Waters shook his head. "We are working on identifying all of the victims in the theatre. A number of them have been identified from their passport and security photos. I do not know if either Tyler is on the list, but we will check."

James sighed and closed his eyes. The video had been horrific, and he could not imagine what the passengers had experienced, helpless and waiting to die. Maybe in all of the carnage, there could be some survivors. He hoped that Temperance Tyler and her daughter were still alive and would survive. All they could do was wait.

CHAPTER TWENTY-EIGHT

The overhead lights shined brightly as Zip inched her way down the interior stairwell closest to the bow of the ship. The carpet on the stairs muffled her steps. The bodies of another young family and two crew members she recognized as servers from the dining room lay in a pool of blood clustered against the wall of the landing as she descended to Deck 8. One of the young men, Daniel, had been their server at dinner for three nights. Daniel had been delightful company, always eager to make sure everyone was having a wonderful time. She recalled how his eyes had shined as he explained to Zip and Reynolds that he was saving money to go to engineering school in New Zealand to provide a better life for his small family. Zip and Reynolds had agreed to give him a $100 tip the last night of the cruise. It was tragic that he would never realize his dreams.

Zip shifted Zoe in her arms. The weight of the pack and the child slowed her progress, forcing her to carefully step around the dead. Sheer panic propelled her forward. It was critical that she reach Deck 4, the emergency station. She understood that reaching the lifeboat emergency station was their only hope. They might not be successful, but she had to move heaven and earth to save her child. Death would be certain if they had remained in their cabin.

She remembered Reynolds describing the recent mandatory training he had received during his company's safety week. Of course, all training in Seattle consisted of the obligatory earthquake and evacuation drills. Seattle was located near the Cascadia subduction zone, where some of the most severe earthquakes in North America had occurred. In fact, five hundred years earlier, a magnitude 9 earthquake had occurred on the Olympic Peninsula. Reynolds had told her that this year the safety curriculum had included guidelines for a workplace shooting event. The takeaway from the consultant delivering the training had been simple: run and/or hide.

Zip considered the sage wisdom for hostage situations. She and Zoe had hidden as long as possible, and she knew it had likely saved their lives. But something told her that their hiding place was no longer safe. Once Alistair's body was discovered, the terrorists would likely have found them. She knew they needed to run.

She continued her descent and made a hairpin turn toward Deck 7. Two more bodies of crew members, still dressed in their white uniforms, were draped across the stairs, obviously fleeing one of the terrorists. A fountain of blood had pooled around the still bodies, dripping through the open stairs below.

She could not allow the child to see the horrific scene.

Zip clasped Zoe as tightly as possible and whispered in her ear. "Sweetie, keep your eyes covered and take some deep breaths."

"OK, Mommy," Zoe murmured.

Zip gave the child a kiss on her hair. "Good girl. Just a little while longer."

Zip continued downward toward Deck 6. Her heart pounded in her chest as she prayed she would not run into one of the terrorists.

Only two more levels and they would reach their goal.

Zip was relieved that the landing on Deck 5 was deserted. It was silent except for the soft music coming from the speaker in the wall nearest the door. She took a deep breath and made the last turn down to Deck 4.

The stairs were empty. To the left, she caught sight of the doorway to the scuba training room positioned beside the exit to Deck 4. The door was partially ajar, held open by the body of the scuba instructor, Jerome. His torso was mangled by what appeared to be a series of bullet holes, and his lifeless eyes were directed toward the ceiling as if he had been caught by surprise.

Zip scurried past Jerome through the exit doors toward their emergency muster station.

She had finally made it. They would be safe.

As she pushed through the double doors, she felt a sense of relief wash over her. Then, just as quickly, she felt the blood drain from her face. There, standing on the exterior deck by the lifeboats was Ruby's friend, Bridget, holding a machine gun. Her face and clothing were spattered with blood. Bridget, obviously surprised to see Zip, quickly raised her weapon.

Zip turned, burst through the double doors, and ran.

CHAPTER TWENTY-NINE

Five leaned against the raised back of the examination table as Lauren wrapped his leg with the gauze and bandages from the medical kit in the infirmary. Secretly, he felt an unexpected deep remorse at the killing of the children and adults in the theatre. Nothing could have prepared him for the disgusting sight of the senseless deaths. And he had been sickened that Lauren, Bridget, Christian, and Jason had seemed elated and invigorated by the mass killings. It was inexplicable, and he was eager for the entire debacle to be over.

Lauren gave him a shot of morphine to dull the pain and enable him to fulfill the mission during what would be the last hour of his life. The gunshot wound had throbbed relentlessly, but the effect of the morphine was almost immediate, giving him a feeling of calm and well-being.

The team had disconnected the ship's Wi-Fi and shut down their cell phones to avoid the relentless emails, texts, and telephone calls they were receiving from the US military. The television was tuned to CNN, displaying images from Facebook and Instagram posted by Cell 53 of the hostage crisis. The Cell 53 Twitter feed scrolled across the screen in large black block letters. The hijacking had become a media circus.

Five watched as the male anchor read a statement from the White House that special forces from the US military were taking coordinated action with the governments of Britain, New Zealand, and Australia to intervene and conduct a coordinated rescue. The British Prime Minister and the governments of New Zealand and Australia had strongly condemned the hijacking attempt. An enlarged digital map loomed behind the anchor showing the region of Oceania.

Five studied Lauren as she packed the wound with gauze and antibiotic cream. When he glanced back at the TV, he was surprised to see the image of his father, Tan, on the screen, standing outside of his impressive residence in the Ampang neighborhood of Kuala Lumpur. The sparkling white house was located in one of the most elite neighborhoods in the city, in close proximity to the homes of diplomats and foreign embassies. Five, his brother, and his sister, Nor, had all attended private schools and had been children of privilege. Five loved his family and, despite the morphine, was saddened by the tears streaming down his father's face.

His father, as usual, wore a suit and tie. His hair was perfectly trimmed, and despite the sweltering heat, he appeared to be cool. "My son was the pride of my life. He was a good boy, highly educated, and a great athlete. I cannot imagine that he would have done this. I do not know what happened—" The camera thankfully pulled away as his father dissolved into sobs.

After a brief commentary, the scene shifted to Five's former wife, Caroline, who was standing beside her BMW outside of their condominium in the Pacific Heights neighborhood of San Francisco. Caroline's gorgeous face grimacing in anger filled the screen. She was clearly trying the escape the cluster of reporters who had corralled her against the exterior wall of the complex.

"I haven't seen Ash in over a year," she barked at a reporter, who shoved his mic at her. Ash was her pet name for him. "We were divorced more than a year ago. The last I heard, he had quit his job and moved to

London." She held up her left hand, displaying a large diamond. "I am now engaged to a doctor, and we are getting married in June. Please leave me in peace," she demanded, slipping her access card to the courtyard into the scanner and slamming the metal door behind her.

The CNN reporter remained in front of Caroline's condominium building, reporting that Five's former employer had declined an interview. Instead, a terse, carefully crafted statement had been released from the pharmaceutical company, stating, "There had been no reason to suspect that he had violent tendencies, and his employment was terminated more than a year ago by mutual agreement."

Five chafed at the statement from his former employer. He had worked very hard and made numerous sacrifices with his long hours of service. It had been one of the issues that had strained his marriage. In fact, when he had given notice, his direct superior had begged him to reconsider his position, offering employer-paid assistance in the form of counseling. His boss had explained that an immigration firm was kept on corporate retainer, so the company could assure Five that he could maintain his green card status and work visa. There was no reason for him to quit. Five had thanked him but insisted that he needed to leave. Life in America was different than Malaysia, and he had ultimately accepted the fact that he would never be able to fully assimilate into Western culture. He was different, and it was time to stop fighting a battle he was sure to lose. Besides, he could not stand the thought of being in the same city as Caroline. He needed a fresh start.

The revisionist history of his former employer made Five angry. It was the last of many betrayals that he had suffered.

The digital clock mounted on the wall displayed the time as 1:25 a.m. At 2:00, they would detonate the plastic explosives in the hull. Nothing would be left of the ship, and they would have served the Cause. Five felt a tingle of excitement that the end was near.

Just as the pain fully subsided in Five's leg from the hefty dose of morphine, a satellite image of the floating *Golden Swan* flashed on the screen. The vessel continued its relentless southern course, and the CNN anchor reported that the ship was traveling at about twenty-five miles an hour. The anchor announced that unnamed sources had informed CNN that the ship must be under the control of a crew member or hijacker because it was not floating aimlessly at sea. The satellite feed was surprisingly crisp, clearly displaying that all of the lifeboats were still in position suspended from the side of the ship.

"There is no indication that any of the lifeboats have been launched. CNN has not yet determined whether there are any hostages or survivors on board the ship after the Good Friday Massacre."

Within moments, the images switched to the Vatican, where the Pope was giving a Saturday prayer before Easter. "He prayed for God's mercy and asked the hijackers to stop the senseless killing."

Lauren grabbed the remote and muted the volume. "Pompous fool," she spat. "As if Catholicism is the *only* religion in the world. I am glad this is the last time I will be forced to listen to him."

Five managed to get up from the examination table and stand on the floor without pain. The effect of the drug was nothing short of amazing. "It worked, Lauren. Now we can get to work."

She gave him a capped syringe. "There is more in here just in case. But be careful. It will make you sleepy. It slows down your vital organs."

He glanced at the image on the screen as he was preparing to leave, surprised to see the visage of one of the passengers. Lauren turned up the volume.

"Look, that woman is one of the women who was friends with Ruby. She was from Seattle and has a child."

Five remembered the woman and her husband. They had been warm and welcoming to Five and everyone they had met.

The anchor, a perfectly coiffed blonde with flawless makeup, stared at the screen somberly. "CNN has just learned that this woman, Temperance Tyler, and her daughter, Zoe, from Seattle may still be alive. Her husband had to return home early for a work emergency. When he arrived in Los Angeles, he received a text message from his wife stating that the ship had been taken over by terrorists and that the two of them were in hiding. There has been no word from them lately, but they have not yet been identified as among the victims of the theatre massacre. Stay tuned. CNN will continue to follow this story and bring you live updates from this ongoing international crisis."

"We should hunt her down and end this," Lauren told Five, as they turned off the TV and left the infirmary.

Five shook his head. "There is no need, Lauren. It doesn't matter. She has no place to go. Within less than an hour, the ship will sink and she and her daughter will be dead. We need to focus on completing the mission."

Lauren smiled. "Of course, you are right. She has no place to go. Let's go find the others and sink this ship."

CHAPTER THIRTY

Zip bounded through a second set of hydraulic doors. Between the weight of the pack and Zoe, she knew she could not outrun Bridget. The bullets from the machine gun shattered the glass doors behind her as she raced into the hall and ducked into the adults-only champagne bar. Her breath was coming in ragged gasps. She crouched down behind the high bar in the darkness and stroked Zoe's hair.

There was no place to run. She had failed to protect Zoe. What could she do?

She could hear Bridget calling to her. "Zip, where are you? There is no place to hide. Come on out and die honorably like your friends Carla and Poppy. I promise I will make it quick, and you will die with honor."

Zip placed her hand over Zoe's mouth and whispered in her ear. "Please be quiet, baby. Please don't say a word. Mommy will protect you."

A blast of machine-gun fire caused an explosion of the mirrors above the bar. A spray of shattered crystal champagne glasses cascaded over them, coating Zip's hair with shards of glass.

The wood and metal bar erupted following a second round of bullets as Bridget crept closer to them. Suddenly, the room was bathed in harsh light as Bridget flipped on the series of canned lights in the ceiling.

"I will kill you and your little girl at the same time if you come out now. It will be preferable to drowning. Do you know that in less than thirty minutes we are going to sink the boat? The hull is lined with plastic explosives ready to be detonated at 2:00. If I do not kill you, you and your little girl will instantly die or drown."

Zoe whimpered, and Bridget released another round of gunfire.

"I know you are here. I can hear you."

Zoe could see the back of Bridget's head above the bar. The woman's reflection was captured in the remaining shards of the ornate mirror over the bar. Bridget was covered in blood spatter, and her facial expression was one of unmistakable insanity.

Zip began to pray as Zoe squirmed in her arms. If only they had left with Reynolds, they would have lived.

Just then, Bridget rounded the corner of the bar. "There you are, you silly goose. Come out now and die with dignity. And please do not beg. Your friend Carla begged for herself and that pouty, spoiled little girl, Poppy. It was a pleasure and a privilege to end her life for the Cause. She was worthless."

Bridget aimed her weapon toward Zoe. "Get up, I said," Bridget shrieked. "You Americans are so weak."

Tears ran down Zip's cheeks, and her hands trembled in fear. If only she had stayed hidden on the balcony.

"And you can take your fucking hand off of your daughter's mouth. She can scream all she wants. I am here now, and I will end it."

As Zip removed her hand from Zoe's mouth, the child raised her hand and let out a bloodcurdling scream. "No, Mommy! No, stop her!"

Bridget dissolved into laughter and began mocking Zoe. "No, Mommy! No, Mommy! You silly girl! Your Mommy is powerless to do anything. Prepare to meet death."

Zip did not catch sight of the man standing behind Bridget until he raised a fire ax over the assassin's head. Zip fleetingly realized that the man was an officer wearing the brilliant white *Golden Swan* uniform. Just as Bridget lifted the weapon to discharge it, the man swung the ax against Bridget's neck, nearly severing her head from her torso. Bridget's eyes bulged from impact, and the gun discharged again, splintering the ornate French cabinet behind the bar, fortunately missing Zoe and Zip.

Instinctively, Zip placed her hands over Zoe's eyes, shielding her from the horrific spectacle. She hugged Zoe as tightly as possible. "You are OK, baby. We are OK now. The bad lady is gone. She cannot hurt us."

Zoe whimpered and buried her head in Zip's shoulder. "I'm scared, Mommy."

Zip stroked her hair and kissed her cheek. "Me too, but it is over. The man saved us."

The man came over and helped Zip to her feet. His brass nametag identified him as Officer Oliver. "Are you OK? Did either of you get hit?"

Zip examined Zoe. "I think we are fine."

"OK, we need to leave. I want you to follow me."

"Where are we going? You heard her. They are going to blow up the ship."

"We are going to launch one of the lifeboats. And we need to do it quickly. We need to get away from the ship."

"Alright," Zip replied numbly. "Do you think there will be others like her out there?"

"I do not know," Officer Oliver told her. "But at least we will be armed."

After he helped Zip over Bridget's body, he reached back and grabbed the machine gun and the ax. Zip, still carrying Zoe and the pack, followed him out of the bar to the outside deck.

CHAPTER THIRTY-ONE

Zip carried Zoe across the threshold of the lifeboat as Officer Green activated the winch to lower the vessel to the water. She and Zoe settled into a bench near the bow. Zoe sobbed softly as Zip cradled her in her lap.

The lifeboat was completely enclosed with square portals on the port and starboard sides. The interior was filled with bench seats. A sign over the door indicated that the maximum capacity was sixty passengers and crew.

Zip scanned the boat, surveying the remaining passengers. It appeared these people were the only survivors of the terrorist attack. People sat silently, huddled in their seats, obviously in a state of shock. They all were wearing life vests. Zip noticed that there were no other children on the lifeboat. Two couples Zip knew were in their late fifties or early sixties from the UK sat in the back and appeared to be praying together. Zip saw two young men from Australia wearing water shoes, board shorts, and soft shirts with sunscreen. Both men were avid divers who had been on the shark cage excursion with Reynolds. They looked shell-shocked. There were two couples in their thirties who had told Zip that they were traveling together on their dream vacation from Omaha Nebraska, and a couple from France who spoke little English. One of the women from Nebraska sobbed softly. None of them acknowledged Zip.

Zip slipped on her life vest and secured the ties on Zoe's. Her heart still pounded in her chest, and her hands trembled in fear. She and Zoe had come so close to death. It was a miracle they had survived.

She noticed a lone female officer wearing a blood-spattered uniform seated across from them. Zip recognized her as one of the attendants in the Fairy Tale Activity Center. The woman came over and sat on the bench beside Zip and Zoe. Her face was swollen, and she had obviously been crying. Her hair, which was usually wrapped in a perfect bun, fell in strands down her back. The young woman was quite beautiful with delicate features. She patted Zoe on the back.

"I am Lisa Reed. I know Zoe from the Center," she said softly.

Zip nodded. "I recognize you." She leaned back and lifted Zoe's chin with her hand. "Zoe, here is your friend, Miss Reed."

Zoe gazed at Miss Reed and managed a weak smile. "A bad lady tried to get us," Zoe said told Officer Reed matter-of-factly. "But a man hurt her and stopped her."

Officer Reed stroked Zoe's hair. "You are safe now, sweetheart. We are leaving all of the bad people behind."

Officer Oliver placed the machine gun and the fire ax, still dripping with Bridget's blood, on a shelf near the bridge. He closed and secured the door after Officer Green had climbed in. Officer Green disappeared into the bridge to operate the release.

"Hold on tight to the railings and seat. This is going to be a hard landing," Officer Oliver instructed the passengers. "The ship is moving, and we have disengaged the winch clasp. This is a dangerous operation, and it is possible that the force of the moving ship might capsize the lifeboat. This operation is usually done while the ship is at anchor."

"Are you telling us we are going to die after we just escaped the hijackers?" one of the men demanded.

Officer Oliver stared back at the man. "The hijackers are going to sink the ship. This is our only option. If you want off the lifeboat and want to take your chances with them, let me know. Otherwise, just hold on. If the lifeboat capsizes, there are some inflatable boats on board, and we will have to evacuate. Now, is everybody with us?"

The man simply shook his head and wrapped his arms around his sobbing wife.

"Alright then. Brace yourselves, and make sure your life jacket is on tight," he told the group.

Zip felt a jolt of fear. After all they had endured, they might still die trying to escape. She felt the sting of tears in her eyes.

Officer Oliver slipped into the seat beside Zip. "Ma'am, I am going to sit next to you to help you secure your little girl on impact." He held on to the seat and clasped Zip by the life preserver. Officer Reed sat on the other side of the bench, grasping the bench with hard knuckles.

Suddenly, Zip felt her stomach lurch as the lifeboat fell one deck down to the water. The jolt from the impact threw her onto the floor. The lifeboat rolled violently in the turbulence from the ship's engines and the wake. The engines on the lifeboat sprang to life and propelled them through the water. Within an instant, they had escaped the violent wake of the ship and were speeding away from the ship.

The shots from the machine-gun fire were muffled by the roar of the engine. Zip did not notice that anything was wrong until she saw one of the men slump over in his seat, exposing a large cavity in his head. One of the engines appeared to sputter as a hail of bullets rained down on them. Glass exploded from the starboard portals, and the cabin was filled with a rush of rain and cold air. The bullets instantly felled the couple from France and one of the Australian divers.

Zip, still clasping Zoe, cowered on the floor and prayed they would be safe. Officer Oliver shielded them with his body. After what seemed to be an eternity, the boat was finally beyond firing range, and the only noise was the dull roar of the engine as the lifeboat sped into the darkness.

CHAPTER THIRTY-TWO

At 1:55 a.m., Five joined Christian, Jason, and Lauren in the Red Shoes Library on Deck 10. Christian had left his post on the bridge and the ship drifted in the current. Five was surprised that only four members of their team had survived. The mission had been more difficult than he had anticipated.

The assembly of electronics programmed to detonate the plastic explosives strategically placed in the hull were spread across the library table. Cell 53 had provided the team with state-of-the-art equipment to achieve the explosion. The sinking of the ship was the last task of their mission.

Christian still carried his machine gun, which was suspended from a strap and slung over his shoulder. As Five arrived, Christian was recounting his attempts to thwart the escape of passengers in the lifeboat.

"Someone killed Bridget—nearly decapitated her. It must have been one of the officers. I managed to shoot one of the engines on the lifeboat," he told them proudly. "They won't get far. With any luck, the lifeboat will sink or catch fire."

Five, still feeling the placid effects of the morphine, surveyed the team. Despite the escape of a few passengers, they had served the Cause well. It was a moment of glory, and he silently praised his God.

"We are nearly ready," he told them. "At precisely 2:00 a.m., we will detonate the explosives." He looked over at Jason. "Have you sent the email?"

Jason had been tasked with sending an email to Cell 53 to confirm that the mission had been accomplished before they detonated the explosives. After the explosion, Cell 53 would announce to the world that they had been responsible for the monumental feat of killing the infidels.

Jason held up his burner phone. "I sent the message at 1:53 a.m. We are prepared for the final stage of the mission to serve the Cause."

At 1:58 a.m., Five, still limping, passed out the detonators to the surviving members of the team. As he clasped the equipment in his hand, he noticed his hand was damp from perspiration, reflecting his excitement at the culmination of the mission.

Christian propped the machine gun against a library chair while Jason pointed out the activation switch to each member of the team. Jason's degree in electrical engineering was critical to ensuring the ship and any remaining passengers were obliterated.

"Remember—press here," Jason told them, pointing to the switch.

Five watched the second hand on his watch for the countdown to activate the equipment. "We will shortly live in glory with our God in paradise. We have served God and the Cause. I love you all," he said.

"Praise God," the group said in unison.

At precisely 2:00 a.m., Five nodded to the team. "It is time," he said simply.

The team activated the switch on each device in unison and then stood quietly, expectantly waiting for the results of their efforts.

Five had not been exactly sure what to expect about the blast. He had initially thought the conflagration would be immediate and their deaths instantaneous. But the ship was huge, and he had been advised that it would not sink immediately. From below, they heard what could only be described as a loud rumbling as the series of explosions began. The ship shuddered as the rumbling continued. Within minutes, the ship had lurched more than sixty degrees to the port side, knocking the team members off their feet. A sheaf of library books cascaded from the shelves, and a large metal lamp fell to the floor. Overstuffed chairs slid from their station toward the list in the ship. The sound of the straining of metal and violent explosions became deafening as the explosives blasted away the hull of the ship. Five was vaguely aware that the ship was no longer moving and realized the engines must have stopped. Smoke poured from air vents in the ceiling. Suddenly, a large crevice appeared in the deck floor. Flames leapt through the crevice, and the air was acrid.

Five knelt down in prayer as he prepared to meet his God. He had served him faithfully. He smiled as he saw a brilliant flash of light and felt a surge of euphoria as he awaited his reward in paradise.

CHAPTER THIRTY-THREE

Officer Green cut the damaged engine and continued to travel south away from the *Golden Swan*. The gunfire had incapacitated one of the engines of the lifeboat, and a pungent smoky smell filled the small cabin. The sea around them was peppered with a spray of bullets. Wind and rain rushed in from the shattered windows. Now that the cabin was open to the outside air, the combined sound of the engine and the wind was thunderous. The tender bounced and rocked violently as it cut across the large waves generated by a low-pressure weather system. It was still dark outside, and there was only a soft light in the cabin.

Officer Oliver scanned the casualties inside the vessel and rushed to the small bridge of the lifeboat. After conferring with Officer Green, Oliver stuck his head out of the bridge and called back to the passengers.

"We are trying to get out of range. One of our engines is useless. It was hit by what must have been a military-grade rocket-propelled grenade. We are leaking fuel. We have turned off our lights so we will not be visible. Hold on and stay low near the floor," he instructed them.

Zip stayed crouched on the floor, holding Zoe as tightly as possible. Together, Zip and Officer Reed tried to shield the child's eyes from the disfigured corpses in the rear of the small vessel. Zip could barely stomach the horror of death that had unfolded in the last few seconds. Her hands trembled violently as she hugged Zoe, trying to stay calm for the sake of her child. Zoe's shoulders heaved as she sobbed softly against her mother's chest.

Marie Anthony, one of the passengers from Omaha, embracing the torso of her husband's body, rocked back and forth in shock. Her face was purple and distorted with agony. She shrieked loudly as she looked at the gaping cavity in the crown of her husband's head, which extended down to the orbital area. A gray substance mixed with blonde hair spattered the rear cabin wall. Death had most certainly been instantaneous.

"Oh my God! William was only forty-two years old! He cannot be dead! William, please wake up! Nooooooo! You cannot be dead, William! How will I live without you! What about our children?" she shrieked unconsolably.

Marie's traveling companions, Becky and Todd Bishop also from Omaha, slid across the floor toward their friend, helplessly watching as she clasped the body of her husband. The couple stayed low to the floor near Marie's knees, trying to avoid the same fate suffered by their friend William.

Becky rubbed her friend's arm compassionately. "Marie, I am sorry he is gone. Please come down to the floor with us until we are out of danger," she begged.

Marie, nearly catatonic with grief, ignored Becky's pleas. She clasped her husband's bloody body and wailed at the ceiling, continuing to rock back and forth.

Becky and Todd watched Marie with helpless concern, and Becky continued to pat her arm.

"Billy is graduating from high school next year! He is captain of the football team! He cannot do this without William! What are we going to do? Wake up, William! Wake up!" she screamed at the corpse hysterically.

Zip looked over at the French couple, still slumped in their bench in the rear of the lifeboat. Zip and Reynolds had had a drink with them one evening in the bar sharing a small table. Juliette and Claude Bocage owned a small rustic restaurant in the eighteenth arrondissement in Paris. The vacation had been a celebration of their twentieth wedding anniversary. They had been lovely and full of life, inviting Reynolds and Zip to visit them on their next trip to Paris. Now, they sat covered in blood and riddled with bullets, hopelessly entwined in death. Juliette's chest cavity had been ripped apart by the gunshots. A fountain of blood spouted from Claude's carotid artery, and the rear of his head appeared to be gone. They were both clearly beyond help.

Zip said a silent prayer for the couple as she averted her gaze and kissed the top of Zoe's head. She wondered if she had deluded herself that they would be safe if they survived the dropping of the lifeboat. She never could have imagined that the terrorists could reach them once they had escaped the vessel.

Officer Reed rested her head against Zoe's back as they huddled on the floor, trying to remain stationary as the boat strained forward across the waves. Zip could feel the woman's fear and clasped her hand. Reed squeezed Zip's hand in acknowledgment, her head bowed as if in prayer.

The surviving diver, Joey Perez, hid near the floor against the starboard wall of the cabin. He covered his face with one hand and held on to the metal stanchion supporting the plastic bench with his free hand. The body of his diving companion, Carl Russell, rested next to him, bleeding profusely.

The two couples from England huddled together midship, their heads nearly on the floor. One of the men, Hunter Campbell, covered the back of his head with his hands. From Zip's position, they all appeared to be alive.

The lifeboat continued to bounce relentlessly across the high seas rushing toward safety. The gunfire appeared to have stopped, and the only sound was the drone of the sole engine and the wind. Except for the wailing of Marie Anthony, the passengers remained silent.

Zip looked toward the stern of the vessel. The small window had been shattered by gunfire. In the distance, she could see a bright orange glow on the northern horizon. As she watched transfixed, the intensity of the light increased until it seemed to completely fill the horizon. It was a curious and beautiful sight against the storming sky.

Officer Oliver stumbled back into the cabin, shouting over the engine noise. "The terrorists have blown up the ship. But we do not know if any of them escaped to a lifeboat. Stay down. We are keeping the lights off until we know we are safe."

Zip turned her gaze back down to the floor and tried to shield Zoe, praying that they would get through the nightmare alive.

CHAPTER THIRTY-FOUR

James silently stared at the television screen as the white text from Cell 53's email came into view announcing that the *Golden Swan* would be destroyed at 2:00 a.m. All 500 passengers and 300 crew members would go down with the ship. There would be no survivors.

The anger and frustration in the room was palpable. The buffet of pasta and salad set up in the room outside of the library remained untouched by the participants in the meeting.

At precisely 2:00 a.m., the satellite feed from the ship's location in the South Pacific was displayed across the screen, showing what could only be a succession of explosions. Fire and light leapt into the dark sky at least a hundred feet and then subsided just as suddenly. The vessel had been badly damaged. Through the flames, it appeared the ship had listed nearly ninety degrees. The crowded room watched in horror as the stern of the ship separated from the hull, rolling in the turbid water before it sank. Transfixed, the group watched as the hull further separated into fragments and within minutes slipped below the surface. Although it was extremely dark, the continued explosions within the hull illuminated the surrounding ocean as it slowly spiraled toward the sea floor 14,000 feet below.

The assembly was eerily silent as they watched the horror unfolding on the monitors in the library. CNN was already reporting that the ship had been destroyed. Within minutes, Ron Parros, a US general, looking weary, stood at the podium and announced that the reconnaissance aircraft sent from Samoa had confirmed the explosion and sinking of the vessel. There appeared to be no survivors, but special forces, including Navy SEALS, intended to sweep the area looking for those passengers and crew who had been brave enough to jump into the ocean to escape the terrorists.

"Of course, the odds are against them," he told the group. "We all remember the stories of the crew from the *Indianapolis* who abandoned ship only to be torn apart by sharks. The Oceanic whitetip sharks in these waters are vicious killers who feed at night, so the odds are stacked against any small groups who managed to get off of the ship. Also, the undertow created by the sinking ship would be strong enough to drag any swimmer under water. The water is more than two and a half miles deep in this area, so we have a *Titanic* situation. Between the rain and seas of eight feet, it is unlikely there are survivors, but we will do everything we can to find them. There is a multigovernmental task force working together to find them."

"What about the lifeboats?" asked one of the women from a British P&I Club. "Are all of them accounted for? Did they sink with the ship?"

The general shook his head. "We cannot say at this point. It would have been very difficult to launch a lifeboat without the cooperation of the crew, especially if the vessel was moving. The military teams in the area thought they heard the signal of an emergency beacon, but it has stopped. It may have simply been from the *Golden Swan* itself. But the lifeboats are painted orange, so if one managed to detach from the ship, it will be more visible in the daylight."

The American foreign service agent stood. "We have been informed that the FBI has cleared Reynolds Tyler, the American who left the ship in Rarotonga, of any suspicion of involvement in the terrorist attack. While it looked suspicious that he had left the ship on the day of the attack, it appears to have been a coincidence. Apparently, he had to return to Seattle for a work deadline. He is frantic about his wife and child, and the government is trying keep him from giving an interview to the press."

The monitor in the corner was tuned to the BBC. A middle-aged reporter held a microphone in front of the neighbor of a couple from the tony area of Chelsea in London. Behind the reporter, a well-tended three-story home with a royal-blue front door was visible. Spring flowers were already blooming in the window boxes. The young man stated that he was a banker who had lived near the Sims family for over two years. Sims, a doctor, had booked a vacation aboard the *Golden Swan* to celebrate his retirement from the practice of medicine.

"It is awful that the trip Dr. Sims and his wife had been so excited about ended in this way. They were charming people," he told the reporter. The show then switched to other reporters who were interviewing friends and families of the passengers and crew aboard the *Golden Swan*.

James felt sickened by the death and destruction from the tragedy. He knew the chances of survival of anyone from this disaster were unlikely, but he hoped at least a few people had escaped. Further, he understood well that this was a public relations nightmare. Simply from a legal perspective, there would certainly be as many as five hundred wrongful death lawsuits from this casualty. Insurance limits would be strained, and the reputation of the Paradise Line would be destroyed. Few people in the future would be willing to entrust their lives or the lives of their families to a Paradise Line ship for fear it would happen again. Security systems aboard cruise ships might change forever. He wiped his eyes and leaned back against the soft cushion feeling helpless.

James's boss, Reed Coleman, came over and tapped James on the shoulder. "James, let's get a bite to eat and talk," he told him somberly.

Together, the two men maneuvered through the crowd and walked into the large room outside of the library. Two white-coated servers heaped their buffet plates with pasta and Caesar salad and brought it over to a small table in the corner.

James toyed with his food, but he managed to eat a few bites of salad and pasta. He had never been so close to a marine casualty of this magnitude. The sinking of the *Golden Swan* was a real crisis.

Reed, a marathon runner, had the capacity to consume large amounts of food and remain slender even at the age of forty-seven. He ate a large slice of lasagna and salad before signaling to the waiter to take his plate away. "I did not realize I was so hungry," he told James, almost apologetically.

"Bunny and I ate a big brunch. And after watching all of this, I can barely eat."

"It is fucking awful. I have never been involved in anything like this other than the *Costa Concordia*. This is worse."

Reed took a long drink of his ice water and then signaled to the waiter for coffee. He lowered his voice and looked at James intently. "We have been talking. There is not much you can do here. I want you to go to Los Angeles to meet with Reynolds Tyler. A representative of the Paradise Lines vessel will be there. Tyler is the only known survivor at this point, and as one of the insurers of the vessel and a member of the K&R team, it makes sense for you to go to LA to be supportive."

James thought about Bunny. She probably would not be happy, but she would understand. It was one of the things he loved about her. "Why me?" he asked finally.

Reed cleared his throat. "I have talked to some of the P&I Club representatives, and we think you would be a good choice to do this. You are about Tyler's age and at the same stage in life. We think you can relate to him. He needs support and, of course, plaintiff's lawyers will be coming out of the woodwork. We have arranged for him to stay in a suite at the Peninsula Beverly Hills Hotel, and we will pay all of his expenses. It is unusual, but Lunar Syndicate will cover the costs and share them with the three P&I Clubs insuring the vessel."

James listened thoughtfully and cleared his throat. "What about work?"

Reed shook his head. "We will have someone cover all of your cases. Contact Bunny and let her know. We have arranged for you to leave on the overnight flight. You will be in LA by tomorrow afternoon."

"Good thing I brought my passport."

"We have arranged for a car to take you to the airport."

"When will I leave?"

"The car will pick you up in an hour. Whatever you do not have with you—a swimsuit—or anything, buy it there and we will cover it."

James nodded and picked up his phone. He would need to go to the lobby to get cell service to call Bunny.

CHAPTER THIRTY-FIVE

James arrived at Terminal 2 at Heathrow in the late afternoon for the Virgin Atlantic flight to Los Angeles. Traffic had been lighter than usual, and the ride miraculously had taken only an hour. The driver, who was an older man from Latvia, had been nice enough to stop at an ATM so James could withdraw cash for the trip on his company credit card. He had decided to convert the GBP into dollars in Los Angeles. The syndicate had given him a new SAT phone for the trip.

As he stood by the car while the driver took his luggage from the boot, government vehicles carrying INTERPOL and British Secret Intelligence representatives pulled in behind his car and disembarked. The occupants jumped out quickly and disappeared through the long glass doors in front of the terminal. He recognized one of the British diplomats who had attended the meeting at the Lloyd's library. They had announced they would be traveling to Rarotonga via New Zealand. It would be a long flight.

James reached into his pocket and withdrew twenty GBP and handed it to the driver. "Thank you for getting me here so quickly."

The driver looked at him and shook his head. "It has all been taken care of, sir. But thank you for the effort."

"Are you sure?"

"I am certain. I have been well compensated."

James thanked the driver and carried his luggage into the terminal. In addition to being a first-class passenger, he had a Fast Track pass through security. He spent the short interval before the flight in the Virgin lounge. The Lunar Syndicate had arranged a car to take him from LAX to the Peninsula Hotel, where he would meet Reynolds Tyler. Still full from lunch, he drank only a large glass of orange juice with ice as he checked his messages.

It was nearly 7:00 p.m. by the time he reached Bunny. She answered her cell immediately. "Where are you?"

"In the lounge waiting to board."

"It is a horrible thing! All of those poor people."

"I know. It is awful."

"How long will you be gone?"

"A week or so. This is unusual."

"I miss you already."

"Me too."

"Call me when you arrive."

"I will unless it is too early."

"Big Bunny kiss. I love you."

"Me too," he replied as he terminated the call.

He sent his boss a simple text. "I am in the lounge and ready to go. Will text you when there."

Coleman responded immediately. "Watch the news. New developments."

The television monitor mounted on a table in front of his sofa was tuned to BBC News. James increased the volume and watched intently.

Satellite images of the *Golden Swan* exploding flashed on the screen briefly before the camera panned back to the female reporter standing near the entrance to the port in Papeete. With a crisp, clear delivery, the woman reported the latest developments.

"BBC News has learned that Tahitian government officials have detained two customs officers responsible for loading the *Golden Swan*. It is believed that the men received bribes to smuggle plastic explosives and military-grade weapons onto the vessel. Two engineers vacationing in Bora Bora are believed to have strategically placed the explosives into the hull of the ship resulting in a chain reaction of explosives. These two men cannot be found and are believed to be in hiding after leaving Tahiti two days ago headed for Vancouver, BC. INTERPOL and the Canadian and American governments are collaborating in a manhunt to locate the two men. The two engineers worked in Toronto before moving to British Columbia and are believed to be central operatives of Cell 53, which has taken responsibility for the hijacking and murder of more than eight hundred innocent people."

The London anchor thanked the reporter and promised the audience it would provide updates as developments and information became available. In impeccable English, the anchor announced that there were further developments in Los Angeles. She introduced a reporter standing in front of the FBI building in the early morning light.

"It is midmorning here in Los Angeles, and we are standing outside of the FBI Los Angeles Field Office where Reynolds Tyler, a passenger aboard the *Golden Swan*, is working with American government officials. Tyler left the cruise early when the boat docked in Rarotonga to return home at the request of his boss in Seattle. When Tyler landed in Los Angeles, he had a text message from his wife who reported the ship had been hijacked. There is no word whether Temperance Tyler, known as Zip to her friends, and their five-year-old daughter, Zoe, perished in the blast that sank the luxury cruise ship. They are presumed dead along with more than eight hundred passengers and crew. Authorities are waiting to confirm whether any of the passengers escaped in the lifeboats before the explosion or jumped off of the ship. A massive search is underway near the area of the sinking to locate any passengers or crew in the shark-infested waters. Chances appear grim that there will be any survivors, but we will wait and pray."

The anchor's face filled the screen as she thanked her colleague. "Thank you, Stuart Wells, our correspondent in Los Angeles covering this tragedy. In case you are just joining us, the luxury cruise ship, *Golden Swan*, flagged in Panama and one of the Paradise Line's ships, was hijacked late last night by members of a terrorist cell known only as Cell 53. An explosion aboard the *Golden Swan* sank the vessel, and approximately eight hundred passengers and crew are presumed dead. All of the world is waiting anxiously and praying for the safety of the survivors. BBC News will keep you updated with the developments," she announced somberly before switching to other news stories.

James could not stop thinking of the horror the passengers had suffered when the vacation of a lifetime had turned deadly. Innocent men, women, and children had been senselessly killed. He thought of Reynolds Tyler. James was not sure why the Lunar Syndicate wanted him to go to Los Angeles. Certainly, Tyler would be distraught and fearful that his wife and child had been killed. Coleman had explained that the Lunar Syndicate would pay for a grief counselor, minister, or a psychiatrist to help Tyler. It was likely he was the only survivor of the tragedy, and he would certainly have survivor's guilt.

Numbly, he walked down the concourse and boarded the first-class cabin when his plane was announced. He settled into the seat and ordered a glass of Malbec to calm his nerves. He realized he was tired from the stress and late evening the night before. He decided that after dinner, he would try to sleep on the ten-hour journey to America.

CHAPTER THIRTY-SIX

Zip and the other passengers were transfixed by the explosion illuminating the night sky. Flaming vessel fragments shot into the darkness like fireworks before falling suddenly toward the ocean. Within minutes, the light was extinguished and the northern horizon was dark again.

"Oh my God!" Officer Reed exclaimed in the silent interlude that had followed. "No one could have survived an explosion like that."

Zip thought about Carla, Poppy, and Wilson blown to pieces in the explosion. It was impossible to believe that two days earlier the two couples had enjoyed the day in the Aitutaki Lagoon. Who would have believed that their lives were nearly over? Poppy was just a little girl with a full life ahead of her. It was all so senseless.

Zip scanned the occupants in the small cabin. Marie remained on the bench, still sobbing quietly and rocking back and forth, clasping her husband's torso. Her silk blouse and dark-blonde hair were coated in blood and what appeared to be bone fragments. Becky sat beside her still trying to console her friend. Todd put his arm around his wife protectively and stared out of the open window. The two couples from the UK were now sitting quietly on the bench in the back, whispering softly. Joey leaned forward in his seat; his face buried in his hands. The lifeless body of his traveling companion oozed a river of blood at his feet across the wooden floor of the cabin.

Officer Oliver returned to the passenger cabin, looking shaken but obviously trying to project a confident façade. He sat down on the bench with Zip, Zoe, and Officer Reed. "Are you alright?"

"Yes, we are for now. Zoe is afraid, but it is a miracle we were able to escape this far."

He squeezed Zip's shoulder. "Sit tight. We are trying to make sure no one is following us. We cannot guarantee the hijackers did not take a lifeboat to escape the blast."

Officer Oliver stood up and addressed the group. The droning of the remaining engine was surprisingly loud, and he shouted to be heard.

"We are still traveling on our course. We do not know whether the hijackers have taken a lifeboat. For that reason, we are traveling with only partial running lights until we are sure we are not being followed. Officer Green has put out a Mayday signal. The emergency locator—the EPIRB— was damaged by the blast, so we cannot rely on that for a rescue. And as we explained on the ship, this part of Oceania is not well traveled. We might be out here for several days before we are rescued."

Todd stood up, bracing himself on the railing. His T-shirt and shorts were spattered with blood. A shock of unruly blonde hair fell over his tanned forehead. "Several days! What will we eat? How can we survive?"

Officer Oliver raised his hand. "These lifeboats have provisions, but they are more like military-grade dried meals. So, it will not be the quality of cuisine served on the ship, but it will keep us alive. We also have water. There are a couple of fishing poles and, worst-case scenario, we can catch some fish and cook them on the hot plate. We will need to be careful and ration the food so it will last."

Todd shook his head. "I guess that is better than nothing. At least some of us are still alive."

Officer Oliver stood confidently in front of the remaining group of passengers, clearly trying to remain in charge. "Alright, now as some of you may know, I served in the special forces in the US Navy for twelve years before being hired by the Paradise Line. Officer Green is also a former naval special forces officer. We have all been through something incredibly traumatic. But we need to work together as a team if we are going to survive this nightmare. We need to be precise like a military operation and work on trust. There are thirteen of us who have made it this far, and we are determined that all of us will make it through until we are rescued."

The Australian diver, Joey leaned forward in his seat. Zip estimated that he was not much older than twenty-four. Reynolds and Wilson had been shark-diving with him and his friend Carl. His skin was red, and his long ponytail was tinted orange from his time in the sun.

"Everyone on this boat wants to come out of this alive. What do you want us to do? We are with you."

"First, we need a lookout at all times. We need to be vigilant that we are not being followed, and we need to look for rescuers. We are going to work in teams and take turns. We have a set of small binoculars on the bridge. Officer Reed is going to be in charge of rationing and dispensing the food. Anyone who would like to assist her is welcome to do it. We are going to need to exercise self-control. None of us will be eating as much as we ate on the boat. When it is daylight, I need a couple of volunteers to try to catch some fish," he announced with determination.

Hunter raised his hand tentatively. "My colleague and I enjoy fishing and usually have good luck. We go to Scotland every year to fly fish. It might be a nice distraction."

Officer Oliver nodded, obviously pleased that the group was focusing on the tasks needed to stay alive. "Good. But this is deep-sea fishing. You put a line in the water with bait. The water here is about two miles deep. There are some big fish, but there are many sharks in these waters, so they might try to steal a catch."

Zip raised her hand. "Zoe and I will help Officer Reed with the food."

"I will help too!" called Becky. "And if we catch any fish, I can definitely help cook them."

"Alright. We just need to work together. I will make up a schedule for the lookout." Officer Oliver stood silently for a moment before continuing to address the passengers. "There are some tarps in a hatch in the back. We will need to wrap our friends in the tarps and move them to the back of the boat. We need to preserve their bodies with dignity until we are rescued."

Joey raised his hand. "I want to help. My best friend was killed, and I want to treat him right in death."

Both Todd and Hunter agreed to help with the bodies.

"Thank you both," continued Officer Oliver. "There is also a bucket. When it is light, we can splash some seawater on the deck to clean things up. But first we need to set up the lookout. Officer Reed, please get the binoculars from Officer Green on the bridge. I will need you to take over the lookout. You will need to alternate between the port and starboard side of the vessel. We are looking for any type of light or glimmer or the sounds of a helicopter."

Officer Reed rose from her seat, retrieved the binoculars from Officer Green, and took up a position near the open window on the port side of the vessel. Her expression was purposeful, despite the chaos and death in the cabin.

After Reed took her station as the lookout, Officer Oliver retrieved a bundle of tarps from the hatch. Then, assisted by Joey and Todd, the three men began the grim task of wrapping the bodies of the French couple, the diver, and Marie's husband.

Marie clung to her husband's body. "I do not want him wrapped in a tarp like a piece of garbage," she shrieked at Officer Oliver. "He will stay with me."

Joey knelt down and gave Marie a hug. He sat beside her, clasping her hand and brushing the tears from her face. "I know it is hard," he said softly. "But we want to treat him with dignity. He will just be in the back, and if you want to sit with him, you can do so at any time."

"I love him. He just cannot be gone!" she sobbed.

Joey stroked her hair and continued to clutch her hand. "Let's try to do what is best for him. He is still with you. But we want to protect him from insects and the sun."

"I want to protect him. He is still my husband."

"That's right. We want to treat him with dignity."

Marie nodded her head in understanding, reluctantly releasing her grip on her husband's dead body. She watched, still sobbing, as the three men carefully wrapped his remains in the tarp and placed him against the wall of the stern of the vessel.

Zip watched the poignant scene unfolding in the cabin. Her heart broke for Marie. Zoe had fallen asleep in her arms, and suddenly Zip realized she herself was exhausted. The adrenalin from their escape had taken all of her strength. According to her watch, it was nearly 4:00 a.m. She stretched out on the bench, still hugging Zoe tightly, and fell into a deep sleep.

CHAPTER THIRTY-SEVEN

Zip awoke a little after 6:00 a.m. The eastern sky was tinged with deep rose-ate striations as the sun hovered above the horizon. The salty air was thick with humidity and rushed into the cabin. Through the open window, she could see the anvil of a towering thunderstorm in the distance. The water was littered with whitecaps, and the small lifeboat bounced relentlessly as it continued its southern route.

It was quiet in the cabin as nearly everyone had fallen asleep. Marie was curled on a bench in a fetal position with her eyes closed. Officer Reed was asleep on an adjoining bench. Joey had taken her spot as the lookout at the stern of the vessel. Zoe still slept soundly, her angelic face, buried in a thicket of strawberry-blond hair, turned toward the back of the bench. Zip watched her sleep, praying that if they survived, the child would not be too emotionally scarred from the experience.

Zip surveyed the horror and destruction in the harsh daylight. The wooden floor of the lifeboat was coated with blood, which emitted an acrid, coppery smell. The tarps wrapping the bodies of the four deceased passengers had been stacked carefully against the wall of the stern of the ship. The stern wall was plastered with blood and human debris. The scene was beyond Zip's worst nightmares.

Zip closed her eyes, refusing to allow the horror around her to shake her confidence. She needed to console and protect Zoe until they were rescued. She needed to maintain a soothing, reassuring facade to help the child through the ordeal. She could not allow Zoe to sense her discomfort.

Careful not to wake Zoe, Zip carefully stood up and tiptoed to the head behind the bridge. She was shocked by her appearance in the metal mirror. Her hair was a tangled mess, and her face was coated with a spray of what was apparently dirt and blood. With her fingers, she managed clip her hair back into the ponytail and wash her face, hands, and neck in the sink water marked "nonpotable." When she emerged, she felt somewhat better and surprisingly alert.

She slipped onto the bridge. Officer Oliver had taken over command of the vessel, and he and Officer Green were engaged in an animated conversation with Hunter. They all turned to her as she entered the control room.

Officer Green gave her a weary smile. "You are awake."

"I took a nap. I am surprised I could sleep at all after the night we have had. My little girl is still asleep."

"Are you alright?" Officer Oliver said, looking at her briefly over his shoulder.

"As well as can be expected considering what we have all endured. I am alive, which is more than I can say for so many of the innocent people on the ship. Do you have any idea how many died?"

Officer Green looked at her sadly. "There were 800 people on board with the crew and total passengers. Unless some of the people escaped, they are all dead."

Zip shook her head. "This is unbelievable. It seems impossible."

Hunter touched her arm. "Were you and your little girl traveling alone?"

"We were with friends from Seattle. They did not make it. As we were coming down to Deck 4, I saw them on the staircase."

Officer Green looked at her compassionately. "I am sorry."

"I see you are wearing a wedding ring. Where is your husband?" Hunter asked.

"He had to leave to go back to work in Seattle. He has a jerk of a boss, and he never tires of ruining our plans. For once, though, this was a good thing."

Hunter nodded. "Lucky."

"I know," Zip continued. "It was lucky for Zoe and me. Because Reynolds left, Zoe and I spent a girls' day together. Otherwise, we would have been with Carla, our friend from Seattle."

"I am sure your husband is aware of the situation by now," Officer Green continued. "He is probably frantic."

"I sent him a text message before I came down to Deck 4. For a while, the cell service was blocked, but I managed to send him the text. He was likely in the air from Auckland to Los Angeles at the time. I could only send one text. The hijackers must have blocked the cell service."

Officer Green looked at her approvingly. "That was smart thinking on your part. I am sure your husband reported the text once he reached the states."

"It is horrible in the other room," Zip told them. "I want to help clean it up a bit so we can try to get past this until we are rescued."

"We have a bucket, and we will use some seawater and a mop. It is not ideal, but it will get rid of the stench," Officer Green replied. "I am sure several of the men will help. We need everyone to pull together and not to be too distracted by the dead bodies. We may have a couple of tough days ahead."

"I am going to try to catch some fish," Hunter told her. "When everyone is awake, we are going to slow down a bit and cast a line. There should be plenty of fish in these waters."

At the first mention of food, Zip realized how hungry she was. "I can help cook the fish on the hot plate. In fact, I think we had several volunteers to help cook."

Hunter nodded. "Nothing like fresh fish. I think everyone could use some hot food."

Suddenly, Officer Oliver tapped an electronic gauge on the bridge. "Looks like the bilge is filling up. We need to empty it later."

Officer Green came over for a look. "I think so. Hopefully, we don't have a leak from the grenade."

Officer Oliver shook his head. "We will watch it," he said stoically.

Zip watched the officers with admiration. They were surprisingly unemotional and intent on their task of keeping the passengers alive. It had been sheer luck she had been assigned to Officer Oliver's survival station.

"I want to thank you for everything you did last night. You saved our lives from that killer. She was ready to shoot me and my little girl. And what is worse—she enjoyed the prospect of doing so." She looked over at Officer Oliver and managed a smile. "Thank you."

Officer Oliver looked almost embarrassed. "You are welcome. I know you would have done the same thing for someone else."

"It was brave and selfless," she replied.

"Military training," he said simply. "Special forces—all of that training kicked in."

Zip extended her hand toward Officer Green. "Since we are going to be on the boat together, I should introduce myself. My name is Zip, and my little girl is Zoe."

"Zip is an unusual name," said Officer Green as she shook his hand.

"It is a nickname. My real name is Temperance. I am named after my great-grandmother."

"It is a fun name. Don't hear it too often," Hunter replied.

Zip managed a smile. "Well, gentlemen, I am going to check on my little girl and then we have some work to do. Swab the decks and all of that."

The men laughed as she left the bridge and went into the main cabin to check on Zoe.

CHAPTER THIRTY-EIGHT

Zip washed Zoe's face with the water in the small head behind the bridge. She felt a wave of nausea in the confined space as the boat bounced wildly in the rough water. When they returned to their spot on the bench, she found a covered rubber band in the pack and secured Zoe's hair in a ponytail before smearing her face and arms with sunscreen. The child surveyed her surroundings and then turned to her mother with a somber expression.

"It is a mess in here, Mommy," she whispered. "And it smells bad. I want to go home."

"I do too, sweetheart, and we will get home soon to be with Daddy." Zip caressed her daughter's face, feeling helpless about their circumstances.

Zoe looked over at the sleeping passengers. "Is the bad lady gone?"

"Yes, baby, she is gone for good. No one here will hurt you. They are all scared by the bad people. They are nice," she assured the child.

Zip retrieved two pieces of chocolate candy she had saved from the nightly turn-down service, which she later had stowed in one of the hiking pack's exterior pockets. She counted ten pieces of candy in the pouch. She would have to ration them. Food was going to be scarce until they were rescued. Zip worried about Zoe having enough to eat. Zip had never had a large appetite, but the child needed regular meals. She would have to make sure Zoe had enough to eat at all costs.

She held out one piece of chocolate. The child's face lit up when she saw the golden wrapper with the swan logo. "Open your mouth, Zoe."

Zoe grinned as Zip popped the candy into the little girl's mouth. "Mmm, it's good. I never have chocolate candy for breakfast."

"I know. Now keep your mouth closed," she said, giving her a hug.

Officer Green peeked into the cabin. "Look who is up," he said enthusiastically. "Would you like to come onto the bridge with us? I will let you steer the boat."

Zoe looked at her mother with pleading eyes. "Mommy, please?"

"Of course. You are a lucky girl. Be sure only to touch what they tell you to."

Zoe grinned clasping Officer's Green's hand and following him onto the bridge.

Zip reorganized the pack and sat quietly in her seat watching the storms in the distance. The salty wind blew into the cabin from the open windows. The circumstances all seemed so surreal, but at least, for the moment, they were safe from danger.

By 7:00 a.m., nearly all of the passengers except Marie were awake. George Evans from Brighton, relieved Joey of his lookout duties. His wife, Sienna, and Hunter's wife, Aurora Campbell, took turns going to the head. Becky had given up trying to console her friend Marie. She helped Officer Reed and Zip count the food provisions in the storage locker. There was a surprising amount of dried and canned food. They would need to ration the food carefully for the days ahead. Hopefully, they could supplement the stores with fresh fish. There were five 30-gallon plastic jugs of fresh water on the bottom shelf of the locker. It was enough to last a few days, but certainly not enough for thirteen people spending an extended time on the boat. A case of ginger ale was shoved behind the water.

"For seasickness," Officer Reed explained to Becky and Zip. "You would be surprised how many passengers feel sick when we use the life-boats as tenders to ferry people from the ship to the beach."

"It will be great for emergencies, and it is loaded with sugar," said Becky as she counted the cans. We have twenty-eight containers here."

"We will have to keep track," Officer Reed told them. "I will keep the key with me," she said, as she looped the chain around her neck, concealing it under the blouse of her uniform.

"Is there any powdered clear soup we can make for breakfast?" Zip asked. "I think people could use something warm until we can catch some fish."

Officer Reed retrieved a large pouch of chicken-flavored ramen and filled a container with water.

"This should work," she said, as she handed the pouch to Zip and continued to peer inside the cabinet. Reed located a vacuum-sealed container with thirteen plastic cups, which she handed to Becky before locking the cabinet. The three women set up the hot plate on the shelf near the stern, trying to ignore the stench emanating from tarps concealing the dead bodies of their fellow passengers.

When the soup was finally hot, Officer Reed ladled the thick liquid with rehydrated noodles into each cup. Becky and Zip distributed the soup to all of the passengers, as well as to Officer Green and Oliver. Everyone seemed grateful for the refreshment except Marie, who remained curled up on the bench, in a near catatonic state. Becky and Officer Reed tried to coax her to drink the liquid but to no avail.

"She is in shock," Officer Reed told them. "Hopefully, she will come out of it."

"Let's give her cup to the officers," Zip suggested. "We are counting on them to save us, and they need their strength."

"I think that's a great idea," replied Becky, as she took the extra cup and headed toward the bridge.

After everyone had finished their soup, the women collected the cups and wiped them down with a cloth. They would need to wash them with seawater later; they could not spare the fresh water simply to wash dishes.

Officer Oliver cut the engine back and slowed the vessel to less than three knots before shutting down the engine entirely. The silence was pleasant as the engine noise disappeared. Officer Green explained that they needed to drain the bilge. The vessel was continuing to take on water, probably from the damage to the hull from the grenades. They also needed to conserve fuel. They had consumed over half of the fuel on board fleeing the ship.

"We are going to float for a while. The currents in this area are going south, which is the direction we want to go. It will give us a chance to get organized."

While the officers drained the seawater in the bilge, Joey, Todd, Hunter, and George filled buckets with seawater and washed down the interior of the vessel. The water drained through scuppers in the floor. Joey used a plastic broom to scrub the blood and human remains from the floor and walls of the vessel.

After the vessel had been cleaned as much as possible, Hunter and George opened the hatch near the bridge and dropped two fishing lines into the water. The hooks were baited with a foul-smelling dark-red substance from a small plastic container near the hatch.

Zip sat back against the bench, cuddling Zoe in her arms, enjoying the lap of the waves against the vessel and the empty landscape. The silence was a welcome respite from the constant droning of the engine. She watched the two British men as they stood together fishing from the lifeboat. In spite of their circumstances, the men looked almost content.

"I've hooked one!" Hunter exclaimed as he reeled a large fish onto the deck. He took a pair of pliers and removed the fishhook as the fish struggled violently, slapping its tail against the wooden deck.

What a beauty," acknowledged George over his shoulder. "It must be at least ten pounds, enough for everyone to have a good meal.

"I will clean it," Hunter replied, severing the fish head with a knife. "We can use the heads to make a broth or for bait." Zip watched as Hunter expertly cleaned the fish, making small fillets and carefully placing them on a small plate Officer Reed had retrieved from the vessel stores.

"We have a small bit of flour and oil. We can coat them lightly and cook them in the pan. It should be delicious," Reed told them brightly.

Just as suddenly, George called to the group. "I have one too!" He reeled the fish onto the deck. It was another large fish, even larger than the one Hunter had caught. Proudly, George extracted the hook, severed the head, and began the process of cleaning the fish. Afterward, they washed the deck down with salt water from the bucket.

Zip felt relieved. At least they would have something to eat. After her adrenalin had dissipated, she had been left with a gnawing hunger that she tried to ignore. But more importantly, Zoe would have nutrition to keep her alive. Zip knew from her nonprofit work with the United Way in Seattle that children were particularly susceptible to acute fatal illness from starvation or dehydration. Zip would have to watch Zoe very carefully.

But what if they were not rescued for a week or even two weeks? What if they were never rescued? Survival would be impossible.

Zip tried to ignore the nagging fears of their situation and busied herself cooking the fish with Becky. Sienna and Aurora helped distribute the food around the cabin on a plate heaped with steaming freshly caught fish. Despite the primitive culinary conditions, the fish had a nice brown crust and was fully cooked.

The mood inside the cabin improved dramatically. Everyone held the warm fish in their hands, no longer bothering with utensils, and consumed the meal with gusto. Everyone, except Marie, seemed to have forgotten their desperate circumstances or the dead bodies stacked in the rear of the vessel.

"This is delicious," said Aurora. "Such a fresh taste. Hunter, I am now glad you took all of those fishing trips to Scotland. It came in handy."

Hunter laughed. "Thank you, darling. Probably the best fish I ever tasted, if I do say so myself."

"Watch for bones, baby," Zip told Zoe. "Let me help you." Zip cleaned out the bones and fed Zoe small chunks of the fish. She was pleased to see the child had a good appetite.

In record time, the heaping plates of fresh fish had been consumed. Zip felt deliciously full and surprisingly relaxed.

Becky and Aurora wiped the fish plate down, doused it in the bucket of seawater, and then dumped the seawater on the floor.

Zip sat back on the bench with Zoe's head in her lap. She looked through the open window as a pod of dolphins swam by, frolicking and leaping through the water. Except for the dolphins and the sea creatures, they were alone in the vast wilderness. There was no sign the hijackers were following them.

The air felt close, and as the sky darkened with an approaching storm, Zoe fell asleep. Officer Green closed and latched the hatch as a torrential rain began to fall. The sound of the rain pelting the roof of the small cabin relaxed Zip. Feeling pleasantly sated, she fell into a deep sleep.

CHAPTER THIRTY-NINE

James felt surprisingly refreshed as the jet touched down on the runway and taxied to the LAX terminal. He had slept at least seven hours and devoured the snack of almond croissants, fruit, yogurt, orange juice, and a latte. He had brushed his teeth, washed his face, and combed his hair after breakfast. It was late afternoon in LA, but still early morning in the UK, an eight-hour time difference. Despite the time change, he did not feel jet lagged, although he doubted he would sleep a full eight hours that night.

He sent Reed and Bunny separate text messages letting them know he had arrived. He was fast-tracked through US Customs as a diplomatic courtesy prearranged by the UK and the US prior to his arrival. Within minutes, he walked through the baggage claim area.

He saw a driver holding a sign with his name as he exited the baggage claim area. James was surprised that the driver was in his mid-twenties and dressed in an expensive suit and Italian shoes. He was fit and handsome, probably an aspiring actor working his day job until he was discovered.

"Mr. Brooks?" he asked James in a neutral accent.

"Yes, I am James Brooks."

"Please follow me, sir."

The driver grabbed James's shoulder bag and escorted him to a black stretch limousine in a covered parking area. James had never been in a vehicle so large. The temperature outside was pleasantly cool. As the driver opened the door, James realized it was the night before Easter.

Isaac Grimm and Kurt Incandela, representatives of the Paradise Line, sat on the large sofa across from him inside the limo. The men shook hands and exchanged pleasantries before settling in for the drive. Both men had California glow tans and were dressed in designer business casual attire. They had come to the airport specifically to meet James.

As the limousine exited the garage and entered a crowded freeway, James noticed the milky-white sky from the notorious LA pollution. Golden mountains soared in the distance in the waning light. The vast freeway system with multiple lanes was unlike anything he had ever seen.

Isaac, a man who appeared to be in his late forties, was obviously in charge. He leaned back in his seat nursing a latte in a Starbucks cup. Kurt, who was only slightly younger, had the body language of someone deferring to a superior.

"Might as well settle in for the drive. On a Saturday evening, the traffic in LA is a nightmare," Isaac told James.

"It is amazing. So different than New York. So where are we going first?"

"We are going straight to the Peninsula Hotel. Two lawyers the Paradise Line hired will meet us there. Horace Tweed from San Francisco was instructed by one of the P&I Clubs. Roth Henley from McMinn Wood is national counsel for the Paradise Line and arrived early this morning."

"What about any Club representatives?"

"John Montrose and Gray Keating from the San Francisco offices are with Horace and Roth," Isaac replied. "We have been conferring with them since the event, along with all of the national and international investigators. Most employees of the Paradise Line have been interviewed to find out whether the hijacking was masterminded by someone in the main office. It has been chaos, and we have all been interviewed by a swarm of law enforcement."

"Any leads or targets?"

Kurt shook his head. "If there are, the government is not telling us. National security interests. They also have had forensic computer specialists collect all of the data from the Paradise Line network and have been meeting with the IT employees. They are leaving no stone unturned."

"What about the owners of the line?" James asked.

Isaac nodded to Kurt as if granting him permission to speak. "Greg and Erika Vandeberg are the majority shareholders of the line. They arrived by private jet from their vacation home in Bermuda and are staying in a suite at the hotel. They were celebrating Easter weekend with their extended family in Bermuda. They have been meeting with the FBI, the CIA, the State Department, and the Attorney General, along with their attorneys, for hours. Both of them are beside themselves about what has happened.

"Greg is a savvy businessman. He appreciates the drastic financial implications this event will have on the future of the line. The line will be forever tagged with the name of the Good Friday Justice ship."

James nodded and continued to listen. Although he understood the Vandebergs' financial and public relations concerns, his thoughts were focused on the passengers and crew who had perished in the sinking of the cruise ship.

"Have they found any survivors yet or lifeboats? I checked the news on my phone and the television monitor on CNN when I arrived, but the reports are saying that there is nothing."

Isaac shook his head somberly. "Nothing. We all fear the worst."

"What about the survivor, Reynolds Tyler?"

"He is at the hotel finally trying to rest. He was up all night being interviewed by the FBI, the Attorney General, the Coast Guard, and the

State Department. There is a multidisciplinary task force investigating the events in the US and meeting with Tyler. He is still a person of interest because it is such a coincidence that he left the ship on the day of the hijacking. The Line arranged for him to be seen by a doctor, who gave him a sedative so he could rest tonight."

James shook his head. "Anything else from his wife and little girl?"

Isaac rubbed the sides of the Starbucks cup nervously and put the empty container on the shelf in the limo. "Nothing. They are presumed dead. No one could survive those waters unless they were in a lifeboat. The area is full of vicious sharks that will tear you apart, especially at night. This is like the WWII USS *Indianapolis* sinking where the crew escaped but many were later killed by sharks. But in some of the satellite footage, one of the lifeboats appears to have been launched. There was a brief EPIRB signal, but then it vanished. The militaries from the US, New Zealand, and Australia are conducting a search."

James considered Isaac's report, sitting silently and watching the river of taillights relentlessly moving forward in the twilight down the freeway. It all seemed hopeless.

"As the Lloyd's representative, I would like to be involved in any meetings with the Clubs and government officials. I am a junior member of the K&R task force for the London Market," he said, finally breaking the silence.

"And that is our understanding," replied Kurt. "We will include you in everything we can, but it is the government's show. They are running things, as you might expect."

"And I would like to meet with Reynolds Tyler as well. The task force designated me to be a liaison with him for the insurers.

"I think that is a good thing. He needs an ally and emotional support until this thing with his family comes to a conclusion. There are plaintiff's lawyers coming out of the woodwork to represent him. The hotel actually caught some bottom-feeder attorney dressed in a kitchen uniform trying to deliver room service to his suite. They are like the sharks; they smell blood in the water," Isaac replied.

James nodded his head in agreement and again turned his gaze to the city as the limo slowed and exited the freeway. Within minutes, the vehicle pulled into a beautiful hotel entrance surrounded by lush, manicured grounds. The driver followed James, Isaac, and Kurt into the gorgeous lobby, where James sailed through a seamless check-in. A bellhop gave him his key and advised him that he would put his baggage in the room.

James followed Kurt and Isaac to the door of a conference room on the second floor that was being used as a command center. As they opened the door, he could see more than ten people were clustered around a shiny conference room table in deep discussion. The television screens were tuned to CNN and the BBC. The scene reminded James of the meeting at the Lloyd's library. He took a deep breath and entered the room behind Isaac and Kurt, ready to settle in for more hours of waiting for a shred of hopeful news.

CHAPTER FORTY

The atmosphere in the conference room was similar to the somber mood in the Lloyd's library. Most of the passengers and crew were presumed dead. But the news was not all bad. The latest satellite footage showed what appeared to be a lifeboat that had detached from the cruise ship sailing south before the explosion that sank the ship. The footage provided a glimmer of hope that there might be some survivors. But the EPIRB signal that had been studied by the experts had suddenly disappeared. The satellite images also showed what appeared to be rocket-propelled grenade hitting the stern of the lifeboat, causing a large flash of light. After the blast, the lifeboat navigation and running lights had disappeared. There was speculation that the boat was operating without lights to remain concealed until they escaped the hijackers. But at this point, this was only conjecture, and there was no hard evidence to support this theory.

It was after 9:00 p.m. when Reynolds Tyler arrived at the conference room, escorted by Club representatives Montrose and Gray. He wore jeans, a Tommy Bahama shirt, sunglasses, and a baseball cap, which he removed as the door closed behind him.

James rose and introduced himself to Tyler as he sat down at the table in the chair beside him. He noticed that Tyler's solemn expression was one of defeat and vulnerability. The man was handsome with dark hair, olive skin, and piercing dark eyes.

"I work for the Lunar Syndicate in London. I came over as a representative to show our support during this difficult time. Please let me know if there is anything you need. I am here to help you in any way possible through this ordeal."

Reynolds nodded. "Thanks." He was relieved to see that James, who was about his own age, was here to support him.

"Were you able to get any rest?"

"I can't sleep. I keep thinking of my wife and daughter, wondering if they are alive and what they are going through. I would show you a photo, but the FBI took my phone to image it."

James was glad the man was at least interested in talking to him. "I saw their photos on the BBC in London. You have a gorgeous family."

Reynolds nodded as tears began to stream down his cheeks. He wiped his face with the back of his hand. "They are…gorgeous. Fair skin, red hair, and beautiful features. I cannot believe I may never see them again."

"I can't imagine what you are going through."

"It is awful. I notified the FBI when I got here and read the text. I could not believe it. By the time I arrived, the news was already reporting on the terrorist attack."

"That must have been a shock."

"The worst ever. Then the FBI took me to their building and questioned me for hours. They took my laptop and my phone, searched my wife's Facebook page, and reviewed all of our social media. They acted as if I were the criminal instead of focusing on the terrorists. It is no wonder people hate law enforcement in this country."

"Terrible."

"Yes, as if I were the suspect. It was bullshit! Every minute the FBI wasted interviewing me, they could have been trying to find the terrorists."

James nodded, encouraging Reynolds to continue to vent his anger and frustration. "I would be furious. It seems like a waste of time, especially since they arrested customs officials in Papeete."

"They seem to think it is all an inside job and, of course, it may be. Someone connected with the cruise line may have hijacked the boat. But I was a simple tourist on a dream vacation with my wife and daughter. I had to come back for work because I have a jackass for a boss. It all seemed so unfair at the time, but it is the only reason I am alive." His lips quivered, and his eyes glistened with tears.

"Were you by yourselves?"

"We were with friends from Seattle. Wilson likes to scuba dive, and we had some really great shark encounter dives on the trip. His wife, Carla, is a yoga instructor and a good friend of my wife. Their little girl, Poppy, is the same age as my daughter Zoe. They attend kindergarten at Epiphany School together. I hope they are with Zip and Zoe. Maybe they escaped the boat together, although they are not holding out much hope here there will be many survivors. The waters are full of sharks, and there is nothing around for miles. Unless they are on a lifeboat, they will not get far."

"I understand that there may be a lifeboat out there. If it is there, the search-and-rescue teams will likely find it. I hope your wife and daughter are on it."

"God, I hope so. Zoe was so excited about Easter. The boat had arranged for an Easter egg hunt and an Easter Bunny visit for all of the kids. Zip bought a package that included a giant Easter basket for Zoe. The kid loves Easter, and now she may be dead…"

Reynolds, becoming distraught again, put his head in his hands. James looked away, trying to allow the man beside him to grieve with dignity. He turned his attention to the television screens mounted on the walls.

The images on the television screen tuned to BBC displayed grainy satellite footage of the *Golden Swan* consumed by flames. Photographs of the terrorists crawled across the bottom of the screen. On the other screen, an image of Zip and Zoe filled the giant monitor. A CNN news anchor described the latest news in a clipped monotone.

"The world is watching the terrible drama unfold in the South Pacific Ocean region known as Oceania, shown on the map on your screen. The luxury cruise vessel, the *Golden Swan*, was hijacked and blown up by a terrorist group calling themselves Cell 53. The Cell is calling the hijacking Good Friday Justice. The terrorist group is believed to have originated in Yemen by radical extremists. Some of the terrorists, who were posing as tourists, took over the vessel and destroyed it. At this time, the governments of the US, the UK, Australia, and New Zealand are conducting search-and-rescue efforts in the shark-infested waters of the South Pacific. More than 800 people are feared dead, and it is not known if there are any survivors. One passenger, Temperance Tyler of Seattle, sent a text message to her husband, Reynolds Tyler, that the ship had been taken over by terrorists. It is not known whether Ms. Tyler, known as Zip, and their daughter escaped the vessel. In other news, it is Easter Sunday at the Vatican, and the Pope has condemned the violence in Oceania and the activities of Cell 53. He said a prayer today for those lost and any survivors."

James watched helplessly as Reynolds quietly sobbed, his shoulders heaving and his face buried in his hands. He reached over, grabbed the remote control on the conference room table, and muted the sound. He placed his hand on Reynolds's shoulder. The cluster of people at the other end of the table looked at Reynolds with concern, obviously unsure about how to handle the situation.

"Do you want some fresh air, maybe something light to eat? What do you think about getting out of here for a while?"

Reynolds wiped his eyes. "The news is so bleak. I am losing all hope."

James shook his head. "My fiancée, Bunny, says you should never give up hope. We know your wife was safe when she sent you the text. And the footage from the theatre has been studied and many of the victims have been identified. Zip was not one of those victims. The search and rescue teams believe there are survivors somewhere. Don't give up hope until they call off the search."

Reynolds nodded. "Let's get the hell out of here. There is a place upstairs, The Roof Garden, where we can get a drink and maybe a salad or a burger."

James stood up. "Let's go. The atmosphere in here is too intense."

Reynolds donned his cap and sunglasses, and the two men took the elevator up to the rooftop restaurant to try to relax.

CHAPTER FORTY-ONE

It was still dark when Zip awoke from her nap. A massive thunderstorm loomed overhead. A hard rain fell, and the air was chilly. The boat rocked wildly in the choppy waves. Zip felt a surge of apprehension as she became aware of her surroundings. Without the adrenalin that had motivated her escape from the ship, she felt sluggish and exhausted, and she had a sour taste in her mouth. Her neck was stiff from lying on the bench at a strange angle. She stretched, thinking how wonderful it would be to have a hot shower and brush her teeth.

Zoe was already awake and sitting with Officer Reed on the opposing bench chatting happily about her life in Seattle. The strands of the child's strawberry-blonde hair that had escaped her ponytail were buffeted by the strong wind. She had a piece of half-eaten fish in her hand, and grease had dribbled down her arms.

"Will you come and see us in Seattle when we are rescued?" She gave Officer Reed a guileless smile, as if they were simply enjoying an afternoon outing at a water park.

Reed smoothed the child's hair. "Of course, if it is alright with your parents."

Zip sat up in her seat. "After this, I suspect we will all be lifetime friends. You are welcome to come stay with us in Seattle."

Officer Reed gave Zip a warm smile. "I would love to."

"So, would we."

Zip shivered. She pulled a thin jacket from her pack and gave it to Zoe. "Put this on. The last thing we need is for you to catch a cold."

The sound of the rain coming through the open windows was loud, and occasional bursts of wind blew water into the stern of the vessel. Zip noticed that a pool of water had accumulated around the stack of bodies in the stern. The water sloshed across the floor in waves each time the boat rocked.

Hunter and Aurora had moved to the front of the lifeboat away from the driving wind. Aurora's aqua blouse was stained with blood and coated with fish scales. Her short gray hair was lifted from her head by the wind. Hunter leaned back in the seat with his arm protectively around his wife. They both smiled at Zip.

"Are we still drifting?" Zip asked, noticing the absence of engine noise.

Hunter leaned forward talking loudly over the drumming of the rain on the vessel ceiling. "We have used a full tank of fuel, and the auxiliary engine is empty. We have less than a quarter tank in the remaining tank. So, Officer Green decided to cut the engines for a while. We have traveled a long way since yesterday, and the water is rough. Fortunately, these currents are strong and are moving us down farther south."

Zip nodded, considering the implications of what Hunter was telling her. What if they were not discovered? Would it be possible for them to live on the boat for a month? She turned away from Zoe and Officer Reed, hoping not to be overheard. The child was giggling and playing a guessing game with Reed. She seemed content and was not focused on her mother's conversation. But Zip had to be careful not to alarm the child.

"Will they be able to find us out here? Will they be looking for us this far away from the ship?"

Hunter rested his elbows on the back of the seat in front of him and looked at Zip compassionately. "These lifeboats are orange for a reason, and they stand out in this blue water. We also have flares. And the rescue teams will be using satellite images. We may be stuck on the boat for a few days, but we will ultimately be rescued."

"Do we have enough water?"

"Officer Oliver set up a couple of the empty water bottles in the corner, and we are filling them with rainwater. It should be potable."

"Have you seen the water in the back pooling around the bodies?"

"Yes, it's blowing in from the rain. When it stops, we will bail it out and mop it up."

Zip, now placated, sat back in her seat, feeling relieved that Hunter did not feel concerned.

Aurora handed Zip a plate of fish. "Hunter caught another fish. We saved you a plate. You were sleeping so soundly no one wanted to disturb your rest. You might want something to eat. If the weather does not let up, we might not be able to catch fish today."

"And we will be stuck eating that awful dehydrated food," Hunter laughed.

Aurora screwed up her face in mock disgust. "I can't wait."

Zip accepted the plate of fish, which by now was only lukewarm. But it had a lovely crust, almost as if it had been fried. The fish was surprisingly delicious, and she found she was hungry, no doubt from the terrific strain. She finished her food quickly and immediately began to feel better. She glanced over at Zoe, who was still playing a word game with Officer Reed. She was thankful Reed had made it onto the lifeboat with them. She was a godsend for Zoe.

Zip went to the back and tossed the fish bone out of the window and held the metal dish up to the rain to rinse it. Joey was asleep on the bench, and the Evanses were visiting with Becky and Todd. Marie remained curled in a fetal position in the back, a rosary clasped in her hands. Officer Oliver slept peacefully on a bench in the back, the rain masking his soft snores.

"What did you do back home?" Zip asked Hunter and Aurora when she came back to her seat.

Aurora smiled brightly. "Hunter is a retired surgeon. He retired in December, and this was our celebration trip. I taught school for a number of years until I stopped to raise our two boys, who are now grown and living in London. I like to cook, garden, and read."

Zip enjoyed listening to Aurora and Hunter speak in their lovely English accents. "I like those things too. I went to England once during my college years. It is beautiful, and the weather is very much like Seattle weather: cool but never too hot and lots of rain."

"What about you?" Hunter asked.

Zip smiled, noticing Hunter's hands for the first time. They were small, soft, and delicate, the hands of a doctor. Hunter reminded her of her gynecologist who delivered Zoe. "I am a part-time graphic artist. I have a home office, and I work from there independently. It gives me flexibility so I can take all of the time I need to be with Zoe and take care of the house."

"That is lovely," replied Aurora. "And what about your husband?"

"He works for a big tech company, and he is always engrossed in his work. This trip was our get-away family vacation with friends, but then he had to leave early to deal with a work crisis. There is always a work crisis."

"Well, you and your little girl are safe," Aurora said gently. "And so is your husband. And after this, we will all have a compelling story about how we survived."

Zip sat back against her seat as the boat suddenly lurched to the starboard side, listing badly.

Zoe shrieked, a look of terror on her face. Officer Reed's face paled, and her expression was one of concern.

"Mommy! What's happening? The boat is sinking."

Zip slid over toward her daughter and wrapped her arms around Zoe. The sudden movement had roused the resting passengers, who were now staring at the deep list of the lifeboat.

Officer Green rushed into the room, bracing himself on the backs of the seats as he walked down the aisle toward Officer Oliver, who was furiously rubbing his eyes.

Officer Green stood in the middle of the cabin, talking loudly over the rain. "Is everyone alright?" He surveyed the room noticing that no one seemed injured. "There is water in the bilge and it is causing the boat to list. This was probably caused by the blast from the hijackers. I have turned on the bilge pump, but it does not appear to be working. I am going down to the engine compartment to try to fix it, but I may need you men to help bail water. We have emergency buckets in the forward hatch."

"Are we going to sink?" asked Becky. Zip noticed that her usually placid face had become a mask of terror.

"We are not going to sink. But we do need to fix it," he replied authoritatively.

Joey raised his hand. "I'll help bail water. I do it in my brother's little runabout boat all of the time."

Todd, Hunter, and George all sprang from the benches and agreed to help. Zip noticed they had become a functioning team and not simply a group of strangers.

Officer Oliver rushed to the front of the lifeboat and retrieved two buckets and a tool kit. He gave the tool kit to Officer Green and distributed the buckets to Todd and Joey.

Officer Green walked to the stern of the lifeboat and lifted up a large hatch covering the engine room.

Todd stared at the interior of the compartment. "Jesus Christ! It is nearly full of water."

Joey put the bucket into the water and began to bail.

CHAPTER FORTY-TWO

James and Reynolds sat in the rooftop restaurant until midnight when it closed. They had consumed a bottle of French sauvignon blanc after their lobster salads and cheese platter. James tried to keep the conversation light, so they discussed sports and travel. Reynolds seemed genuinely interested in James's work travel and his life in Cambridge, and James did his best to distract him.

"I don't think I can face sitting in that room downstairs any more. Everyone is very attentive and knocking themselves out, but I need some time alone. In its own way, it is a strain to listen to the news broadcasts 24-7," Reynolds told James after James had paid the check and they rose to leave.

"I know you must be going through agony. I think I will turn in as well. It has been a long day, and there is an eight-hour time difference."

"I still can't stop thinking about them. Here I am in a five-star hotel and they may be drowning in the South Pacific. I feel very guilty," Reynolds said after James pushed the elevator button for their floor. The hotel had arranged for the group to stay on the same floor.

"It is very possible they made it to the lifeboat that was launched from the ship," James said as the elevator doors opened on the fourth floor.

"I am almost afraid to hope," Reynolds replied, as they walked down the hall, stopping in front of Room 412. "This is me."

"I am in Room 419. Don't hesitate to call me or send me an email or text any time. You have my card. I am a light sleeper, and with the time change, I am sure I will be up early."

The two men shook hands, and James walked down to his room. He could hear the door open after Reynolds activated the key card to enter his room.

The hotel had booked James into a suite with a spacious and beautifully decorated living room area, large bedroom with a king-sized bed, and sumptuous marble bath. Both rooms were appointed with 85-inch flat-screen televisions. The suite was the ultimate luxurious space, available only for the uber-rich. There was an adjoining balcony with a comfortable sectional. He noticed the bellhop had unpacked his suitcase and that his shirts and slacks were hanging in the closet. There was a printed note card advising that his shirts had been pressed courtesy of the hotel.

James took a hot shower and brushed his teeth with the toiletries provided by the hotel. Afterward, he put on the terry cloth hotel robe and went out onto the balcony for some fresh air. Suddenly, he was no longer tired.

He sent Bunny and Reed each text messages. Bunny responded immediately. "Love and miss you to the moon and back. Come home soon! Happy Easter!" She included a heart emoticon, a rabbit, and a smiley face with a kiss on its cheek.

Reed's response to the text message was simply to call James on the phone. He was from the telephone generation. James knew his boss preferred direct communication over text or email.

"I am glad you are awake. I just finished breakfast at the Four Seasons, and I thought I would go back over to the Library. It's been raining pretty hard this morning. My wife is having Easter lunch with my daughter, her husband, and their children at their home at Sevenoaks. The Easter egg hunt for the kids may be rained out. How is it going?" Reed asked him.

James could not help but think of the irony of Reed staying at the Four Seasons, which had recently opened in a historic building at Ten Trinity Square. James had been booked at the hotel across the street.

"Reynolds is upset but glad to have someone to talk with who is not affiliated with law enforcement or the cruise line. I think he was feeling almost suffocated by the American lawyers and the cruise line representatives. He is, as you would expect, beside himself about his wife and child and panicked about the situation. We went to dinner together, and it was a good distraction."

"Well, it does not look good. It has been almost thirty-six hours since the takeover of the ship and everyone is feared dead. The search-and-rescue teams are still looking for the lifeboat, but they are coming up empty. While the satellite footage indicates that a lifeboat was launched, it was a dangerous-as-hell effort because the ship was traveling at full speed. The lifeboats are designed to be launched when the ship is moving at a maximum speed of five knots."

"Did the EPIRB ever activate again?"

"No, and the lifeboat may have sunk or been incapacitated by either the launching or gunfire from the hijackers. According to the information obtained by INTERPOL from the customs agents, the ship had rocket-propelled grenades onboard, and plastic explosives had been placed throughout the hull. They still can't rule out that the hijackers might have escaped from the ship before it was destroyed. The customs agents did not know if this was a suicide mission or if they had escaped."

"Why did they cooperate in something so horrific?"

"They were each paid $100,000 American dollars. None of these people could have ever hoped to have that much money at one time in their lives."

James listened to Reed as he described the details of the investigation. The news was disheartening. It was quite possible that no one had survived and that all had perished.

"The teams have located ship debris in the area of the explosion. There were one or two bodies found clinging to debris and half-devoured by the sharks. There is not much left: metal fragments and plastic floating on the surface. The ship now appears to be resting on the ocean floor."

"How long will they continue to search?" James asked finally.

Reed paused. "Probably another forty-eight to seventy-two hours—or until there is no hope."

James sighed. "I am not sure how Reynolds will react when the search is called off."

"Does he have family? Parents or siblings? Anyone?"

"Apparently not. He told me his father died when he was young. He was raised by his stepfather and mother in New Jersey until they both passed away. He was an only child. His wife and child were everything to him."

"Christ."

"He mentioned going back to Seattle. He wants to go home. He said it will make him feel closer to his wife and little girl to be in their own home."

"Go with him and stay close by. The man needs support, and we want to help him."

"I am willing to go to Seattle. I have never been there. I hear it is beautiful."

"Do what is necessary. I am sure he will be contacted by lawyers who are dying to bring suit. He is vulnerable and in pain."

"Alright."

"The plaintiff's lawyers will be worse than sharks. The family members of some of the American passengers identified in the theatre have already hired lawyers. After the search is called off, the cruise line will probably file a limitation action to marshal the lawsuits. I am sure there will be an avalanche of litigation."

James was becoming annoyed with the discussion of litigation. It was easy to be cynical and detached working on files in a beautiful office in London. Under those circumstances, it was easy to lose sight of the significant pain of the victims' families. James's job up to that point had been all about numbers, insurance reserves, capping legal defense costs, and claims resolutions. The meetings, global investigations, and his dinner with Reynolds had given James a front seat to human tragedy. The man was faced with the fact that he might never see his wife and child again. James was becoming involved in the tragedy, which gave him a different perspective.

"It is a disaster for the cruise line. And the representatives admitted that as much when they picked me up at the airport."

"It is a nightmare. A billion in primary and excess limits is probably not enough to cover it," Reed replied. "And it is a tragedy for the passengers. The entire event will probably revolutionize security on cruise ships, just like 9/11."

"It is awful, and I am watching it firsthand."

Reed's tone softened, as if he understood what James had been feeling since he arrived in LA. "I am sure it is difficult, and we appreciate what you are doing. You are a good man. You should get some rest," Reed replied, his tone conveying that understood the difficulty of James's position.

"I will call you later."

"Speak then," Reed said as he terminated the call.

James plugged his phone into the complimentary telephone charger and flipped on the television, watching an old episode of *Law & Order:*

SVU until he could no longer keep his eyes open. Finally, he flipped the button on the nightstand and extinguished the lights. Almost instantly, he fell into a dreamless sleep.

CHAPTER FORTY-THREE

Hunter, George, Joey, and Officer Oliver continued to bail long after sunrise while Officer Green worked on the bilge pump. The vessel remained in a 30-degree starboard list, making it difficult to move around the cabin. The pleasant mood had dissipated into palpable anxiety. Zip noticed that Officer Oliver's expression was grim.

The rainwater that had been carefully collected from the storm had splashed across the floor due to the vessel's list. The containers were now less than one-third full.

By late morning, most of the water had been bailed out and the vessel had been righted. The water that had puddled around the bodies had been mopped up. Through it all, Marie had remained curled up on a corner bench.

The rain had stopped, and a high-pressure system had come through the area. The salty air felt clean and fresh, but the air inside the cabin was oppressively hot. The seas were calm, and the water was no longer turbid. Through the open window, Zip could see a number of sharks swimming about fifteen feet below the surface. The scene gave her the chills. Despite the startling beauty of the ocean, the water was clearly dangerous.

Officer Oliver had finally repaired the bilge pump, which sprang to life. Everyone gave him a round of applause. Joey and Todd whooped in excitement. The somber mood had turned more hopeful, and relief was evident.

The small assembly watched in fascination as the bilge pump drained most, but not all, of the water from the engine room and compartments below. Afterward, Officer Green replaced the hatch cover and went to the front cabin to speak with Officer Oliver.

Zip and Zoe returned to their bench in the front of the cabin. Zip had noticed that the bodies of the deceased passengers had begun to emit a foul odor, and she was eager to escape the stench. If anyone else had noticed the odor, none of them had said anything.

From her position on her bench, Zip saw that the two officers had turned toward the bow away from the passengers and appeared to be having an animated discussion. They were speaking in low tones, so Zip could not hear their conversation. After a time, Officer Reed joined them on the bridge.

Finally, the three of them emerged from the bridge into the cabin. Their expressions were serious. They stood together in the middle of the cabin facing the passengers.

Officer Oliver addressed the group. "We have a leak in the stern of the lifeboat. The force of the grenade gouged a hole in the metal. It is not a huge hole, but it is enough to cause a problem. Officer Green bolted a steel plate in front of the hole, but it is far from watertight. There is not much we can do except to run the bilge pump and hope for the best." He paused and scanned the faces of the group.

Joey spoke first. "What is that going to mean? What can we do to help?"

Officer Oliver did not break eye contact with the group. Obviously, he had been accustomed to dealing with disaster head-on. "We will try to control it as much as possible, and we will pump and bail the water. If the bilge pump stops working again, we will have a problem. We will deal with it as best we can."

"And if we can't?" Todd asked, the concern etched in his face.

Officer Oliver's tone remained even and controlled. Despite the circumstances, he seemed confident. "Worst-case scenario is that we might have to evacuate to the inflatable boats. We have three of them. Each boat has a small outboard engine. They are bright orange. Unfortunately, they are not covered, but it may be necessary to do that to stay alive."

Hunter stood up from the bench he shared with Aurora near the window. His voice was calm. "How likely do you think that is?"

Officer Oliver cleared his throat. "We hope we can keep the lifeboat afloat and control the problem until we are rescued. The EPIRB was destroyed, but we have continued to put out a Mayday call on the radio. There is no reason to not believe that we will be rescued before the worst happens. I am sure there is a search for survivors of the explosion. The only fact working against us is that this is a remote, desolate area."

Hunter nodded. "So, hopefully it might not be necessary, but you are saying we need to be prepared."

Officer Green spoke up. "That is correct. I do not want to unnecessarily alarm anyone, but we need to be realistic. The list earlier this morning was a real problem, and we need to be vigilant about how much water we are taking on. I think we need to be prepared to bail every hour, or even every half hour if necessary. But if we have a rapid water incursion, we will have to evacuate immediately. We might have only minutes to evacuate safely, so we need to prepare."

"How? What should we do?" Todd asked.

"I want to inflate the small boats and tether them to the lifeboat. Then, if we need to evacuate quickly, we will be prepared. We will also need to wear life vests at all times."

"What about food and water?" Aurora called from her spot next to Hunter.

Officer Green nodded. "I want to put some provisions of food and water by the head. In an emergency, we can transfer them to the small boats quickly. Again, this is just a precaution, but we need to be prepared for anything."

"Will we all fit in the boats?" Becky asked, obviously shaken by the news.

"There are thirteen of us, so there would be five people in one boat and four people in each of the other two boats. We would tie the boats together so no one is separated," replied Officer Green.

Officer Oliver scanned the group for a reaction. "So, who is ready to help launch the boats? Then maybe Hunter can catch us some more fish. I, for one, have worked up an appetite."

The men helped Oliver and Green retrieve the three boats from the stores. Zip and Zoe watched as the men removed the boats from the plastic containers and used an air pump to inflate them. The outdoor motors were affixed to the back. Afterward, the men tied the boats to the side of the lifeboat with plastic rope so they could be towed from behind.

Once inflated, it was apparent how small the boats were and how they had really been intended only for a quick transport between the lifeboat and shore. Zip tried to squelch a wave of dread that they might be forced to evacuate from the lifeboat.

Zoe, on the other hand, was fascinated with the little inflatable boats. "Look, Mommy, at the tiny boats. I hope we get to ride on them."

Zip squeezed her daughter. "Maybe so."

Zoe seemed happy at the prospect and clapped her hands. "Good."

After the boats were set, Officer Reed and Becky stacked provisions and encased them in a plastic net. Then, Hunter and George put out their fishing lines. Within minutes, they had pulled in three large fish. Becky and

Aurora helped Reed prepare and cook the fish. The appetizing aroma of cooked food filled the cabin.

The group ate silently now that order had been restored. But it was evident to Zip that everyone was concerned about the size of the inflatable vessels and the fear of leaving the security of the lifeboat.

Afterward, the metal dishes were washed in seawater. Zoe napped peacefully with her head in her mother's lap. Zip could not sleep in the heat and stared out of the window into the vast blue wilderness.

Joey's shriek suddenly pierced the silence as he called into the cabin. "We have lost one of the inflatable boats. It was ripped apart by the sharks."

CHAPTER FORTY-FOUR

Joey helped Officer Green pull the remains of the inflatable boat into the cabin while Officer Oliver retrieved a repair kit from the sealed pocket. They stretched the orange plastic across the floor of the stern and set about trying to repair the damage.

"It is more of a puncture, and I think it is fixable," he said to Officer Green as he worked intently.

Officer Oliver squatted down next to Officer Green. "Perfect imprint of two shark bites. They probably thought it was food and were disappointed."

The men worked tirelessly with adhesive patches and glue for the next half hour until the small inflatable boat appeared to be repaired. When they finished, Officer Green sat back on his haunches, surveying the repairs.

"We will need to let the glue dry, and then we can try inflating it. Looks OK to me," he said.

Joey bent down and inspected the work. "Looks great to me. Good job. Fingers crossed that it will hold air." He stood up and stretched.

Becky leaned over and looked at the partially inflated boat and blinked back tears. "How are we going to survive in those boats? What if a shark attacks them while we are in them? We will all die," she shrieked.

Todd rubbed his wife's back and embraced her protectively as she cried on his shoulder. "We are not going to die," he assured her. "Not after everything we have been through. The little boats are just a safety net."

"She's right. I am worried too," chimed in Sienna. "We are in the middle of ocean surrounded by sharks, and we don't stand a chance."

Aurora nodded her head in agreement. "I am not leaving this lifeboat unless it is going down."

Zip watched the drama unfold from her bench in the front of the vessel. She had been badly shaken by the shark damage to the inflatable boat. Aurora, Sienna, and Becky were right. They were in a perilous position. She felt a surge of panic and helplessness. How could she possibly keep Zoe safe if they had to evacuate the lifeboat? She had to get a grip on herself and remain strong for Zoe. They had to stay alive until they were rescued.

Officer Oliver stood up in the center of the cabin. His formerly starched white uniform was now grimy and coated with dirt and blood. Like all trained leaders, he tried to regain control over the situation. "There is no reason to be alarmed. These inflatable boats are used in shark-infested waters all over the world. What happened is unusual. We are all safe now, and Officer Green, Officer Reed, and I are going to do everything we can to make sure we all get out of this alive. Remember, we are a team here. We have taken out the lifeboats as a safety precaution. Everyone needs to keep a clear head. We are in this together."

Joey, still standing by the repaired dinghy, nodded in support. "He is right. I have been in these inflatable boats while diving off the coast of Australia in great white shark territory. Everybody knows how dangerous the waters are around Australia. I have never seen this happen before. This was unusual."

"Good to know," bellowed George, obviously wanting to stymie the mounting wave of hysteria building in the cabin. "Hopefully, this pump will continue working and we will be rescued soon. I, for one, could use a hot shower, clean clothes, a big meal, and a soft bed."

Hunter gave a forced laugh. "You are not the only one. And I want a big steak. I have had my fill of the beach vacation for a while."

A few of the men laughed in response. The group had been pampered aboard the ship, in sharp contrast to the oppressive heat and the filth inside the lifeboat.

Sienna and Aurora bowed their heads in silence, obviously unwilling to get into a pointless argument. Even Becky seemed somewhat mollified by the comments, lifting her tearstained face from her husband's shoulder and wiping her eyes.

Zip felt slightly comforted by Officer Oliver's comments. At the moment, they were safe, and they might never need to leave the safety of the lifeboat.

The tension in the cabin seemed to lift briefly. The only one who was oblivious to it all was Marie, who had not moved for hours. Clearly, the stress of the last forty hours and her husband's death had broken her. Zoe felt a deep compassion for the woman who had suffered so much. Marie and William, like nearly all of the passengers on board, had been on their dream vacation with friends. What had happened to all of them was inconceivable. She wished there was something she could do for Marie, but right now, she had to focus on taking care of her daughter.

She watched Zoe sleep soundly despite the loud voices and commotion in the cabin. Zip realized with sadness that today was Easter Sunday. According to the pre-cruise literature, the crew of the *Golden Swan* had planned an extravagant Easter celebration for the children, including an Easter egg hunt, a visit by the Easter Bunny, and a large Easter basket in the suite of every child on board. It seemed almost impossible to believe that fewer than two days ago, she had been looking forward to watching her daughter's special Easter celebration. Now, instead of chocolate candy and special entertainment, they were confined to a dirty lifeboat in shark-filled waters with only MREs and fish to eat.

Zoe finally awoke from her nap. She sat up and rubbed her eyes with her fists. Her hair was a frizzy, tangled mess. Zip softly pulled it back into a ponytail and kissed the top of the child's head.

"Mommy, is today Easter?"

"Yes, sweetie. I think today is Easter."

"Did the Easter Bunny come?"

"No, he did not have a way to get here because he does not swim. But I am sure he will leave you a surprise at home."

"But isn't he magic?"

"He is magic, sweetie. He sent me a text message saying he is leaving your basket in Seattle. Your Daddy will take care of the basket until we get home."

Zoe looked at her mother with an expression of delight and amazement. "You got a text from the Easter Bunny?"

Zip nodded and kissed Zoe again on the head. "I did."

"Can I see it?"

Zip hugged her little girl. "It is a magic text and only adults can read it. Even if I tried to show it to you, you could not see it."

"Can we call him?" Zoe persisted.

Zip tried not to sigh. She hated to perpetuate a lie about a fantasy, but the child deserved to have a positive distraction from their dire circumstances.

"I tried while you were asleep, but his number is blocked. And he is busy delivering baskets all over the world."

Zoe nodded her head with comprehension. "Like Santa Claus," she mused.

"Exactly," Zip assured her. "And we will look forward to seeing your beautiful basket when we get home."

Zip gave her daughter a squeeze and made a mental note that as soon as she got off the boat, she would have to tell Reynolds that they needed an Easter basket in Seattle waiting for Zoe when they returned home. She knew from past experience that the child would not forget about the basket.

Zoe, now pacified about her Easter gift, looked at her mother with concern. "My tummy feels funny, Mommy. I need to go potty."

Zip took Zoe to the head to relieve herself. Much to her surprise, the child vomited uncontrollably into the toilet. Within minutes, her stomach was obviously empty, but she was left with dry heaves. When Zip felt sure the child could vomit no more, she carried her out and laid her on the bench.

"Lie on your back," she told her, watching her child writhe in pain.

"My tummy hurts bad, Mommy."

Officer Reed came over with a canned ginger ale, encouraging the little girl to drink. "This might help to keep her hydrated."

Zoe sipped some of the soda but was still fidgety. Zip watched with helplessness, realizing there was nothing she could do. Did the child have food poisoning or was this something more sinister?

Officer Reed retrieved the medical kit. "I think we have something for nausea."

Zip watched the woman searching the kit, hoping there would be something to make her little girl recover.

Officer Reed found an anti-nausea medication, which she had Zoe swallow with a swig of soda. After a while, the child relaxed and fell into a deep sleep. Zip watched her daughter with concern, praying they would be rescued soon.

CHAPTER FORTY-FIVE

After a hot shower and shave, James dressed in a pair of casual slacks and a sports shirt before he walked down to the conference room, his laptop in a leather case over his shoulder. Reynolds had sent him a text earlier that morning saying he planned to work out and swim for about an hour. James promised to meet him downstairs with the group from the Paradise Line.

By 10:00, everyone except Reynolds had assembled in the hotel conference room. CNN was visible on one of the flat-screens, although the sound had been muted. A headline in white bold text crawled across the screen: "Search-and-Rescue Efforts Have Not Located Any Survivors in the Forty Hours since the Hijacking of the *Golden Swan* in Oceania—All Aboard Are Feared Dead."

James was relieved that the ongoing diatribe and speculation about the incident, the endless commentaries on marine safety and survival, and the rehashing of past terrorist hijackings had been muted. He realized that with each passing hour, survival in that remote region of the world was becoming less likely. But the rescue teams had committed to continue the search for at least five days, so there was still a glimmer of hope that some survivors might be located.

An elaborate brunch from The Belvedere had been brought in and laid on a table in the corner. Hot food steamed under solid silver chafing dishes. A carafe of freshly brewed coffee with hot milk was placed near frosty pitchers of juice and strawberry smoothies. A bowl of chocolate Easter eggs wrapped in gold foil sat in the middle of the table.

Lawyers Horace and Roth, each now joined by a younger attorney from their respective offices, ate heartily. The two P&I Club representatives sat across from the lawyers they had instructed; they too appeared to be enjoying their meal. The group conversation focused on vacations and upcoming work commitments.

It was obvious to James that the tragedy unfolding was simply a plum instruction and profitable work for the attorneys in the room. The sinking of the *Golden Swan* assured these attorneys large fees and a busy calendar for the next three or four years. These were men at the top of their game, whose primary focus was an avalanche of continued good work and exorbitant fees to maintain their high standard of living and bolster their investment accounts. They had set up their laptops, iPads, and iPhones, all plugged into the electrical outlets on the table and at the ready. They then moved on to discuss the proper venue to file a limitation action and the merits of a legal demand made on behalf of a victim identified in the theatre massacre that a Florida lawyer had communicated to them.

One of the younger attorneys from New York stood in a corner talking on his phone to a junior associate and barking instructions for a Lexis case search. He seemed indifferent to the fact that the associate on the other end of the phone was trying to enjoy a family Easter celebration. He directed the junior associate to go to the office to meet with a team that was assembled there and to plan to work for the remainder of the day and likely well into the evening.

"This is what happens in an emergency. You put your life on the back burner and rise to the occasion. It is too bad about your Easter plans. If you are not interested, there are plenty of other Ivy League graduates who would jump at the chance to work at the firm," he snapped.

The response of the junior associate on the other end of the phone was inaudible. "That is what I thought," the more senior attorney quipped. We will await your memo."

With that, he terminated the call and glanced over at Roth for approval. His boss seemed more intent on his Easter morning breakfast and ignored the younger attorney.

James recognized that these lawyers were already working on damage control, and it was evident they were only mildly interested in the rescue of any survivors. As Horace had explained to James out of the presence of Reynolds the night before, survivors would have details of tremendous pain and suffering that would impact the public's perception of the cruise line, whereas the deceased were always silent.

John and Gray were less sanguine. Although concerned about the tragedy, they were focused more on the insurance implications of the claims that had been presented and would certainly continue over the next few days. To these men, although the hijacking of the *Golden Swan* was highly unusual, it was all part of the job. The sinking was an insurance numbers game: trying to keep the value of claims suppressed to lower the "calls" on members of the mutual insurer. It was obvious to James that these men had worked closely with all of the attorneys in the room and knew them quite well.

James felt disgusted by the dynamics in the conference room. The fact that these professionals simply viewed the tragedy as an opportunity to suppress damages was not admirable. In his entire career, James had never been involved in a death or personal injury claim. His entire focus had been property damage, vessel damage or loss, and business interruption claims. It was easy to be detached about property loss, but the loss of life was haunting to him. This morning, in the cold hard light of day, he was eager to stay away from the lawyers and P&I Club members.

Isaac and Kurt from the Paradise Lines somberly sat in the corner in deep conversation, barely touching the huge feast prepared for them. The two men were obviously concerned about their future employment with Paradise Lines, a closely held corporation that might not be able to withstand the tragedy. The evening before, James had overheard Kurt telling Isaac that he might need to start brushing up his résumé.

The Vandebergs were noticeably absent and, according to Kurt, were upstairs in their suite "resting." Their personal lawyer had delivered a scripted but heartfelt statement to the press that they were devastated by the loss of life and sinking of the *Golden Swan*. It read, "The Vandebergs are cooperating with law enforcement and the rescue efforts to locate survivors of the tragedy and are praying for the families of those victims tragically lost in the terrorist hijacking of the cruise ship." The statement had been posted on a number of Internet news sites and was circulated to broadcast news around the world.

James served himself a plate of hot food and an almond croissant. He set them down at the end of the table and returned to pour himself a cup of coffee and orange juice. The food was, as expected, delicious. Despite his jet lag, he felt invigorated by the coffee and good food.

Reynolds arrived after James had finished breakfast. All of the lawyers rose when he arrived, greeting him with overly solicitous concern. Reynolds spoke politely to the group before serving himself a cup of coffee and selecting a seat beside James. This morning he looked dejected and solemn. It was clear to James and everyone else that the ordeal was taking its toll on Reynolds. James sat beside the young man, allowing him to eat undisturbed. He could not imagine the grief he was feeling over his wife and child after waiting forty hours for good news.

At about 11:00, two senior-level FBI investigators, three members of the US State Department, a staff member of the New Zealand embassy, two men from INTERPOL, a US member of the US Foreign Services, and an MI6 representative assembled in the adjoining conference room. They declined the offer of the Easter brunch spread, asking instead to meet with Isaac, Kurt, and the Vandebergs.

The most senior FBI investigator instructed Reynolds not to leave the room because they intended to speak to him in due course. Reynolds blanched slightly but assured the investigator he wanted to cooperate fully. "I want you to find my family," he told the investigator in a tremorous voice.

Kurt called Greg, asking him and his wife to join them downstairs. The couple appeared a few minutes later followed by two well-dressed men who James guessed were their personal counsel. Greg, who appeared to be in his late sixties, ignored everyone in the room and walked directly over to Reynolds.

The older man grabbed Reynolds's hand in a firm handshake. "I am so sorry for what you are going through," he told Reynolds. "My wife and I are devastated about this. We are praying for your wife and little girl."

Reynolds's eyes filled with tears and he grimaced. He nodded his head and thanked the man in a soft voice.

Erika followed her husband and patted Reynolds on the shoulder. "We are here for you and praying for your family. We are so crushed about this," she told him in a slight Scandinavian accent.

Isaac took Erika by the arm and escorted her and her husband into the room with the law enforcement and state department officers. Their personal counsel followed them into the room. When Horace and Roth tried to accompany the group into the adjoining conference room, the senior FBI investigator stood in front of the entrance.

"This is an international investigation," he told Roth in an imperious tone. "You are liability lawyers and do not have authority to participate. We cannot let you join us," he said unapologetically.

"I represent the cruise line, and you are interviewing employees of the line," Roth persisted.

"This is a matter of national and international security," the investigator barked. With that, he closed the door.

Roth, clearly angered, sat down at the table in a huff, his face turning bright red. Clearly, as a prominent Wall Street lawyer, he was unaccustomed to being treated without complete deference.

"Arrogant fuckers," he muttered to Horace.

Horace leaned back in his chair, turning toward the P&I Club representatives. "If this is a criminal investigation, I wonder if the Clubs should instruct white-collar representation. Those Miami hacks representing the Vandebergs are just grandstanders and would be incompetent in defending a criminal investigation if it bit them in the ass. Now, my firm has a couple of white-collar lawyers, one from the Justice Department and the other one is a former US Attorney. They are only a phone call away. Would you like me to give them a call?"

Roth's expression turned into rage as he realized that Horace was trying to turn his humiliation at the hands of the FBI into additional work for his own California law firm. Not to be outdone, Roth walked over to John and Gray.

"We have world-class white-collar lawyers with international experience. I can have them here today. We cannot take a chance that there is a prosecution or interviews of the Paradise Line owners or employees when they are not represented by qualified counsel."

John rubbed his eyes in thought before responding to the competing lawyers. James knew John was in a tough spot.

"The Clubs do not have any authority over the Vandebergs' choice of personal counsel. But we can instruct white-collar counsel for the employees. You can each bring one lawyer from each firm but no associates," John told the two men.

Horace and Roth immediately rushed from the conference room to make their respective phone calls in private. The two men were focused on making another dollar for their firms and to generate additional money for their personal revenue columns.

James looked over at Reynolds with concern. It was terrible for the grieving man to be exposed to the underbelly of the legal and insurance world in his time of grief. In desperation, James fired up his computer.

"Feel like watching a movie to pass the time? I've got a spare set of earbuds in my case, and I loaded a couple of British films."

Reynolds looked relieved at the offer of a distraction. His mouth turned up with the hint of smile. "That would be great. Thanks."

With that, James handed Reynolds the earbuds and started the first film. The two men, ignoring the ugly scene in the room and the drama playing out in the adjoining conference room, began watching the film.

CHAPTER FORTY-SIX

Zoe slept peacefully while the group finished yet another dinner of fish caught by Hunter, George, and Joey in the late afternoon. Sunset in the tropics was abrupt, and the sun quickly slid down below the horizon. The moon lit up the sky around them in a soft glow and sent shimmers of silver ribbons across the lapping waves. It was no longer oppressively hot in the lifeboat, as the air became tolerably cool in the tropical night.

The bodies of the four murdered passengers had begun to emit an overpowering stench, causing all but Marie to move to the benches closest to the bow of the ship to escape the odor. The women clustered together in the front while the men stretched out on the benches to nap.

The mood in the cabin was subdued but still hopeful of a rescue. Everyone was exhausted from the stress, fear, and grime of the boat. Zip noticed that even Officer Oliver and Officer Green were exhibiting strain from the last two days.

It had now been forty-eight hours since the hijacking of the *Golden Swan*. It was tacitly understood by the group that they might be alone at sea for another few days. Everyone was simply trying to stay positive and survive the ordeal.

When Zoe finally woke, Zip noticed that the child's breath was sour and had a metallic smell. It was not a good sign. Zip gave her the remaining can of warm ginger ale that had long since gone flat. She also gave her the second pill for nausea that she had saved in her pocket. Zip was concerned that the child was becoming dehydrated. Children were especially susceptible to dehydration and death in circumstances that most adults could survive. If Zoe died, she would never forgive herself.

Zip was rested but groggy. Officer Reed found an MRE of chicken soup that she hydrated with the remaining rainwater. Zoe finished her cup of soup, and the nausea appeared to have passed. None of the other passengers were interested in sharing the soup, so Reed put it aside for Zoe to eat later. All of the female passengers, who were mothers themselves, recognized the danger of dehydration and had clustered around Zip and Zoe to offer their support.

Zoe slipped under her mother's arm, resting her head against Zip's shoulder. She fell asleep again, probably from the pill Zip had given her.

The women began to converse in soft tones, sharing bits of their lives from before the cruise. Zip shifted against the hard bench, finding a comfortable position, and began listening to the discussion. It was a pleasant diversion to listen to the women talk about their lives and the pleasant prospect of returning to what was waiting for them when they were rescued.

Officer Reed, settled in beside Zip and Zoe on the bench, also quietly listened to the conversation. A bond had developed between Zip and the female officer over the past two days. Zip realized that this was an indication of the arbitrariness of life. But for the sinking of the boat, they would never have known each other.

Becky, her long blonde hair now a tangled mess, explained that Todd and William had been business partners in Omaha.

"They run an insurance agency for a big company," she explained. "They were so successful that the company awarded them this trip because they were the highest grossing sellers of insurance in the region. We were all so excited, especially Marie. We went on a shopping trip overnight to Chicago to buy suits and clothes for the guys. And Marie planned all of the shore excursions. She spent hours on the Internet, researching the best snorkeling spots and the best things to see on the trip. She has lived, eaten, and breathed this trip since January."

Sienna shook her head. "Such a tragedy. Are you two close?"

Becky coiled her hair around her fingers and tied it in a lose bun, chewing on the side of her cheek. "We are friends, but Marie is always busy so we do not talk every day. Marie is always a bundle of energy: super-mom, best wife, fanciest house, latest fashions, best tennis player in her league. She has many friends, but I do not know that she is 'close' to any-one. William and their son are her life, and I am not sure what she will do now that William is gone." Becky's voice cracked slightly as she glanced over at her friend who had refused to eat and had remained in a fetal posi-tion for nearly two days.

Sienna placed her hand over Becky's arm and gave her a squeeze. "She will survive and be fine, especially for their child. When you are my age, you learn to accept what life gives you and to deal with it. Life goes on."

"Tell us about your life back in Omaha. When I think of Omaha, I think of good beef, rolling hills, cold weather, and Warren Buffet," Aurora prompted her, trying to steer the subject away from William's death.

Becky fleetingly smiled, obviously thinking of better times. "Omaha has cold winters, but it is clean and friendly. The summers are warm and lovely. Todd and I have two boys, John and Thomas, who are twelve and fourteen old. They play hockey every winter and tennis in the summer—typical boys. And what appetites they have! I cannot imagine what they are going through now. I am sure they think we are dead." Her voice cracked, and her face crumpled as she sobbed.

"Who is with them now?" Aurora intervened.

"My parents came over from our hometown in Champaign, Illinois, to stay with them. My dad had a small pharmacy that he recently sold, and they now fully enjoy their life. They love John and Thomas."

"Good, then they are taken care of, and you do not have to worry," Aurora said softly.

"What do you do with your time when you are not taking care of your family?" Sienna asked, rubbing Becky's arm. The touch of another human seemed to have worked its magic as Becky composed herself.

"I like to garden. I have a beautiful flower garden. Vegetables are too much trouble, although Todd does grow tomatoes. And I have two Arabian horses that I board at a farm right outside of the city. I try to go every morning in the warm months after the kids are out of the house."

"Does Todd like to ride?" Sienna continued.

"Sometimes he comes with me. But Todd is so busy. He's always working to provide a good life for us. He tells me he works hard so all of us can enjoy the good things in life."

Becky glanced over at her husband and gave him a warm smile. Todd, his back propped against the port wall of the boat, blew her a kiss from his bench two rows behind them. Becky positively beamed with the attention.

"What about you, Sienna?" Zip asked softly. "Tell us about your life in England with George."

The older woman gave Zip a wan smile. Zip estimated that she must be over seventy. Her short hair was bright silver, and deep crevices ran through her deeply freckled skin. Sienna had all of the hallmarks of someone who had spent her life in the sun without protection. Her cornflower blue eyes set off her pleasant round face.

"George is a retired solicitor. He worked in the London office of a large international law firm until he retired last year. We live across the street from Hunter and Aurora, and we have been friends for many years." She paused and gave her friend a hug with one arm. "We planned this trip together when Hunter retired from his job. George and I have a holiday house in southern Spain near Malaga, and we have started spending several months a year there."

"We talked about going there when Hunter retired in December," Aurora interjected. "But I had the bright idea to do something special, like going to French Polynesia and the Cook Islands."

"Well, it was wonderful for a time. And who could have predicted that some crazed terrorist group would take over the ship?" Sienna chided her friend. "And besides, we had a trip planned to New Zealand after the cruise, and after this nightmare, I think that we all should go. I know that George and I plan to finish the trip if I have to drag him by his ears to the South Island," Sienna told them with obvious resolve.

Aurora laughed. "I agree. We will all need a vacation after this. Life is too short to be ruined by a terrorist attack. And where Sienna and George go, Hunter and I will go too."

Zip listened to the women with interest. She admired their resolve and determination, even though they were surrounded by death and floating helplessly at sea. "That's the spirit! Ending everything on a high note," Zip exclaimed.

Even Becky giggled. "You ladies are amazing! I am so glad we have gotten to know each other! You absolutely have to come see us in Omaha when this is all over!"

The women all shared a good laugh. Zip was glad the mood was lightening in the cabin. Everyone needed a bit of levity after what they had been through.

Becky turned around in her seat to face Officer Reed and smiled. "Officer Reed, you are so quiet, and you have done everything to take care of us. Tell us about yourself and share a bit about your life."

Reed clasped her fingers together shyly and faced the cluster of women. "I live in Manila. My husband is in the military, and my daughter and I are living with my mother. We are saving for a nice house. I make good money with the Paradise Lines, and we would have saved enough to buy our house after this cruise."

"How old is your daughter?" Zip asked.

Officer Reed sat up a little straighter when she talked about her little girl. It was obvious she was very proud of her daughter. "She is seven years old. She is a good student and likes math and science. My mother says my daughter wants to be a doctor when she grows up."

"It must be hard to be away from her when you are on the ship," Becky observed.

"It is, but it provides us a good life. I grew up poor without many opportunities. My life has changed dramatically working for the Paradise Line. And I love working with the children. It is a dream job."

Zip patted Officer Reed on the shoulder. Obviously, this woman had a great deal of inner strength and was willing to do whatever it took to take care of her family. Surely, none of it had been easy.

Just then, Hunter leaned toward the group of women. "Ladies, I am so glad you are relaxing and bonding, but it is getting late. And as the only doctor on board, I think we should all try to get some rest. It will be six thirty before you know it, and who knows what tomorrow will bring. Doctor's orders."

The women giggled in response. Zip noticed that Hunter's voice was firm but soothing. No doubt it was his bedside manner developed over a lifetime of working with patients.

"Aye aye doctor," Aurora mocked her husband. "But reluctantly, I agree. This has been a long day, and I need to get some sleep."

The women settled down, and soon there was a chorus of soft snoring from the men on the boat. Zip cuddled Zoe in her arms and, after a time, fell into a deep sleep. They had survived another day.

CHAPTER FORTY-SEVEN

Zip and Zoe were awakened when they were violently thrown against the port side of the vessel, perilously close to the open window. Zoe was screaming. The passengers were shrieking in fear. Now fully awake, Zip realized that the vessel was listing again, nearly rolling onto its side.

Officer Green, hanging onto the handholds along the wall, managed to make his way into the cabin.

"Wake up, everyone! The bilge pump must have run out of battery power, and we are taking on water fast. The boat is listing at eighty degrees and is going to sink in less than half an hour. We need to abandon the vessel and get into the other boats. Make sure your life vest is secure. Officer Oliver and I will get the food and water. Get out now!"

Zip shoved her pack over her back and grabbed Zoe, who was crying uncontrollably. Zip and Officer Reed helped each other climb over to the entrance to the lifeboat. Officer Oliver had already lined up the inflatable boats and suspended a nylon rope safety ladder down the side of the entrance. With Reed's help, Zip climbed down the rope across the partially exposed hull and settled into one of the inflatable dinghies alongside Zoe. Officer Reed joined them two minutes later. The inflatable boats were shallow, and the women had to wedge themselves into the bottom. Soon, Joey climbed in and put his arm protectively around Reed.

Todd and Becky crawled into the boat behind them with Hunter and Aurora. Zip noticed the tears streaming down Becky's face. She was clearly terrified. Todd also looked ashen and resigned to their fate.

One by one, Officer Oliver assisted the passengers down the safety ladder. It was a perilous evacuation as the boat rocked and shuddered. Finally, Officer Oliver climbed down with Marie on his back and positioned himself in the last inflatable ship with Officer Green, George, and Sienna. When they had all safely evacuated, Officer Green cut the nylon rope securing the little flotilla to the lifeboat, setting them adrift. It was eerily quiet as the current gently swept the little inflatable boats out to sea.

The moon had set, and a wedge of light was visible in the east. Zip checked her watch. It was almost 6:30.

Officer Oliver started the outboard motor of his zodiac and pulled the three inflatable boats away from the lifeboat at a slow speed. By the time the sun had sprang up above the horizon, Oliver had cut the engine, and they had floated more than a half a mile from the lifeboat.

The group was transfixed by the scene unfolding before them as the lifeboat, which had been their safe refuge for over two days, shuddered and gently rolled over upside-down, exposing the bare metal hull that was covered with sea slime. Fewer than five minutes later, the stern disappeared under the water, and the bow soared into the air before slipping under the surface.

Instantly, Marie began screaming. "We have to go back! William is in the boat! We have to save him!"

Before Officer Oliver could grab her, Marie had dived into the water, paddling furiously toward the submerged lifeboat. Officer Oliver stood up to go after her when suddenly he paused, staring at Marie in the water.

As the group watched in horror, two large sharks grabbed Marie and pulled her under the blue waves. Her arms were flailing wildly above the surface as one of the sharks, holding the back of her life vest, dragged her through the water. Marie wailed.

Zoe screamed. "Mommy, something bad has that lady! Help her! She will die!"

Zip covered Zoe's eyes and pulled her close in a hug to protect her from the horrific scene unfolding before them.

Within seconds, the water around Marie's submerged body turned crimson as her hands disappeared under the waves. A minute later, her empty life jacket sprang to the surface, the straps floating aimlessly on the surface.

Zip was shocked at the speed of the attack. She held Zoe tightly with one arm, stroking her sobbing child's back with her free hand.

"Jesus Christ!" exclaimed Joey. "I have never seen sharks act like that."

Officer Oliver, his face grim from the spectacle, simply cranked up the outboard motor and towed the flotilla toward the east.

Zip clutched Zoe as the wind whipped around them. For the first time in two days, she accepted the fact that there was a real possibility the group might not survive.

CHAPTER FORTY-EIGHT

Officer Oliver gave the outboard motor a full throttle, towing the little flotilla northeast. The little motor strained with the weight of pulling two additional inflatable vessels. Progress was slow but steady. The inflatable boats careened wildly as they skimmed across the small waves. The boats were designed so that passengers could sit comfortably on the inflatable gunwales. Except for Officer Oliver and Oliver Green, the passengers and Officer Reed remained seated on the bottom of the boats rather than the sides lest they fall over into the treacherous sea surrounding them.

Zip held onto Zoe with one arm and grabbed onto the rope hand-hold ribbing the side of the boat. Officer Reed seemed nervous, clasping the crucifix dangling from her necklace in her left hand and gripping the rope handhold with her right hand, facing into the wind. Joey's hair, now free from its clasp, brushed his shoulders and whipped in the wind. He stretched his legs out in front of him and leaned back against the gunwale, his fingers loosely curled around the handhold. After ten minutes, Officer Oliver cut the motor and allowed the convoy to again drift in the waves.

"We need to conserve fuel," he explained, his voice even and controlled. "These are small motors designed for short distances, so we can run for a while and then drift. Fortunately, we have three motors, so we can switch between them."

"We have flares aboard all of the boats, so we can attract attention if we see anyone," Officer Green told them. "I am sure a rescue effort is still underway. It has only been a couple of days. We cannot lose hope. They will find us soon, and eventually this will all be a distant memory."

Officer Oliver took over again. "Look, there are a few things we need to address as a group. As awful as this has been, we have all survived, and we have been lucky. But now we need to ration the food and water so we can survive this ordeal. We have MREs, which are not as tasty as the fresh fish we have enjoyed over the last two days. And we do not have any way to heat the food when it is hydrated. But it is nourishment, and it will keep us alive." He waited for a few seconds before he continued.

"We also have water. You can live for days without food if you have fresh water. We can catch rainwater again. No matter what, do not try to drink the seawater. It will make you violently ill. So, Officer Green and I will be rationing the water. It is important for everyone to remain hydrated and have his or her fair share of water. We will do our best to ration everything equally. In addition, each boat has a survival neoprene blanket inside the pocket on the port side—that would be left for you nonseafarers. This will keep you warm if we encounter a rainstorm, so you will have to share the blanket."

Their comments were met with silent resignation from the exhausted group. No one challenged their judgment, and everyone accepted that Officer Oliver and Officer Green were in charge. Fear and hopelessness were palpable, and it was clear that all of the passengers were wondering whether they had endured so much only to perish in the inflatable boats.

Officer Oliver cleared his throat. "Now, I have one more thing to say. As a practical matter, nature will call, and everyone will need to relieve himself or herself. The only thing you can do is sit on the side of the boat and do your business over the side. If you have to go, just let everyone know and everyone will turn away. We need to be respectful of each other and make sure no one is embarrassed. This is like a military operation. We are all living in close quarters, but we are alive and together. We have worked closely as a team so far, and we will continue to do so until we are rescued."

Officer Oliver scanned the faces of the group of dejected passengers. Most of them simply nodded in comprehension and then turned away to stare at the blue wilderness surrounding them.

"OK then. It appears we have a consensus," he said, as he retrieved a small set of binoculars on a lanyard from his pocket. He sat ramrod straight on the side of the little boat and scanned the horizon obviously looking for a rescue.

Zip ignored the rumbling in her stomach. She was willing to do without food as long as she and Zoe made it through the ordeal alive.

She scanned the horizon in the silence, praying that they would see a boat or a plane searching for them. Fortunately, neither Joey nor Officer Reed were interested in small talk. The group appeared to be beyond the need for any social interaction or support now. They were all in survival mode.

Zip thought about Reynolds and whether her text message had been delivered to him. Surely, he believed she and Zoe had perished with the *Golden Swan*. She could not imagine his pain when he learned that Zoe—the light of his life—might be dead. As she pondered their circumstances, her thoughts turned to Marie, William, and their now orphaned son. The death and devastation caused by the small group of terrorists was unfathomable.

There was a pleasant light breeze, and the sky was crystal clear. But as the sun rose high in the sky, the air temperature became hot and humid. The sun's intensity was relentless. Zip retrieved the tube of zinc oxide from the pack and slathered it on her face, neck, and arms. She did the same with Zoe before offering the tube to Officer Reed.

Reed shook her head. "I don't really need it. I seldom burn. You and Zoe use it."

"Are you sure? Well, it is here if you need it." She reached across and offered the tube to Joey. His skin was ruddy and weathered from his years in the Australian sun.

Joey shook his head and managed a smile. "No, thanks. I appreciate it, but my skin is used to it. But you and Zoe look like you need it given your red hair and pale skin. If it gets too bad, I might need some on my face later."

Zip felt relieved. The tube was nearly half empty and had to last them as long as they were on the water.

There was no conversation as the group floated across the aquamarine water, jostled by soft waves. Most of the passengers and remaining crew seemed sobered by the events of the last few hours. Marie's death had been horrific and was a constant reminder of the ever-present danger they faced from the proliferation of sharks in the area. Their chances of survival had been reasonable as long as they were in the sturdy lifeboat. They were protected from the elements and could catch and cook fresh fish. They could stretch out and sleep, and there had been a primitive head onboard. Zip wondered if Officer Reed had managed to bring the first aid kit onboard with them. What if Zoe or one of the older passengers succumbed to illness? What would they do?

Zip stroked Zoe's hair and tried to use her body to shield the child from the burning sun. Their situation now was dire and precarious. She had to face the cold reality that they could not survive for long in the inflatable boats. She was sure the others felt the same way.

She looked back at the boat tethered behind them. The Bishops and the Campbells were holding hands in a small circle with their heads bowed. Todd was speaking softly, leading the four of them in prayer. In the leading boat, George had his arms around Sienna, who was sobbing. Officer Oliver and Officer Green remained perched on the gunwales, appearing to study the sea conditions and the horizon.

Suddenly, Joey broke the silence. "Dolphins!" He pointed over the starboard side of the boat about fifteen feet from the flotilla as a large dolphin breached the surface and leaped into the air. The pod encircled the boats, sailing through the air in flips before diving beneath the surface. The group was large, probably consisting of at least forty large mammals.

Zoe sat up on her knees and giggled with excitement as she watched the dolphins' antics. They showed no fear and seemed fascinated by the fleet of inflatable boats. The mood of the group lifted as they enjoyed the attention of the friendly creatures.

Joey grinned at Zoe. "They are beautiful, aren't they? And they seem to like humans. They chase away the sharks. Maybe they will stay with us for a while. In Australia, we think of dolphins as good luck."

Zip appreciated the distraction it provided for Zoe as she watched enthralled by the magnificent pod swimming around them. Zoe shrieked in delight as two of the dolphins breached the surface, leaned back, and looked inside of the boat. They were obviously curious and intelligent. Another dolphin came so close that Zoe managed to reach over the side and lightly touch its skin with her finger.

"They are soft and slippery," Zoe observed. "They are like the dolphins in Bora—but prettier."

"Yes, like the dolphins we saw in Bora Bora. They are beautiful," Zip replied, relieved that her daughter would have some pleasant memories of the trip if they survived. Zip worried that after everything her daughter had witnessed, she would be in therapy for the rest of her life.

The dolphins stayed for hours, lifting the spirits of the group. By the time they swam away, it was late afternoon. Officer Green, assisted by Officers Reed and Oliver, hydrated three packets of chicken noodle soup with the rainwater they had collected, and poured it into the small plastic cups from the lifeboat.

The soup was tasteless and only partially dissolved. Zip managed to coax Zoe to consume her soup before eating her own. After they finished the soup, Officer Reed stacked the cups in the corner. As the sun edged lower on the horizon, Zip helped Zoe relieve herself over the side of the vessel. The group took turns relieving themselves, averting their heads to allow as much privacy as possible. Afterward, they settled into the bottom of their boats as the sun set, plunging them into darkness. An hour later, the moon rose, and the sky glimmered with brilliant stars and the Southern Cross. It was a gorgeous sight.

After a time, Zoe fell asleep and dozed peacefully in Zip's arms. Officer Reed and Joey lay across from Zip and Zoe, braced against the side of the inflatable boat. Gentle waves undulated beneath them, and the air cooled to a delicious temperature. The passengers in the three boats were silent.

Zip stared at the sky trying to fall asleep. She realized that it had now been two days since the hijacking. For the second time that day, she prayed for their safety and rescue.

CHAPTER FORTY-NINE

Tom Denton, the white-collar attorney from Horace's law firm arrived at the hotel in fewer than two hours after getting Horace's call. Fortuitously, he had been spending Easter with his family and parents in Los Angeles. Nonetheless, he was more than willing to sacrifice his family time to work on the high-profile case. He appeared to be in his late forties and had the self-important air of one who had spent years working in the Justice Department. After receiving intensive training with the US government, he had gone to the *dark* side representing corporations and individuals against federal prosecutions. It was a specialized niche in the legal profession, and Tom could demand excessive hourly rates for his services. Most of his clients were high-net-worth corporations and individuals who universally would pay anything to avoid a criminal conviction.

Tom walked over and shook Horace's hand. "There is a crowd of reporters near the hotel entrance," he told Horace. "Someone must have alerted the press that the meetings are being held here."

Horace smiled broadly and placed his hand firmly on his partner's shoulder. "Thank you for coming, Tom. I know today is your daughter's birthday, but we have a crisis here." Horace did not bother to introduce

Tom to anyone else in the room. Instead, he escorted him over to the conference room.

Tom knocked on the door loudly and then brusquely opened the door, announcing that he was there to represent Kurt and Isaac. James caught a glimpse of the Vandebergs speaking in hushed tones with their personal attorney. Kurt and Isaac sat across from the Vandebergs. Their faces were ashen, and even from nearly thirty feet away, James could see they were uncomfortable. Within seconds, Tom closed the door behind him and disappeared into the conference room.

Roth looked annoyed by Tom's arrival. He and his associate left the room to talk in private. It was obvious they were anxious for the white-collar attorney from their New York law firm to arrive and take charge. Roth was obviously convinced that his partner was eminently superior.

James was mildly disgusted by the American lawyers' competitive display under these circumstances. In the ten years he had worked in the London insurance market, he had worked with many American lawyers. In his experience, they had always been pleasant, deferential, and eager to obtain the best result. James decided that the real problem here was the fact that the P&I Club representatives, John and Gray, had instructed two correspondent firms to investigate the casualty. James questioned their judgment as that tactic appeared to simply escalate the costs and decrease efficiency. Legal representation was not free, and he was certain that the Club and other insurers on the risk would be faced with a huge legal expense.

He made a mental note to send Reed an email that afternoon about the proliferation of attorneys handling the crisis. He would definitely want an update.

While the interview with the cruise line representatives took place, James and Reynolds continued to watch a couple of British films on James's computer. Although Reynolds had initially seemed eager for the distraction, James noticed that he was becoming increasingly restive, tapping his fingers on the table and staring at the door of the adjoining conference room. He was clearly preoccupied and fixated on his missing daughter and child.

CNN and the BBC News were still dedicating considerable news coverage to the search-and-rescue mission of the passengers of the *Golden Swan*. Although the sound was muted, photos of the *Golden Swan* and images of the explosion were shown every hour. News crews had been flown to American Samoa and New Zealand, where search-and-rescue operations for survivors were centralized. The news was grim, and most of the passengers and crew were presumed dead.

James was surprised to see video footage of Tom Denton as he entered the hotel, avoiding a crowd of reporters clustered around the entrance. Horace grabbed the remote and turned up the volume. The news anchor, speaking in a deep monotone, informed viewers that the Vandebergs and cruise line counsel were staying at the luxurious five-star resort during the crisis.

"CNN sources have confirmed that a prominent California white-collar attorney believed to be representing the cruise line was seen entering the hotel earlier this afternoon. He did not provide us with a comment. In French Polynesia, we know that two customs officials were arrested for allowing stevedores to load military-grade weapons and explosives onto the *Golden Swan*. As of this time, there is still no word whether any of the eight hundred passengers and crew survived the sinking. Sources have also informed CNN that Reynolds Tyler, a passenger who left the day of the sinking, is still cooperating closely with federal authorities at the luxurious Los Angeles resort. Reynolds's wife and child were believed to be on the vessel at the time of the sinking and are presumed dead."

Reynolds put his head down on the conference room table. "Oh God!" he sobbed. "They are really gone!"

Roth walked over and grabbed the remote and shut down the televisions, glaring at Horace. "How the fuck could you have done that? Did your firm leak this to the press to get publicity? The fact that the Vandebergs and the cruise line representatives are staying here was supposed to be confidential. This puts the cruise line in the worst possible light: while people might be fighting for survival, the owners are holed up here in luxury. Not to mention that Reynolds Tyler is here grieving and waiting for any word about his family. You are a heartless, self-promoting motherfucker!"

Horace's face bloomed a deep purple. He had obviously been caught in conspiring to leak confidential information.

"You prick. How dare you speak to me that way! You can never prove that. Tom Denton is a very prominent attorney in California. The press simply put two and two together." His loud voice tremored with anger, but his protestations had a hollow ring.

James, badly shaken by the disturbing scene in front of him, stood up. As a client and insurance representative, he sensed he would have the upper hand.

"Both of you, stop," he said authoritatively. He turned to Horace. "Mr. Tweed, not only do we have the cruise line's reputation and liability to consider, but this man here is a victim of a crime. You are not showing him the least bit of consideration or sensitivity. I think it might be helpful if you and your associate go back to your suite to work. We will let Tom, Kurt, and Isaac know where you are when they come out."

Roth sneered with victory. "That's right asshole. Go up to your room."

James, incensed, glared at Roth. "Both of you need to cooperate here and act like adults. You are acting like children. Don't think for a minute that I will not be reporting this to all of the insurers. You were hired to do a job, not to outdo each other."

The threat that James would be reporting the pettiness between the two lawyers instantly brought about an attitude adjustment. Complaints about their handling of this high-profile case could be devastating to their careers.

Roth spoke first in silken tones. "Mr. Tyler and Mr. Brooks, my sincerest apologies for my behavior. I was simply reacting to the news coverage. We want the cruise line and Mr. Tyler to be placed in the best possible light. I assure you that an outburst like that will not happen again. I have known Horace for many years, and we have served on a number of Maritime Law Association committees together. We work well together, and we can put this behind us."

The anger Horace had exhibited was gone. He stood up and shook Roth's hand with a smile. "That is right. I apologize. We are all working for the same team here. This is a stressful situation for us all."

Roth walked over to Reynolds and patted him softly on the back. Reynolds continued to sob uncontrollably. Roth sat beside him and waited for him to compose himself.

"Mr. Tyler, it is important not to give up hope," he said softly. "My wife and daughter were in a catastrophic automobile accident a few years ago. My daughter was not expected to live, and I spent ten days and nights in the ICU waiting room praying for their recovery. It was one of the darkest times of my life. But the doctors never lost hope, and today both are fully recovered. Your wife was resourceful. We know she was not in the theatre. She may have managed to get off of the boat."

Reynolds lifted his head and rubbed his eyes. He nodded. "Thank you. I guess you understand how horrible this is."

Roth put his arm around Reynolds and gave him a squeeze. "The everyday uncertainty is the worst. But there is always hope."

Horace cleared his throat. "James had a good idea. It is almost 9:00 o'clock, and none of us have eaten since brunch. Let's get out of this room and go up to my suite and order dinner. Sitting in a windowless room day after day is oppressive. I can send Tom a text."

"I agree," replied James, as he shut down his computer and slipped it inside its leather pouch. He helped Reynolds to his feet. The now amiable group trooped upstairs to Horace's suite to relax and have dinner as the interview with the Vandebergs, Kurt, and Isaac continued endlessly in the downstairs conference room.

CHAPTER FIFTY

By the time the multidisciplinary government interview had concluded with the Vandebergs, Kurt, and Isaac, Reynolds, James, and the attorneys had consumed a light dinner in the privacy of Horace's suite. It had been a relief to all of them to be out of the conference room downstairs.

James, who had been feeling jet lagged, was refreshed after a Dungeness crab salad and grilled salmon. He drank a decaffeinated latte and a large glass of strawberry lemonade. After dinner, he managed to send Bunny a text message and composed a short report to Reed updating him on recent events. Although the relations between counsel seemed improved, it was important for Reed to understand the dynamics and to evaluate how many attorneys were actually needed on the casualty.

Roth and Horace had tried to steer the conversation to lighter subjects. They encouraged Reynolds to talk a bit about himself and his life in Seattle. Reynolds revealed that he had grown up in New Jersey, the stepson of a chemical engineer. He had chosen Stanford for college to get away from the northeastern winters. He had earned a B.S. in electrical engineering and software development and programming. He had received a master's degree in electrical engineering and computer programming, and had landed a plum job in Seattle at one of the many burgeoning tech companies.

"This disaster has been a real wake-up call for me," he announced to them with candid resolve. "If Zip and Zoe make it through this, I am going to spend as much time with them as possible. I now know what is important."

The group returned downstairs by 11:00 p.m. The FBI agents, men from INTERPOL, and MI6 representatives were waiting impatiently for the group to return. Phillip Thompson, the New York white-collar crime lawyer, was seated in the corner with Isaac, Kurt, and Tom conversing in hushed tones.

Phillip rose and introduced himself to Reynolds, James, Roth, Horace, and Horace's associate, shaking hands with all present. James found him to be much more polished than Tom.

"The Vandebergs and their attorney have gone upstairs. It has been a grueling day for them. I think Kurt and Isaac will probably turn in as well," he told them.

The FBI agent came over to Reynolds. "Mr. Tyler, we would like to speak to you a bit before you go to sleep if you don't mind."

Reynolds paled slightly and followed the investigators into the adjoining conference room where the representatives from MI6, INTERPOL, the State Department, and governments of New Zealand, the UK, and Australia awaited him. One of the men from INTERPOL walked over and closed the door firmly behind Reynolds.

The group of lawyers decided to go upstairs. Despite their earlier conflict, Horace and Roth walked out together, conversing amiably. James, John, and Gray were left alone in the room.

Although he was exhausted, James decided to wait for Reynolds as a show of support. He returned to the conference room table and opened a bottle of cold Fiji Water.

"What the hell are they doing?" John asked Gray, who was reclined as much as possible with his head against the back of his chair.

Gray sighed and sat up. "Beats me. But since he was the only survivor from the boat they can ask about the hijackers, they probably have a lot of questions."

"They should leave him alone after what he has gone through. He wife and daughter are certainly dead, and I am sure he is devastated."

"They don't give a rat's ass about him. This is all about locating Cell 53."

"Do you think we should wait for him?"

Gray sighed again. "It's almost midnight, and I am exhausted. I am going to my room to get some sleep. I need to call my wife. She had big Easter plans for the family. She was a good sport about this, but I need to check in with her. Give me a call if anything earth-shattering happens."

John stood and stretched. "I think I will turn in as well." He looked over at James. "Are you staying here?"

James nodded. "I'll stay. I might stretch out on the sofa and take a nap. It is now almost 8:00 a.m. in Cambridge, so I am tired."

"It may be awhile," Gray replied, as he picked up his case and wrapped up the cord for his computer charger.

"I am OK. I'll see you both tomorrow morning."

Gray and John each shook James's hand before leaving the room.

James was relieved to have time alone. He sent Reed a long email report detailing the events of the past day and sent Bunny a text. He checked his unread emails and forwarded messages that were time sensitive to Reed so someone could cover them at the office. Finally, when he was so tired, he could no longer hold his eyes open, he stretched out on the contemporary sofa in the conference room and took a nap.

James slept soundly until the conference room door finally opened. He checked his watch. It was nearly 2:00 a.m. He sat up and rubbed his eyes, realizing he was beyond exhausted.

An INTERPOL agent with an inscrutable expression escorted Reynolds back to the conference room. The remaining government and international law enforcement officers followed closely behind. Reynolds nodded briefly to James before taking his jacket from the back of the chair and headed out of the room. Two FBI agents followed Reynolds, walking in the direction of the lobby. James noticed that Reynolds seemed oddly subdued, and it was odd that he did not seem to want James to accompany him.

James stood up and grabbed his case. "Everything alright?" he asked the middle-aged MI6 agent.

The man shrugged. "Can't really say at this point."

"Any word from the search-and-rescue teams?"

"Nothing. It does not look good," he said somberly.

James shook his head and walked toward the elevator. As he reached his floor, he glanced toward Reynolds's room. He was surprised to see both FBI agents standing in the hall near the door to the Reynolds's suite. A third man in a cheap suit, who James had never seen before, was seated in a chair in the hall. There was a telltale bulge in his suit coat from his holster. One of the FBI agents looked at James pointedly. Something about the demeanor of these men told him they did not want to be disturbed.

Perplexed, James headed down the opposite end of the hall toward his suite. It had been a long day. The king-sized bed had been turned down and looked invitingly comfortable. Quickly, he undressed, tossing his clothes on the floor, and crawled between the sheets. Within a minute, he was fast asleep.

CHAPTER FIFTY-ONE

James was roused from a deep sleep by the persistent ringing of the land-line in the suite. The bedside clock read 11:00 a.m. He glanced at his cell phone, which had a low-battery reading on the screen. He had been so tired the evening before that he had failed to plug in the charger.

Groggily, he picked up the receiver, hit speaker, and laid back against the down pillows. He recognized the voice on the other end was Reed.

"Were you asleep?"

James yawned. "Yes. It was a late evening."

"Have you heard?"

"No."

"Turn on the TV. They found the lifeboat."

James sat up, now fully awake and felt a surge of hopefulness. "Any survivors?"

"None. The boat is under water. There are some satellite images of what appears to be the sinking of the boat. There might have been some inflatable boats with some survivors, but it is not clear. And the weather is deteriorating because there is a storm in the area. So even if they evacuated the lifeboat, they are in trouble. Time is working against them. No one can survive in a little inflatable boat like that for long under these conditions."

"But now they know where to look."

"They have sent drones in. If they are alive, they cannot be too far away. They are intensifying the search."

"I think I will shower. I need to go downstairs."

"I'll be in touch," Reed told him as he rang off.

James reached for the remote control and flipped on CNN. A news anchor with flowing red hair reported on the location of the lifeboat. The screen was filled with grainy images of what appeared to be a large metal lifeboat careening on its side, the stern submerged, and the bow flipping in the air until it slipped under the surface. The early morning light was dim, and the image of the vessel was cloaked in shadow. Nevertheless, the shape of the lifeboat was unmistakable.

"A boat believed to have been one of the lifeboats of the *Golden Swan* has been spotted in the South Pacific two hundred miles south of Rarotonga in a remote area of the South Pacific. The boat apparently sank about 5:00 a.m. on Monday. Search-and-rescue efforts continue to look for survivors. The search teams are racing the clock because there is a dangerous storm approaching the area. Stay tuned throughout the day and CNN will bring you the latest details."

James continued listening to the news account as he made a cup of Nespresso coffee in his suite. The beverage was tasteless, but it gave him a much-needed caffeine jolt. He took an electric-blue power drink from the suite refrigerator and drank it in nearly one gulp. He then turned up the volume of the news channel before going into the marble bath to shower and shave. He quickly finished his morning routine, dressed, grabbed his computer, and headed out of the suite.

As he exited his suite, he noticed a team of men wearing bootees, gloves, and hairnets leaving Reynolds's suite. The chair that had been propped against the wall near Reynolds's suite was now empty, lying on its side. An INTERPOL agent was standing beside the chair speaking to two men James had not seen before. Phillip and Roth stood nearby watching the scene unfold.

Curious, James walked down toward the group of men clustered in the hall. Roth waved at James and met him by the elevator bank. Phillip followed closely behind.

"My boss called me about the lifeboat. What is happening here?"

Roth shook his head. Phillip stepped forward, speaking in a hushed tone. "Reynolds killed the FBI agent guarding his room this morning. Shot him with his own gun. He shot the second agent in the chest, and he is in surgery now."

James stared at Phillip in shock. "Why would he do such a thing?" It seemed inconceivable that Reynolds—the man who was grieving the likely death of his wife and child—would have killed anyone.

"Two agents were interviewing him this morning and confronted him with the latest evidence discovered about the hijacking. The shooting occurred when they were trying to arrest him."

"Arrest him for what? He was a victim here. His wife and child were likely killed in a terrorist attack."

Phillip looked at James soberly. "FBI forensics discovered communications between Reynolds and Cell 53 on the dark web. The communications were found on an encrypted server popular to send anonymous emails on a laptop under a floorboard in his home. The team also interviewed his boss at the tech company where he has been employed for the last seven years. Reynolds's boss gave a sworn statement that there was no work emergency. He claims he never demanded that Reynolds interrupt his vacation to return to Seattle. When this inconsistency was discovered, Reynolds came under suspicion. When his laptop was scraped, the communications between Reynolds and Cell 53 were discovered. He was following and directing their movements while he was on the ship. When he was confronted today, he overpowered one of the agents and killed him with his own gun. He shot the other agent point-blank in the chest."

James was stunned by the news. "He was a subversive involved with a terrorist cell?"

Phillip nodded. "He was apparently the mastermind of the hijacking. He left early before the attack to save his own hide."

"The coward left his wife and daughter to die on the ship," Roth injected.

James tried to comprehend the impossible revelation. He had spent the last two days with a terrorist. It seemed impossible. "There is nothing on the news," he said finally.

"Because it is an international terrorist matter and involves national security, the government will keep it quiet," Phillip told him. "Reynolds Tyler and his parents were actually Syrian refugees who were in the US illegally via Canada. He has been using a fake name and a false Social Security number that was issued to an eight-year-old child in Greenville, Mississippi; the child had died in a car accident more than twenty years ago. Tyler's father was investigated for terrorism by the FBI and deported. Tyler's mother changed their name, and the two of them moved to the New Jersey coast. His mother remarried. Tyler blamed the US government for breaking his family apart."

James looked down momentarily, trying to grasp this strange turn of events. "This is unbelievable."

"It certainly is. To think that we have been eating and talking with him for the last two days. The only good news is that this absolves the cruise line of any wrongdoing," Roth added.

"And we felt sorry for him. Where is he now?"

"He disappeared after the shooting," Phillip replied simply. "He won't get far. There is a manhunt underway."

"I need to call my boss. He needs to know this." James pulled out his phone.

Phillip put his hand on James's arm. "Not yet. There is plenty of time to report this. The FBI wants us to keep this under wraps until they find him. We do not want to jeopardize the search. Right now, let's just focus on the search and rescue of the possible survivors."

James nodded and put his phone back in his pocket, deciding that he would find a time to slip out and call Reed in private about the astounding developments. He followed Roth and Phillip downstairs to the conference room to await reports from the search-and-rescue team.

CHAPTER FIFTY-TWO

Zip was having difficulty sleeping in the inflatable boat. After a few restless hours, sleep continued to evade her. Wide-awake, she lay on her back with her head propped against the gunwale of the tiny boat, staring at the sky and being careful not to wake Zoe. Joey was snoring softly next to her and appeared to be resting peacefully. Zip could see the outline of Officer Reed's face leaning against Joey's chest.

There was no sound coming from the other boats. From all indicia, she was the only one who was awake.

The star-studded canopy that had been so spectacular earlier that night was now obscured by a layer of ominous dark clouds. The full moon had vanished behind the curtain of clouds. A brisk wind buffeted the small flotilla over the waves, tilting Zip's boat at a fifty-degree angle each time it crested a wave and dropped down to the crevasse below. The erratic movements of the boat made Zip fearful that it would capsize. Even with a life vest, survival in the deep dark water would be nearly impossible. Every so often, she felt a bump against the bottom of the inflatable hull. She prayed it was not a shark.

The air was noticeably cooler now, causing her to occasionally shiver. There was a strong odor of ozone in the air, which reminded Zip of the smell that always preceded thunderstorms during her college days at the Rhode Island School of Design. Thunderstorms were rare in Seattle, and she had almost forgotten the pleasant aroma of ozone and the clean feeling after a passing storm.

Although the bulky life vest provided some warmth, her legs and arms were bitterly cold. She wanted to pull out the solar blanket, but she did not want to disturb the others.

Zip had a bad taste in her mouth, and she suddenly felt parched. She realized she had not urinated in many hours and did not feel the urge now. She was clearly becoming dangerously dehydrated. She worried even more about Zoe. She decided that the moment Zoe awoke, she would make sure she drank some water.

As she stared at the sky, she began to wonder how many more days the group could survive. The Campbells and Evans were seniors. Although they were vibrant and energetic, it was unlikely they could survive long with very little food and water.

Were they all going to make it through this? Was this her last day on Earth? After everything they had been through, is this how it would end?

She was losing hope and now realized that death was a very real possibility. Although the boats were orange, they were certainly not as visible as a thirty-foot lifeboat. They could easily be overlooked in a search. It was also possible the search might have already been abandoned, and everyone was presumed dead in the explosion. There were no guarantees anyone was looking for them at this point.

As her mind wandered, she thought about Reynolds. Had he already lost hope that they were alive? For the first time since he had left the ship, she realized she was angry with him. What job could be more important than spending time with his family? Reynolds should have been there with them to protect her and Zoe. Why had he abandoned them?

A fierce gust of wind suddenly lifted the bow of Zip's boat in the air, and just as quickly, dropped it on the crest of the wave. The boat lurched wildly as it slid down the mountainous wave. She looked down at the valley between the waves, feeling that she might fall forward. Zip grabbed onto the nylon rope handhold and held Zoe firmly with her right arm. She managed to loop the straps of Zoe's life jacket to her jacket so they would not be separated.

As the flotilla settled into the smooth water between the waves, she heard Becky scream from the boat tethered behind them. "Oh God. We are going to fall out!" she shrieked.

Zip turned toward the sound. In the dim light, she could see the Bishops' small boat crest the wave at a ninety-degree angle, nearly toppling the inhabitants into the dark water.

Aurora and Hunter both screamed as the boat pitched wildly and dropped into the cavern below. Zoe, now awake, whimpered in fear. Zip clung to her daughter and the nylon rope for dear life. Joey and Officer Reed were now awake, both scrambling to brace themselves as the little boat was helplessly pummeled by the waves. The waves were growing higher, spraying salt water over the short gunwales, drenching Zip and Zoe. The forceful spray was chilly and stung her arms.

Over the wind, Zip could hear Officer Oliver screaming to the group. "There is a storm coming. We are going to have to untie the boats and use our motors until it passes. It is too dangerous to stay tied together like this."

Zip watched as Officer Green untied the rope that tethered the third boat to the flotilla. Officer Oliver cranked the outboard motor of his boat.

"We need to stay horizontal to the crest of the waves. Try to stay together," he called to the group. "Follow me—quickly!"

As he sped away, a hard rain began to fall, pelting them with large drops. Visibility had dropped precipitously. The sound of the rain was deafening.

Joey quickly untied the nylon rope connecting their boat to the Bishops and Campbells' boat. He tossed the rope into the well of their boat and cranked the outboard motor. The motor sputtered and died. Undeterred, Joey cranked the motor again; the engine suddenly roared to life. Sitting on the stern gunwale, Joey, his expression surprisingly placid but purposeful, steered the vessel across the water.

"Hold on," he told them as the boat mounted a large wave, skimming the surface as it sped away in the darkness. Hunter manned the second boat, which followed them at a safe distance.

When they caught up to Officer Oliver, he motioned to them to reduce their speed. Joey cut back the motor and steered the boat toward Officer Oliver's group.

Zip clasped Zoe toward her chest and looped her hand through the nylon handhold. She bowed her head to shield her face from the stinging rain. Officer Reed huddled beside her, holding onto her crucifix with her free hand and staring ahead into the darkness. Zip felt tears of fear and grief slide down her cheeks as the flotilla of boats sped aimlessly into the darkness.

CHAPTER FIFTY-THREE

The sun edged over the horizon less than an hour later revealing the boiling ocean wilderness surrounding them. The rain had finally stopped, leaving them cold and wet. Zip, Zoe, and Officer Reed wrapped themselves together under the emergency blanket, trying to stay warm and keep their body heat regulated.

A line of advancing thunderstorms was visible in the distance. The outboard motor on Officer Oliver's boat sputtered and ultimately died. Peering over the edge of the blanket, Zip watched the boat spin helplessly across the waves, dipping beneath the horizon and suddenly appearing on the crest of the waves. It was a terrifying site.

Joey shook his head. "They are out of gas. We have more fuel, but we might need to conserve it. More bad weather is coming in, and we may need it," he told them as he cut the engine back to idle.

Hunter brought his boat up behind them. "Out of fuel, I think," Hunter told them. "I am going to cut it back for a while too and drift. Let's do our best to stay together."

"I agree. There is safety in numbers."

The boats idled across the crest of the waves. Officer Reed retrieved the remaining MRE packets of split pea soup and dissolved them in two small plastic containers of water. She handed one of the containers to Joey, who passed it along to Hunter.

"We need to have some sustenance while there is a lull in the weather. We can get more from Officer Oliver's boat later."

Hunter encouraged Becky and Aurora to drink the cold soup. When they had finished their share, they returned the half-empty container to Hunter. He drank a bit of the soup, offering it to Todd, who declined. Zip was shocked at his appearance. Despite his sunburn from the previous day, he was deathly pale. Listlessly, he lay on the bottom of the boat with his eyes closed.

"He is seasick," Becky told them, caressing Todd's face with her free hand.

Hunter handed Becky the remainder of the soup. "Try to get him to drink something. He needs to stay hydrated. Remember, I am a doctor."

Todd angrily shoved Becky's arm away as she tried to coax him to drink the soup. "I don't want it."

Hunter shook his head in resignation. Becky shrugged and drank the remaining soup.

Zip managed to get Zoe to drink some of the nasty green liquid. The child was pale and seemed to have no energy, sure signs of dehydration. Officer Reed had explained that the MREs were specially formulated with vitamins and minerals for survival under harsh conditions. After Zoe drank as much as she could, Zip forced herself to drink the soup. Normally, she hated peas above all other vegetables, but found herself actually enjoying the taste of partially dissolved cold soup. When she finished, she passed the container to Reed and Joey. Afterward, the four of them shared a container of water. The water felt fresh and clean, quenching Zip's thirst.

Officer Reed replaced the bottle of water into the boat pocket, and the four of them huddled under the blanket. She could hear Aurora singing hymns over the drone of the idling motor in the next boat. The music was soothing. Zip clutched Zoe, stroking her hair and kissing the top of her head.

"I am so tired, Mommy," Zoe murmured. "I am going to take a nap."

"OK, sweetie. Go to sleep and listen to the pretty music."

Within minutes, she could hear the child's rhythmic breathing under the blanket. Zip knew the child was sleeping too much. It was not a good sign.

When the wind subsided, the sea conditions levelled off, and both Joey and Hunter cut the outboard motors. The boats drifted like synchronized swimmers in the troughs between the waves. Zip leaned against the gunwale and studied the waves. Every so often, she caught sight of the boat carrying the Evans couple, Officer Oliver, and Officer Green, drifting about a quarter of a mile away. Zip spotted a towering wall of water on the horizon, rapidly advancing toward the third boat.

"Look over there!" she screamed pointing toward the water. As the group watched helplessly, the rogue wave lifted the third boat fifty feet into the air. The boat perched on the wave crest briefly before capsizing, dumping Officer Oliver, Officer Green, George, and Sienna to their deaths. Their boat disappeared below the surface as the wave crashed down with extreme force.

"We need to see if they are alright!" Aurora told Hunter.

"Rogue wave. We need to let the danger pass. There may be other waves behind that one. Then we can go and search for them."

Transfixed, the group watched as a second and third wave with equal force battered the sea in front of them. They had been fortunate to be out of the path of danger.

After thirty minutes, the sea conditions subsided enough to allow them safe passage to search for the third boat. The tattered remains of the boat floated just below the surface. There was no evidence of Officer Green, Officer Oliver, or the Evans. Zip realized with deep sadness that the two men who had kept them alive and saved their lives over the past few days were now gone.

How could they possibly survive now?

CHAPTER FIFTY-FOUR

In the early afternoon, a vicious thunderstorm drenched the two remaining dinghies. The wind howled and churned the ocean around them. A waterspout sprang up fewer than a hundred feet away from a tornado produced by the thunderstorm. Zip watched in awe as the waterspout danced across the ocean surface, spinning like a top, approaching dangerously close to the little flotilla. Hunter and Joey increased the speed of the outboard motors to escape the path of the tornado. If the boats were struck by a tornado, death would be certain.

Hunter and Joey ran the outboard motors at a speed low enough to control the boats. Meanwhile, Officer Reed and Aurora opened their water bottles to capture much-needed rainwater.

Zoe had slept through most of the storm, huddled underneath the blanket. Zip was becoming increasingly fearful. The child was listless and sleeping far more than was normal. She was deathly pale. Clearly, the harsh elements were taking their toll on her. She had noticed Zoe had stopped urinating, and her eyes were glazed. Zip tried to coax her to drink water, but Zoe shoved her arm away.

"I wanna sleep, Mommy."

"Please, sweetheart, take a drink."

"No, I am tired."

Officer Reed met Zip's gaze with concern. "When the storm passes, we need to make her drink," she told Zip.

Zip nodded. If she had to, she would force Zoe to drink. As Officer Oliver had told them, even without food, they could live for several days with just water. What Zip did not know, though, was how long a child could survive with only water.

As the boats rose on the waves, Zip could see Todd still lying on the bottom of the other boat, his face covered by his arm. Becky sat beside him, huddled under the blanket with Aurora. Hunter sat on the gunwale studying the ocean intently, seemingly oblivious to the driving rain.

By the late afternoon, the sky had cleared, and the air was hot and humid. The large waves had gradually subsided, and the ocean was reasonably placid again.

The return of decent weather was fortuitous. Both boats were out of fuel, and they drifted lazily across the deep-blue water. The mood had turned bleak. Everyone realized that without the outboard motors, the boats were simply at the mercy of volatile sea conditions.

Zip and Officer Reed stowed the blanket and watched the western sky turn a brilliant shade of magenta. Within minutes, the golden disc slipped below the horizon, and they were again shrouded in darkness. But as the full moon rose, they were bathed in a soft light. The gentle sound of the ocean lapping the side of the boat was peaceful.

After the storm had passed, Zip and Officer Reed had managed to coax Zoe into drinking a large quantity of rainwater. Afterward, the child seemed more animated, and within a half an hour, she had urinated in the bottom of the boat. Neither Joey nor Reed seemed to care about the urine or the smell. The small group was simply focused on survival.

Zip looked over at Hunter. "She urinated."

Hunter nodded. "That is a good sign. We know her vital organs are working, which is key. We just need to keep her hydrated. She will be OK."

Zip managed a weak smile and kissed Zoe on the top of her head. "Hear that Zoe? Doctor's orders: You need to drink a lot of water."

Officer Reed checked the side pocket to assess the food situation. "We have one MRE left to share between all of us," she announced. "I suggest we save it until tomorrow. Does everyone agree?"

"And what delicious meal will we have next?" Joey asked, trying to inject some levity into the situation.

"Beef stew, my favorite."

"A feast," Joey countered. "I can't wait to have it tomorrow."

"Anyone else feel that they can't wait to eat until tomorrow?"

"I think we are fine," Hunter responded. "We need the calories tomorrow."

Satisfied that there was a consensus, Officer Reed put the MRE away. Afterward, she settled back into a comfortable position, nestled by Zoe.

After a while, Aurora resumed singing her hymns. Both Hunter and Becky joined in the singing of "Amazing Grace" and "Rock of Ages." Hunter had a surprisingly beautiful baritone voice that complemented Aurora's soprano and Becky's alto. Zip, Officer Reed, Zoe, and Joey sat back against the bottom of the boat, humming along with the hymns. It was a welcome distraction. When they finally stopped singing, Becky recited Psalm 23 and the Lord's Prayer. Afterward, she said a prayer for them all.

"God, thank you for saving us. Please help us be found. Rest in peace, Officers Oliver and Green, who helped save us all. God bless George and Sienna."

When she finished, everyone joined in an "Amen."

When the group fell silent, Zip drifted off to sleep. Her dreams were vivid and unpleasant. By the time she awoke, a sliver of bright light illuminated the eastern sky. Zoe, Officer Reed, and Joey were still asleep. Zip felt desperately thirsty and lightheaded. The skin on her face and arms was tingling from sunburn, despite her religious use of zinc oxide. She felt an overwhelming sense of exhaustion. She could feel herself giving up.

As she peered over the side of the dinghy, she noticed that the other boat had drifted more than one hundred feet away. She wanted to call to them but did not have the energy.

Officer Reed and Joey finally stirred as the sun climbed in the sky. Joey took out the sole paddle fastened by nylon netting on the gunwale and began paddling toward the other boat. Officer Reed busied herself by rehydrating the beef stew. Each packet was intended to feed no more than three people. It would be a meager last meal for a group of eight.

Zip watched Officer Reed attempting to mix the dry MRE. She had very little appetite now, and it was frightening to think that this might be the last meal she would ever eat. She closed her eyes and drifted back to sleep, oblivious to the relentless rays of the sun.

She was jolted awake as Joey's whoops of excitement pierced the silence. "I see a drone!" He pulled out the flare gun from the pocket of the boat and fired it into the air.

CHAPTER FIFTY-FIVE

Within hours of Reynolds's disappearance, his body was discovered by a hotel maid in a linen closet. He had a single gunshot wound to his temple—an obvious suicide. His body was taken to the morgue for an autopsy.

"A coward right up until the end," Roth commented to James and Phillip that evening over dinner in hotel's Belvedere restaurant.

"There is nothing in the news about his involvement in the hijacking," James replied.

"And there will not be," Phillip told him. "His involvement in the hijacking was an international conspiracy and threatens the national security of the US. He was a US citizen, and the cooperating governments will continue to investigate his involvement in order to locate the other members of Cell 53. Ultimately, there will be a press release saying he killed himself because of his grief over his wife and child, who are believed to be dead."

James shook his head. "What a cold, calculating person he was to set this in motion and attempt to let his wife and child die. And he was a great actor. I actually felt sorry for him."

"We all did," replied Roth. "He was a pro, and he deceived many people. And the troubling thing is that he fit the profile of the typical cruise passenger of the Paradise Line: affluent and educated. No background check could have ever detected his involvement."

"And he clearly had no connection with the Vandebergs. He is a new kind of terrorist and does not fit the profile of a mass murderer. Even if law enforcement had known of his Syrian heritage, they might not have been suspicious. The US is home to many former Syrian citizens who left to escape oppression." Phillip folded his napkin beside his empty plate of Dungeness salad.

James contemplated the situation as he finished his poached salmon and parsley potatoes. Contrary to Roth's request, he had notified his boss earlier that day after Reynolds's body had been found. Reed had been shocked, but he had asked James to stay a few more days, at least until the investigation was over or the search-and-rescue efforts had been called off, with or without finding survivors.

James was disappointed that Reed wanted him to stay. He missed Bunny and their life together. But he was pleased that Reed had selected him to represent the Lunar Syndicate in Los Angeles. He knew intuitively that many of his colleagues would have been delighted to spend a few days in the Peninsula Hotel in Los Angeles. It was a prized—albeit depressing—assignment.

After dinner, James returned to his hotel room to catch up on emails. He sent Bunny a text telling her about his extended stay and that he missed her. He decided he would talk to the concierge in the morning about buying Bunny a nice present to bring back with him. Perhaps a new Prada handbag; Bunny loved handbags and would be delighted with a gift. His long absence would be immediately forgiven, and Bunny would be happy for days.

He managed to watch a few minutes of Jimmy Fallon before he turned off the TV and fell into a deep sleep.

The following morning, he took a long hot shower before dressing in casual clothing and going to breakfast in the dining room. He found a table close to the window. He lingered over a large latte, enjoying the solitude after the intensity of the last few days. Before returning to the conference room, he stopped by to speak with the concierge, who promised to put him touch with an exclusive shop on Rodeo Drive that sold lovely handbags. It would all be painless. James would provide his credit card details, and a gift-wrapped handbag would be sent to the hotel and placed in his room.

Within a few minutes, a woman from the shop called James and made some suggestions. James took her recommendation and gave her his credit card details. Afterward, he went to the conference room and ordered another latte.

A few minutes before twelve, Gray rushed into the conference room with an announcement. "Eight survivors have been found. They will be brought to Rarotonga and then to LA tomorrow."

James sat back in his chair. It was miraculous. He immediately pulled out his phone and dialed Reed's number to give him the good news.

EPILOGUE—ONE YEAR LATER

James received a promotion at work after the hijacking claims were finally settled. He resigned from the Kidnap and Ransom team. At his request, he was assigned to handle only property damage claims now. His promotion was accompanied by a large raise, which enabled him and his new wife, Bunny, to buy a small thatched-roof cottage in Sevenoaks. His commute was far easier, and he could spend more time at home. This was important now that Bunny was pregnant.

Paradise Lines was ultimately sold and absorbed by another large cruise line. The last James had heard, the Vandebergs had retired to Nassau and invested in a luxury hotel.

On occasion, James was haunted by the thoughts of Reynolds. Reynolds's involvement as the mastermind of the hijacking had remained secret. James thought there was a certain justice that his wife and child had endured the nightmare and survived. He had learned that the survivors had sold their story to a Hollywood producer and, in two years, a major motion picture would be released loosely based on the hijacking of the *Golden Swan*. Of course, Reynolds would be portrayed as a victim.

The public would never know the real truth of what had happened. James decided that was probably best.

* * *

Zip closed her contracts hornbook and shut down her laptop before pulling on a heavy cotton nightshirt. Zoe was sound asleep in the adjoining room of their spacious townhouse in Arlington, Virginia.

When she and Zoe had arrived at the hotel in Los Angeles, the FBI had informed her that Reynolds had committed suicide. There had been scant details provided, other than he was despondent and felt guilty that he had not remained with them on the *Golden Swan*. Naturally, she had been devastated, but she was determined to be strong for Zoe.

She could not bear to stay in the Madrona house because there were too many memories of Reynolds and their happy family life before the cruise. Within two months, she had sold the Seattle house for a substantial profit and taken Zoe to Denver for a long visit with her family. Between the money from the house and the settlement from the cruise line, she had no financial worries. She also had received money for the sale of their story to a Hollywood producer. After taking the LSAT, she was admitted to Georgetown University Law School. She paid cash for the gorgeous Arlington townhouse and enrolled Zoe in a private school. Because of the amount of her settlement, she was free of the burden of student loans. They had begun a new life.

Zip and Zoe were both undergoing therapy and, as expected, had been diagnosed with PTSD. For months after they were rescued, Zip experienced panic attacks every night. School had been an unexpected diversion and, once again, she was finally looking toward the future. Zoe had also improved and seemed to be adjusting well in school.

Zip stayed in touch with the Bishops, the Campbells, Joey, and Officer Reed, who she now called Lisa, by email and Facebook. The Campbells had invited Zip and Zoe to visit them in Brighton the next year. But Zip's therapist cautioned her that seeing the other passengers might trigger another episode of PTSD. Zip decided to wait and see how things developed.

She had learned one important thing from the hijacking: It was impossible to know what the future held. But after everything she and Zoe had been through, it was unlikely they would ever endure anything so horrific again. She took confidence from that thought and knew it would carry her through her new life.

$4 \overline{)24}$

7 − 11 − 7 − 11